MAR 0 8 1992

NOV 16

FEB 03 19

OUT OF

"I know you would rather die than let me know it, but you're upset about something, aren't you?"

"You know perfectly well what I'm upset about—you dirty rat!"

"Now hold on a minute. Jim called me last night and told me what happened, and I want to apologize to you—"

"Save your breath. I don't appreciate your implying to your friends that I'm a loony tune, Mr. Tremayne, so just stop it! And don't even talk to me. Not ever again!"

FOREVER AFTER

"Can I kiss you?"

"No!" he refused guiltily.

"If I really thought for one minute that you loved Elaine, I wouldn't dream of doing what I'm about to do."

"This is miserable. You're supposed to respect my state of engagement . . . ."

"That's just what your engagement is—a miserable state. How long is it going to take for you to realize it?"

Other Leisure Books by Lori Copeland:

PLAYING FOR KEEPS/A TEMPTING STRANGER
OUT OF CONTROL/A WINNING COMBINATION

THE BEST OF
LORI COPELAND

OUT OF THIS WORLD
— & —
FOREVER AFTER

LEISURE BOOKS ▪ NEW YORK CITY

A LEISURE BOOK®

May 1991

Published by

Dorchester Publishing Co., Inc.
276 Fifth Avenue
New York, NY 10001

OUT OF THIS WORLD Copyright© MCMLXXXVI by Lori Copeland
FOREVER AFTER Copyright© MCMLXXXV by Lori Copeland

All rights reserved. No part of this book may be reproduced or transmitted
in any form or by any electronic or mechanical means, including photo-
copying, recording, or by any information storage and retrieval system,
without the written permission of the Publisher, except where permitted
by law.

The name "Leisure Books" and the stylized "L" with design are trademarks
of Dorchester Publishing Co., Inc.

Printed in the United States of America.

OUT OF THIS WORLD

To the girls on my Monday night bowling team:

Annavee Duncan, Jan Burlison,
Billie Murdock,
Jocelyn Klein, Mona Gillihan, and
Kay McClelland.

CHAPTER ONE

A small economy car pulling a U-Haul trailer turned down Fallow Drive and slowed to a crawling pace. The large elm trees shading the street were a pleasant and welcome sight to the young woman who had driven nearly nonstop for the last twenty-four hours to reach her destination.

Her eyes scanned the street numbers intently as the car crept along. The houses on Fallow Drive were at least twenty years old, their lawns boasting neatly tended flowerbeds and well-trimmed shrubbery. Massive old trees lined the sheltered street, their boughs nearly touching each other and forming a canopy of green.

Toni Cameron drew in a long, cleansing breath of the perfumed May air. In another few weeks, people had told her, Texas would be dry and almost unbearably hot, but for today it looked like sheer heaven to her.

Forty-seven sixteen. This was it.

Braking carefully, she pulled alongside the curb and brought the car to a halt. Her eyes surveyed the homey-looking vine-covered cottage before her, and she heaved a sigh of relief.

The rental agency had assured her that the duplex she had rented sight unseen would be suitable for her needs, but she had worried all the way from Iowa that she had made a mistake. But now, without even seeing the inside, she knew it was right.

Restarting the engine, she pulled forward until the end of the trailer had cleared the drive and then stopped again. Backing trailers was not exactly her area of expertise, but at the moment she had no other choice than to attempt the feat.

Slipping the transmission into reverse, she closed her eyes, prayed for skills she knew she didn't have the slightest hope of possessing, took another deep breath, and then began.

She had no idea how she accomplished it, but within twenty seconds the trailer was sideways in the drive and the car was butted straight up against it. Shaking her head disgustedly, she put the car into low gear and pulled forward again.

This time she didn't make it ten feet before the trailer wheel hit the curb, throwing her head forward and bringing her to a jolting, abrupt halt.

Rubbing her neck painfully, she grimaced and jerked the car back into forward. The trailer thumped loudly over the curb and left a black streak of rubber as it shot back out onto the street.

She knew that every dish she owned had just been wiped out, but what could she do?

Grumbling irritably under her breath, she yanked the car back into reverse and gunned the trailer back over the curb, leaving a trail of blue smoke as it bounced up in the air and landed in the middle of one of the tidy, manicured flower beds that lined the twin drives.

And there went all her other fragile objects, including the glass refrigerator shelves! she thought impatiently.

Zackery Tremayne glanced up from washing his car and watched the dirt and pieces of rosebushes spewing up in the air with amazement as the wheels of the trailer tried to dig their way out of one of *his* flower beds.

Once more the squeal of rubber filled the air as the trailer shot back out onto the pavement and came to a screeching halt.

Woman drivers! He shook his head in amusement and turned his attention back to what he had been doing.

But a few minutes later, it became hard to ignore the sound of bushes being snapped off and ground under the tires of her car as she once more made a wild stab at getting the trailer backed into her drive.

Grumbling good-naturedly under his breath, he pitched the soapy sponge into a bucket of water, then jumped the small hedge that separated the two drives and walked over to where she was sitting still, now with the motor idling.

"Hi."

Toni had been so lost in thought as to what she was going to do next that the sound of his voice startled her.

"Sorry," he apologized, noting the way she had nearly jumped out of her skin. "I didn't mean to scare you, but I thought you could use some help." His gaze discreetly surveyed the car, which was now jackknifed around the trailer, and then came back to her as he stuck out his hand in a friendly greeting. "Zack Tremayne. You must be my new neighbor?"

"Hi. Toni Cameron, and yes, I sure could use some help," she accepted gratefully as she slid out of the driver's seat and turned to face him. "I'm afraid I'm not very good at backing trailers."

He was bare-chested, barefooted, and wearing a pair of white tennis shorts, but he looked like a six-foot-one, hazel-eyed angel of mercy to her.

"They're tricky," he admitted, and flashed her a winning smile if she had ever seen one. "I'll be glad to do it for you."

Sliding behind the wheel of the car, he eased it forward, and within a few minutes he had the car gliding smoothly up the tree-lined drive.

Toni stood back and shook her head in awe, envying the ease with which he handled the car. Eventually she would have managed to get the trailer where she wanted it, but she shuddered to think how long it would have taken her.

While the task was being finished, her gaze unthinkingly focused on the handsome white knight driving her car. She certainly couldn't have asked for a more attractive liberator.

He was at least a head taller than she was, and his hair was brown—no, actually, it was more of a dark blond—and it had a little bit of natural curl to it, which gave it a look of controlled disorder that Toni had always found appealing. He had a nice tan that set off his eyes, which were a most attractive and unusual shade of green, and she had noticed a deep

12

dimple on his left cheek when he grinned at her. And it certainly wasn't hard to see that he was in fine physical shape. He wasn't muscle-bound, but he had that nice firm look about him that bespoke masculine strength and power.

One of those real heartbreakers, she thought absently, the sort of man she planned to avoid from now on.

By now he had the trailer backed neatly to the side porch and was getting out of the car. "There, that ought to fix you up." He smiled. "The trick is turning the wheel in the opposite direction you want the trailer to go."

"I can't thank you enough." She smiled, then frowned apologetically. "I hope I haven't done too much damage to the neighborhood—and your flower bed."

He smiled back. "I don't think so. You new to the area?"

"Yes, I just drove here from Des Moines."

"Des Moines, huh? What brings you such a long way from home? Your husband get transferred to Texas or something?" With male appreciation, his gaze ran lightly over the attractive blonde standing before him.

She wasn't very tall, but she was definitely well built. His eyes were reluctant to move away from the snug-fitting T-shirt she was wearing, although he was careful to maintain a polite decorum while he looked. Her hair was long and the rich color of honey, but she had chosen to pull it away from her face into a ponytail; somehow, the carefree style made her look much younger than he guessed her to

13

be. She had laughing blue eyes, a perky little nose that tilted ever so slightly when she grinned, and a most sensational pair of legs.

He could have done a whole lot worse in a new neighbor, he quickly decided, forcing his gaze to safer territory.

"No, I'm not married," she corrected. Funny how that thought still seemed to rankle her, even now. "I just decided I needed a change of scenery."

"Well, I hope Texas treats you well." He stuck out his hand once more and shook hers. "Let me know if I can be of any further help."

"I will, and thanks again, Mr. Tremayne. I'll get that flower bed back in order as soon as possible."

"Hey, I promise I won't call you Ms. Cameron if you won't call me Mr. Tremayne. Let's make it Zack and Toni." He grinned again and jumped the hedge to his side of the drive.

"That sounds fair to me, Zack." She watched as he walked back to his shiny red Mazda RX-7 and went back to work.

Turning her attention back to the enormous job of unloading the trailer, she found herself unwilling to face the task as total fatigue closed in on her. Perhaps she would go inside and explore her new home and rest a few minutes before she tackled the awesome job.

The duplex, with its shiny new coat of fresh white paint, had a side entrance, and she quickly decided this would be the door she would be using the most often. Stepping up the three concrete steps that led to the side porch, she inhaled deeply and delighted in the smell of the dark crimson roses that were climbing up a large trellis beside the door. Their sweet perfume floated lightly on the air as she unlocked the door and stepped into the cool interior of the living room.

It was only a three-room house, but the rooms were large and airy, and they looked very comfortable. There was a set of French doors off the living room, and the realtor had told her they led to a small backyard.

She wandered over to the doors and opened them, then walked out into the afternoon sunshine. Like the front of the house, the backyard was shady and inviting. There was even a tiny patch of dirt sitting over in the corner where the sun peeked through. It looked as if someone had once had a garden there.

Tomato plants and pole beans, she quickly decided. That's what she would plant. And she could watch them grow and produce and then harvest their bounty all summer long.

She stood in the lush, freshly mown grass a few more moments savoring the warm rays of sunlight on her face before she finally turned and went back into the house.

The bedroom proved to be the smallest room in the house, but it was more than adequate for what little furniture she had brought with her. It had a lovely covered window seat where she could sit and look outside. She would like that. The house she had lived in before had very few windows, and she had missed the outside light.

In view of the fact she had only a bed, a sofa, a portable television, two end tables, one lamp, a refrigerator, a card table, and two kitchen chairs, she really didn't need a lot of space. It wasn't very much to show for a woman who would soon be thirty-one years old, but she consoled herself with the thought that she was still young and could start over again.

Only this time, she would be more careful.

The kitchen was cheerful, even though it, too, was compact. There was a large window overlooking the driveway that would provide a cool breeze and a pleasant view. Coupled with the fact that she would only be twenty minutes away from the county courthouse, where she would start her new job as a court stenographer first thing in the morning, the house was more than suitable for her needs.

Now her only problem was to get the trailer unloaded and back to the rental agency before she had to pay another day's fee. She knew she could manage everything but the sofa and refrigerator herself; those two heavy items would present her biggest challenge. Friends had helped her load them onto the trailer in Des Moines, but she didn't have those friends to help her now.

An hour later, she was still wondering what she would do as she set the last box on the card table in the kitchen and looked around her. She was all finished, except for the two heavy items remaining on the trailer.

A soft rap on the side door interrupted her musings; she dusted off her hands and went to see who it was.

"Hi, again." Zack Tremayne stood on the small porch and smiled politely at her. He was now dressed in a pair of dress slacks and a sport shirt, and he looked much more presentable than he had earlier. Even this early in the season, he had a dark tan and a healthy look about him that most men would envy. The gentle breeze that drifted by him caught the very pleasant scent of his soap and after-shave.

Toni found herself extremely happy to see him again. Brushing absently at a stray wisp of honey-brown hair, she opened the door wider. "Hi there. What brings you over the wall again?" she said teasingly.

He chuckled. "I've been watching you unload that trailer for the last hour, and although you've done an amazing job of wrestling those boxes around by yourself, I honestly don't see how you're going to manage that refrigerator and sofa."

She laughed at his astute assessment of her latest predicament. "Would you believe I don't know how I'm going to, either?"

"Then you wouldn't object to my offering my help once again?"

She looked at him thoughtfully. "Are you sure you really want to? You look as if you have more important things to do than help me move." He looked spit-shined and polished, and every stylish dark blond hair was in place. She knew a man as good-looking as he was must undoubtedly be antici-pating a more stimulating evening than moving fur-niture.

"I have a few minutes before I have to keep an appointment," he assured her.

"Well, if you're sure you have the time, then I'll admit I sure could use the help."

He stepped back as she opened the screen door

17

and slipped out to stand beside him. "I really do appreciate this," she chattered as they walked off the porch together. "I have to have the trailer back to the rental agency in another hour, and I hated the thought of having to try to hire someone to unload it in addition to having to pay another day's rent on it."

In a few minutes they were standing at the trailer, and even though there were two of them now, the chore of getting the refrigerator unloaded still seemed monumental to her.

"I don't know—what do you think?" She looked up at him hopefully.

"Looks pretty heavy," he conceded.

"You think we can handle it ourselves?"

"Nope."

"No?"

"No, that's why just before I came over I took the liberty of calling a good friend to come over and give me a hand," he confessed. His eyes traveled over the tan shorts and red T-shirt that he had admired earlier. Red had always been his favorite color, but she made it even more appealing. "Your muscles are much prettier than Jim's, but I'm afraid his are more suited to moving refrigerators than yours are."

Toni let out a sigh of relief. "Thanks again. I don't know if my back would have held out or not."

Seconds later, a bright red Pontiac Fiero pulled up in front of Zack's house, and the driver tooted its horn playfully.

Placing the tips of his fingers in the corners of his

18

mouth, Zack let out an ear-piercing whistle. "Over here!"

Toni's ears were still ringing as the driver jumped out of his car and bounded over the hedge. "Hey! What's happenin', Tremayne?"

"Not much, Howerton. You made good time."

"Yeah, traffic was pretty light." The new arrival looked at Toni, and his grin widened as he stuck out his hand in a friendly gesture. "And this must be the beautiful damsel in distress?"

"Toni Cameron, this is my good friend, Jim Howerton. Toni's my new neighbor," Zack explained.

"Lucky you." Jim punched Zack in the ribs knowingly, then shook her hand energetically. "Toni, nice to meet you."

"Hello, Jim. It's very nice to meet you, too."

"So this is what we have to unload." Jim's pleasant brown eyes surveyed the refrigerator and sofa thoughtfully. "No sweat. It shouldn't take us but a few minutes."

Toni stood back as Zack climbed into the trailer, slipped a dolly under the refrigerator, and strapped it down tightly. Within half an hour, the trailer had been unloaded and the articles neatly placed in their new positions.

"I can't thank you two enough," Toni said again as she walked back outside with them. "I don't know what I would have done without you."

"No trouble," Zack assured her.

"None at all," Jim seconded. "Say, I'll bet Toni hasn't eaten yet. Why don't we all go grab a sandwich somewhere?"

"Sounds like fun, but I have an appointment at

seven," Zack declined apologetically. "Maybe some other time."

"Oh? Well, I guess Toni and I could survive without you." Jim grinned at her. "What do you think? I know a great little Italian place that makes delicious meatball sandwiches."

Toni smiled ruefully. "That's very nice of you, but I'm afraid I can't make it, either. I still have to get the trailer to the rental agency, and then all I want to do is come home for a hot bath and a good night's rest. I haven't been to bed for close to thirty hours, and I'm exhausted."

She walked with the men to the hedge and paused to express her gratitude once again.

"Really, it was no trouble at all," Zack reiterated. "If anything else comes up that you can't handle, just raise your kitchen window and give me a holler."

"Thank you. I will."

"The same for me," Jim offered. "I'm in the phone book and not more than twenty minutes away."

"Thank you. I'll keep that in mind."

A few minutes later, Toni stood on the porch and watched Jim and Zack go off in their separate cars. She gave them both a friendly wave and watched their cars disappear down the street.

For a moment the ever-familiar feeling of loneliness washed over her as she thought about the fact that she was in a new town where she knew no one but the two men who had just driven away. And they were only very polite strangers.

The loneliness will get better, she reminded herself, but it wasn't the first time she had had to make an effort to believe it.

It simply had to.

A soft breeze sprang up and gently kissed her cheeks as she turned and walked back into her house. It was as if the breeze had decided to be her friend just when she felt she had none. The scent of roses still perfumed the air, and the massive old elms still shaded the tree-lined street; but somehow none of those things were as comforting to her as they had been a little earlier.

It was nearly nine o'clock by the time she returned the trailer to the rental agency and stopped at a fast-food chain for a hamburger and soft drink. On arriving home, she found the box with the bed linens and made her bed. That accomplished, she took her eagerly anticipated hot bath and slipped into a lightweight cotton gown.

A cooling breeze rustled through the leaves of the tree next to her bedroom window. She sat down on the corner of her bed and absently ran a brush through her hair. The sound of the leaves was particularly pleasant, since there had been no trees close to the house where she had lived before.

Strolling over to the window while she rubbed an almond-scented lotion onto her arms, she let her gaze absently wander to the shadowy yard beside the house. The house next door was dark and quiet. It was still early, and her new neighbor, Zack, had not returned from his "appointment" yet.

She had to smile when she thought about how nice he had been to her. Not everyone would have offered their help the way he had. And Jim wasn't bad, either.

Switching off the lamp beside her bed, she sat down on the window seat and gazed upward at the stars. The night was crystal clear, and she could see the Big Dipper stretching across the sky in a brilliant display of heavenly lights.

In a little game she had played ever since her father had taken her outside one starry night when she was just a small child and pointed out all the interesting things that were in the sky, her eyes began to search for the Milky Way, and then they traveled slowly across the diamond-lit sky to search for satellites orbiting the earth. If by chance she were able to locate one, then it would become a different game to try and guess if it was the United States' or Russia's. Someone had once told her there was a difference in the two superpowers' satellites, but no matter how hard she tried, she had never been able to distinguish between them.

She yawned and stretched as exhaustion threatened to overtake her now. The hot bath and the quiet moments were beginning to relax her. Casting one last glance toward the starry heavens, she slid off the window seat and stood up.

Suddenly, a bright object in the western sky caught her eye. Ever so slowly, she leaned closer to the window and sought to make out more clearly the tiny dot of glowing light that seemed to be picking up speed and traveling in her direction.

She stood for a moment and watched the strange light grow steadily brighter.

She climbed back up in the window sill and tried

to focus her sleepy gaze on the object. It was moving fast, still picking up speed and coming her way.

A plane, or some other kind of low-flying aircraft, she reasoned. That's all it was. Her shoulders drooped with relief. For a minute she had thought she might have spotted one of those UFO's that had stirred up such a controversy several years ago. She chuckled to herself at her wild imaginings and started to stand up once again, but something made her cast another quizzical glance out the window.

No, wait. No plane would be moving that fast, she realized. The object hurtling toward her was growing larger now, and its speed was hard to determine, but it was not a plane. She was sure of it.

Her eyes widened as the object came steadily closer and closer. As if in a daze, she slid off the window seat and crept through the darkened living room, pausing at each window to see if it was still there. Each time it was, only it seemed to grow larger by the minute.

Her breath came in short spurts as she opened the side door and slipped out onto the porch. The smooth concrete felt cool to her bare feet, and she realized that she had forgotten to put on her slippers, but it didn't matter. The glowing object was nearly over Zack's house now. As it approached, it paused, then cut back for a few minutes and hovered about a hundred feet off the ground. She guessed the craft to be about fifteen to twenty feet in diameter, and it had red, green, and yellow lights rotating around the rim.

Her heart was hammering so hard, she could feel it beating in her chest. She stepped over the low hedge and cautiously peeked around the corner of the house where the craft was now stationary directly over Zack's backyard.

She could hear no sound coming from the vessel; only the eerie flashing of lights told her it was there. The neighborhood dogs started barking, the only noise to break the uneasy silence that seemed to cloak the earth now.

As she huddled behind the house, a bright yellow beam shot out of one of the portholes of the saucer-shaped object and scanned the yard and the tops of the trees for a few minutes. It paused periodically on the lawn furniture, and then it suddenly turned around and focused an unusual amount of attention on Zack's odd-shaped barbecue grill.

After a few moments it traveled on slowly about the yard, then turned around abruptly once more and came back to the grill, pausing once again as the shaft from the light enlarged. Toni could see particles of dust swirling in the light, as if they were being suctioned up into the body of the ship, as the beam riveted on the grill and stayed there.

She was mesmerized by the strange object, and she couldn't tear her eyes away from the sight, although she was about to faint from fright. She could see the branches of a nearby tree swaying, and the light poles and wiring surrounding the house were aglow with a peculiar bluish light.

There was something about the grill that fascinated the object. Its lights continued to focus on the spindly red kettle until Toni decided it would never move on.

Five minutes later, its curiosity apparently satisfied for the moment, the beam of light swung back over the house. She hurriedly ducked her head back around the corner and held her breath until the ray disappeared back into the body of the craft moments later. Then, as suddenly as it had appeared, the thing shot upward in a rush of wind and back into the ebony sky.

Crawling on her hands and knees, she rounded the corner of the house and sat transfixed as she watched the glowing object move away from her at a speed that could not be comprehended, and grow smaller and smaller in the distant sky.

Reaching up to touch her face, she could feel the wetness sliding down her cheeks as the wind from the strange object still tossed her hair about in wild disarray. Numb, in a state of shock, she reached up to wipe away the tears of fright—or were they tears of wonder?—as her gaze continued to follow the ship until it completely disappeared into a black void.

Then an awesome quiet descended over the backyard.

It was several moments later before the tree frogs and cicadas started up again. The wind made a gentle rustling sound through the leaves of the trees as she sank weakly down onto the dew-covered grass and listened.

It was as if the last fifteen minutes had never taken place.

Rising to her feet slowly, her gaze still refused to leave the brilliant heavens, hoping for one last sign of the unexplainable object. But whatever it had been, it was there no longer. Only tiny diamonds twinkling back at her from a backdrop of black velvet met her gaze as she scanned the sky one final time.

Good heavens! Had she gone completely bananas, or had she just seen a flying saucer?

Her feet suddenly sprouted wings as she found herself racing back to the safety of her house. Surely an object that big would have been seen by other people. If so, then the police would have reports of it.

Her hands were shaking so hard, she could hardly find her car keys, but she finally did, then raced back out the front door. Since her phone was not in working order yet, she would have to go down to the one on the corner that she had seen earlier today to make a call.

Ten minutes later, she was standing outside her car, still dressed in her housecoat, her nerves strung tight as a fiddle's as she dialed the operator. There were several long, agonizing rings before a woman's voice came on the line.

"Operator."

"The police—give me the police station, please."

"One moment, pleeeeze."

A new series of rings began, promptly followed by a male voice. "Police Department."

"Yes—uh, my name's Toni Cameron, and I live on Fallow Drive."

"Yes."

"Yes, well, I was wondering—have you had any reports of a strange object being in this area tonight?" she prompted hopefully. "Say, in the last fifteen minutes?"

"Strange objects?"

"Yes, strange, glowing objects," she encouraged, "objects that sort of make the trees and the power lines look kind of—bluish." Even as she spoke the words, she knew how ridiculous they sounded.

"Bluish, huh? Just a minute, ma'am. I'll check."

Moments later he was back on the line. "No, ma'am. We haven't had any reports of bluish objects in your area."

"Oh, dear, you haven't?"

"No, ma'am. Are you wanting to make one?"

"Me? Oh, no thanks. I was just wondering."

She replaced the receiver on the hook, then immediately jerked it back off and punched the operator button again. *Surely* someone had seen what she had and reported it.

"Operator."

"I need the local newspaper office."

"One moment, please."

It took a few minutes to get through to the news desk, but the answer was the same. No such report had been turned in, but the reporter had laughingly asked her if she had seen a flying saucer, which she had promptly denied.

She had the same result when she called a couple of television and radio stations. Apparently she was the only one who had seen the strange object, and she wasn't about to admit to such an occurrence if no one else had seen it.

Casting one last exasperated look upward, she slid back into her car and started the engine.

If this had been the work of her imagination, then it certainly was up for an Academy Award this time.

CHAPTER TWO

The sound of birds singing in the trees awakened her the next morning. It was a comforting, normal sound, and she assured herself that it was okay to wake up and face the new day.

Had she actually seen a flying saucer, or had she only dreamed she had?

Rolling over onto her side, Toni forced her eyes open just as a new and beautiful dawn was breaking. Sunshine was streaming through the leaves of the tree outside the window, casting a pretty, symmetrical pattern across her bed.

She felt groggy and listless. As tired as she had been last night, she still had not slept well. Her mind kept reliving the incident that had taken place earlier, and, try as she might, she had not been able to relax and go to sleep until the early hours of the morning.

It had occurred to her that she might confide in her new neighbor what had taken place in his backyard, but she hadn't heard his car pull into the drive until close to two this morning. Besides, he would probably never believe her. And who in his right mind could blame him? Even she wasn't sure it had really happened.

Perhaps she had been more mentally exhausted than she had first thought. The last three weeks had been enough to test anyone's sanity.

Sliding out of bed, she reached for the light robe on the end of the bed and slipped it on.

Breaking up with Skip had taken a lot out of her. Not that she wouldn't eventually get over him, given enough time, and she thought she was doing pretty darn well, considering the traumatic experience. Coming out of a relationship she had nurtured and cherished for the past two years still fully intact was just one more thing to be thankful for.

Maybe she was still a wee bit shaky, but it was getting better all the time.

Oh, at first she had fallen apart. After all, she had spent the last two years of her life living with Skip Harden, always with the promise that marriage was in the near future for them. But it had never taken place, so she had finally made the inevitable break.

Now, after the initial shock of the separation had worn off, Toni was beginning to see that what had happened between them was probably for the best.

Even months before the breakup had actually occurred, she had toyed with the idea of severing the relationship. As far as she could see, they were getting no closer to the altar than they ever had been.

But somehow she hadn't found the strength to actually give up on him. She loved him dearly, and Toni Cameron was no quitter, although she had always felt that living together was wrong. A firm believer in the sanctity of marriage, she had wondered at times what had possessed her to commit to such an arrangement. But she had no plausible answer except for the fact that she was in love.

Now that it was over, she could see how naïve and gullible she had been, but she had loved the man and had believed every pretty word he said. And he had certainly said enough of them.

"If you'll just be patient and wait until my job is more secure, then we'll get married. We have plenty of time, babe," he had argued. "We have a good thing going for us. Let's not spoil it by getting married."

Or, "Let's get the car paid off before we jump into marriage." Then, "Wouldn't you love to have our furniture paid for first?" On and on the excuses went.

But his excuses soon became old hat to her, and she grew tired of granting him reprieves.

And to add to her misery, her parents were on her case constantly. They made no bones about how disappointed they were in their only daughter, whom they had raised in a home that exemplified love and commitment, and they could not understand her wanting to live with a man without marriage.

So after two long years, Toni couldn't stand the pressure any longer or her own feelings of wanting more from this man. So she had demanded marriage —now or never. Skip had panicked like a cornered animal and chosen never. No doubt this had made her parents ecstatic, but she couldn't say it had done a whole lot for her happiness.

Now she was starting over in a new town with

new surroundings and a totally new outlook on life. She could only hope she wasn't as "tainted" or as "bad a judge of character" as her parents had suggested, and that someday she would find the sort of man she had thought Skip to be when they first met: dependable, trustworthy, and a man of his word.

Maybe, just maybe that was what the problem was. She had just been under too much emotional pressure lately, and she had only imagined that she'd seen that flying saucer last night. She supposed that was possible. The mind could play strange tricks on you at times, and this undoubtedly was one of those times.

She hurriedly made the bed and started for the shower, reminding herself that she wanted to arrive at her new job early today.

It was truly a glorious morning as she stepped out of her side door an hour later dressed in a tailored, light blue linen suit and matching blouse. Her high-heeled navy blue leather pumps made a tapping sound on the concrete drive as she stepped along jauntily. Her mood was much lighter than it had been earlier as she got into her car.

Starting a new job and a new life would be enough to restore anyone's faith in mankind, she reasoned as she tossed a friendly wave to her neighbor, who was just staggering out his back door to retrieve his morning paper.

Her eyes unwillingly paused to study him for a moment. She was a bit taken aback by his appearance this morning. Actually, he looked somewhat like an unmade bed. He was wearing faded pajamas, an old robe with the ties trailing down his sides, and scuffed slippers. His hair looked like he had thrown it up in the air and jumped under it. His eyes were bleary, and he had the sleepy, dazed look of a man who had stayed out too late the night before and now had to pay the piper.

"Good morning," she called out brightly as she put the car in reverse and backed out of the drive. "Beautiful day, isn't it?"

Squinting painfully in the bright sunshine, Zack waved lamely and turned to go back into the house.

She grinned as the car started down the street. Yes, he must have had a big night.

The drive to the courthouse was enjoyable. The town was just the right size for her, and Toni found herself glad that she had picked this area to begin anew. She had chosen the town for no particular reason other than the fact that she had visited a friend here many years ago and had liked the region. It had worked out that the town was also the county seat for Pios County. She found herself wistfully regretting the fact that her friend had moved to California shortly after her visit; at least if Margo still lived here, she would have known someone in town.

Parking proved to be no problem, and shortly after seven thirty Toni was climbing the steep, polished marble stairs of the old courthouse. The building was at least a hundred years old, majestic in design and steeped in Texas history.

Even though the hour was early, the halls were already bustling with activity. The smell of fresh-brewed coffee permeated the air as Toni walked down the corridors looking for the room that housed the Small Claims Court, where she would be working this week.

When she had located the room, she cautiously peeked through the double oak doors and saw a woman dressed in a blue uniform standing behind the judge's bench sorting through some papers. She paused and tapped softly on the door.

Glancing up from her work, the woman smiled. "Yes?"

"Hi, I'm Toni Cameron—the new stenographer?"

"Oh, yes! Toni, come in."

By the time the hands of the old clock behind the judge's bench were approaching nine o'clock, Toni was seated behind her stenographic machine and eager to begin her new job. The fact that she had always possessed exceptional typing skills, along with an unusual love of the judicial system, had made her decide on her profession. Actually, she had dreamed of becoming a judge herself someday, but the idea of law school scared her, so she contented herself with just being in the courtroom with all the action.

The bailiff entered the courtroom and in a deep baritone voice commanded, "All rise."

The small gathering of people did as they were told as he continued. "Court of Pios County is now in session, the honorable Zackery Elsworth Tremayne presiding."

Toni's eyes shot up in surprise as the door to the judge's chambers opened and her new neighbor, looking considerably more presentable and a whole lot more intimidating in his long black robe than

33

when she had seen him earlier in the morning, entered the courtroom.

"You may be seated." Zack picked up a folder of papers lying before him and opened it. "Morgan versus Parks." He paused as he noticed Toni's presence in the room for the first time. A flicker of surprise registered on his face, then he flashed her that cute smile he had before he quickly turned his attention back to his papers.

The morning flew by with amazing rapidity, and Toni was almost disappointed when the noon recess was called. The cases she had heard had been interesting and varied, and she had been completely engrossed in her work.

Somehow, her new neighbor's being a judge still surprised her. Not only was he a judge, he seemed to be a very good one, intent on hearing all the facts of each case no matter how lengthy and how boring they might be.

Walking out into the corridor, she paused and tried to decide which direction the coffee machine would be in. She was not particularly hungry, so she decided to eat the apple she had stuck in her purse that morning and have a cup of coffee during her break.

Locating the women's room, she washed her hands and retouched her makeup, then went in search of the coffee and a comfortable chair.

The vending machines proved to be downstairs, and a long line had already formed in front of them. The smell of sandwiches being heated in microwaves filled the air as she stood and waited her turn.

"I don't know why I put myself through this everyday," the flashy blonde ahead of her muttered as she withdrew a filter-tip cigarette from her purse and lit it. Inhaling deeply, she grumbled again. "The sandwiches taste like they're made out of goat meat when you finally get them."

Toni smiled faintly. "That bad, huh?"

The woman eyed her contemplatively. "You're new around here, aren't you?"

"Yes, this is my first day."

"Then take a tip from me, kid. Stay away from the pastrami. It'll kill you."

A few minutes later, the line seemed to have ceased moving at all, so Toni dropped out and decided to try for coffee again a little later. She found a deserted chair in a quiet corner out in the corridor, where she ate her apple and read the newest issue of *Vogue,* which she had bought earlier.

The crowd around the vending machines had finally cleared out when she rose thirty minutes later and rummaged around in her purse for change.

"Please, allow me."

Toni glanced up to see Zack grinning at her, and her pulse suddenly accelerated for no apparent reason. She certainly hoped she wasn't going to develop a case of adoration for him just because she had always had a thing for judges! she thought irritably. A case of hero worship would be the last thing she needed to complicate her life right now.

"Hi!"

"Hi. Cream or sugar?"

"No, black."

Zack dropped a couple of quarters into the machine and punched a button. A paper cup dropped down and immediately began filling with coffee. "Want to hear how surprised I was at seeing you there in my courtroom this morning?" he prompted.

Toni grinned at him. "I'll bet you weren't half as surprised as I was when I saw you take the bench. Why didn't you tell me you were a judge?"

"Why didn't you tell me you were a stenographer?" he countered.

They both laughed. "I suppose one doesn't run around announcing their profession to their new neighbors, do they?"

"I suppose not." He handed her a cup of coffee and inserted two more coins into the machine. "How was your first night in your new home?"

Her mind immediately conjured up the strange scene in his backyard, but she quickly discarded any idea she might have of telling him about it. "Uh, fine. And how was your appointment?"

"Okay." He smiled and picked up his cup and took a cautious sip. "Things going all right on your first day?"

"So far, so good."

"Well"—he glanced at his watch; Toni noticed it was a very attractive gold Rolex—"I have to run."

"It was nice to see you again," she said sincerely. "See you in court."

He smiled at her again, and she noticed the small dimple on his left cheek again. The unbidden notion that it looked very kissable shot through her mind. She chastised herself immediately for her errant thoughts as he said good-bye, then turned and disappeared back down the corridor as quickly as he had appeared.

Good heavens! She had been so flustered, she hadn't even thanked him for the coffee, she thought irritably.

The afternoon didn't go by nearly as fast as the morning had, but still the day seemed short. She left the courthouse late that afternoon, stopped by a market to purchase a few groceries, then made her way home through the evening rush-hour traffic.

As she stepped out of her car, her eyes unwillingly wandered over to Zack's backyard. She paused and bit her lower lip thoughtfully. Switching the grocery sack to her other arm, she glanced toward his drive cautiously. The Mazda wasn't in the driveway, so he must not be home yet.

Then, before she lost her nerve, she cast one more apprehensive glance around and hurriedly stepped over the hedge and headed around the corner of his house.

This was silly, and she knew it. But if there had been something in his backyard last night, it surely would have left some sort of indication that it had been there; something that big couldn't just come and go and not leave a sign of its visit. If she couldn't find anything unusual, then she would know for sure that it had all been an illusion, and she would dismiss it from her mind once and for all.

Setting her sack down beside the barbecue grill, she bent over and began to carefully examine the area where she thought the object had appeared.

There was nothing irregular there at all. The grass was a lush green, with no evidence of having been exposed to any sort of heat. She had once read an article on flying saucers that said they sometimes radiated great heat; the correspondent told stories of various injuries, ranging from eye damage, burns, radioactivity, partial or temporary paralysis, and various types of physiological disturbances that had occurred in people who had had extraterrestrial sightings.

She shuddered and quickly withdrew her hand from the ground at the thought of radioactivity.

The article had also said that often there was a repulsive odor, like rotten garbage, that lingered for hours after one of their visits. She sniffed the air apprehensively, but there was nothing in the air but the pleasant scent of a lilac bush blooming next to Zack's back porch.

Dropping to her knees, she began to crawl slowly around the perimeter of the yard, pausing to closely inspect the leaves on the bushes for any signs of searing or wind damage. Again, there was nothing to indicate any visitors from outer space.

So preoccupied was she with her mission, she failed to hear the car pull up in the drive.

Minutes later, she had completely circled the yard and was now crawling around the barbecue grill to see if there was anything out of the ordinary there. For some reason, the thing had expressed a great amount of interest in this particular item. Granted, she would have been a little curious about it herself if she hadn't have known what it was.

She lay down flat on her back and stared at the body of the grill. Apparently this had been a home project on Zack's part in his high school days, because it did look rather strange. The round, flat, saucer-shaped kettle had a huge smokestack and sat on four spindly legs that looked almost anorexic. He had not painted it the usual black, but instead had chosen a flamboyant bright red to grace his new creation. No doubt he was proud of it, but it was very funny-looking, even to this earthling's untrained eye.

The sound of someone clearing his throat caused her to quickly snap out of her musings. From her position on the ground, she could see a pair of expensive, immaculately polished men's loafers next to her, and she felt her heart sink as she raised her eyes sheepishly to meet Zack's puzzled stare.

"Oh, hi." She waved at him limply.

He hesitantly waved back. "Hi."

"You're home a little early, aren't you?"

"A little. Are you all right?"

"Sure. Why?"

"You're lying on the ground."

"I know."

"Are you hurt?"

"No, why?"

He knelt down beside her. "No reason. I was just curious about why you were out here lying under my barbecue grill."

Springing to her feet guiltily, she wiped off the seat of her skirt and felt her face flaming with color. "Oh, that. Well." She knew she had to think fast, but her mind wouldn't cooperate. "I was just resting a little before I went home." She grinned weakly. "I hope you don't mind. You have a lovely backyard."

"No. No, I don't mind at all. But wouldn't you rather come up on the porch and rest? I could get us something cold to drink."

"No, no thanks," she refused hastily. "I really have to go in now."

She snatched up the discarded sack of groceries and rushed over to the hedge. "Oh, by the way, thanks a lot for the coffee this morning," she tossed over her shoulder as she lifted up her skirt and straddled the hedge carefully so as not to snag her pantyhose.

Zack watched with anticipation as a slender expanse of leg was bared, then modestly covered back up again.

"My pleasure," he replied.

He stood in his yard with a mystified frown on his face as she scurried up the side porch, unlocked the door, and slammed into her house.

CHAPTER THREE

The following weeks passed swiftly, and life began to settle down to a normal pattern. She loved her job, and she was sure it would only be a matter of time before her loneliness for Skip was a thing of the past.

Somehow, he had found out she was living in Texas, and he had called to see how she was doing. The sound of his familiar voice had brought a fresh round of pain surging through her heart, but when the brief, stilted conversation had ended, she was still relieved that the affair was over.

She had seen very little of her new neighbor in the previous two weeks. She had only been in Judge Tremayne's courtroom twice since she had started work, and since he was practically never home, their paths rarely crossed.

Now that she was finally unpacked and more organized, today would be a good time to repair the damage she had done to his flower bed, she thought matter-of-factly as she stood at the kitchen window Saturday morning and drank coffee. The two deep tire ruts running through Zack's smashed petunia beds were a real eyesore in his otherwise immaculate yard.

He had been very nice and had not said one thing about restoring the flower bed the few times they had talked, but she really felt she should do something about putting it back in order.

A quick trip to the area nursery provided her with the plants she needed to complete the job, and by ten o'clock she was dressed in an old pair of shorts and a halter top busily digging in the warm Texas soil.

Evidently, Zack was still asleep, she mused as her hands energetically tore away the old plants and tossed them aside. And no wonder. The hours he kept would be exhausting to anyone. She had heard of carefree bachelors, but Zack Tremayne was a Superman when it came to his social calendar.

Not that it was any of her business what he did, but living right next door to him, it wasn't hard to keep track of his irregular hours of coming and going.

And the women she had seen going in and out of his house! Whew! They ranged from sophisticated to questionable, in her opinion.

Many nights she had heard the tinkle of ice in glasses and feminine laughter floating out the open living-room window next door as she lay in her bed and tried to get to sleep.

But it was no wonder that he attracted the ladies. He was young, uncommonly nice-looking, sexy, and highly successful.

She even had to admit she was beginning to feel a

certain attraction to him herself, which she found surprising.

In a way, it was an encouraging sign, maybe she was finally getting over Skip. But the last thing she needed was to get involved with a man like Zack, a man who was *obviously* enjoying his freedom.

She had to laugh at her wild imagination, and it suddenly occurred to her that it felt good to laugh again, even if it was at herself.

What in the world had ever made her think Zack Tremayne would be the least bit interested in her in the first place? Although he had been extremely nice to her on their chance meetings, he had never indicated that he wanted to go out with her, let alone get serious about her!

But regardless of how he felt, he had been a good neighbor, and she couldn't complain. She knew he had to be wondering about her after catching her lying under his barbecue grill.

The sound of a screen door banging shut broke into her thoughts. She glanced up and saw Zack stepping off his porch with a cup of coffee in his hand. Fresh from his morning shower, he was dressed in a pair of blue cutoff denims and a white T-shirt that said "Here comes da judge."

"Good morning."

"Hi!"

He surveyed her busy hands. "What's up?"

"Not much. I just thought this would be a good time to work on your flower bed."

Zack yawned and reached up to rub the kinks out of the back of his neck. "That's awfully nice of you,

43

but it isn't necessary. I was going to take care of that myself."

"You shouldn't have to," she dismissed brightly. "I was the one who tore it up."

"Well, I suppose it would go more quickly if we both worked at it." He set his coffee cup down on the ground. "Move over, and I'll give you a hand."

For the next hour they worked alongside each other and chatted first about one thing and then another. She found him to be a very pleasant person, highly intelligent, and with a sense of humor that had her giggling like a schoolgirl from time to time.

". . . and so I asked the defendant why she had spit in the man's face, torn his shirt off, and broken his collector's album of the Beatles over his head, and she told me it was none of my business!" Zack related as he sat back on his heels and rested for a moment.

"And what did you say?" Toni asked, laughing.

"I told her it *was* my business, and then I ordered judgment for plaintiff."

"You didn't!"

"Well, my judgment wasn't based solely on her nasty attitude," he admitted with a chuckle. "The plaintiff had a strong case in his favor."

Toni laughed again, then paused and looked at him, undisguised admiration shining in her eyes now. "You must have a very interesting job." She sighed.

"Yeah, I kind of like it," he admitted.

"Are there any other judges in your family?"

"Yes, my father, and my grandfather, and his father." He grinned. "It's a good thing I like what I do, because I was doomed to follow in their footsteps."

She sighed again and went back to puttering with the new plants. "I thought I wanted to be a judge at one time."

"Oh? Why didn't you?"

"Oh, law school sort of scared me, and I really like being a court stenographer. I think my parents were disappointed that I didn't go on with my education," she confided. "They say I don't have enough get up and go, but that isn't true. I just believe a person has to do what makes them happy, not what someone else wants them to do."

"I agree." He handed her a trowel and wiped his hands on the side of his shorts. "You seem like a pretty smart lady."

"Hah, no, I'm not smart," she confessed, thinking about all the costly mistakes she had made in her life. "But I'm getting more experienced every day."

"Well." Zack stood up and reached for his discarded coffee cup. "It's been good visiting with you again. I'm afraid I have to desert you now. I just have time to mow my lawn, then keep a tennis appointment at one."

She wondered if it was the racy blonde or the flamboyant redhead who would have the pleasure of his company today. "That's okay. I appreciate your help." She stood up and dusted off her hands. "It looks pretty good, doesn't it?"

He surveyed the colorful flower bed with a critical eye. "Yeah, it does. Even better than before," he decided.

He helped her gather up her tools and then walked over to the hedge with her. "Your lawn always looks nice," she complimented. "I don't know where you find the time to keep it in such good shape." And that was the truth, the whole truth, and nothing but the truth; she really didn't know how he did it with his schedule.

"Thanks. I like working in the yard."

They paused at the hedge, and she glanced over his shoulder into his backyard. For a moment, she could still see the strange spaceship hovering . . . glowing. . . .

"That's a nice barbecue grill," she murmured, standing on her tiptoes now to see around his large bulk. Her eyes studied the bright red object intently.

"You think so?" He turned and grinned proudly. "I made that myself in shop when I was a senior in high school."

"No kidding? I don't think I've ever seen one quite like it," she mused. "The legs are so"—she groped for the right word to describe the emaciated gobs of iron—"so creative."

"Yeah." His gaze traveled wistfully over what he obviously considered to be a magnificent work of art. "I was about out of material when I got to the legs, but I think they look all right, don't you?"

"Oh, yes. They're very nice." If—and it was still a big if in her mind—she actually *had* seen something in his backyard that night two weeks ago, then for some reason that thing had been interested in his grill, she was nearly sure of it. But why?

Noting her unusual preoccupation with his grill,

he turned around more fully and followed her gaze with bewilderment. "Something wrong?"

"Wrong?" She quickly blinked to shake her stupor. "Oh, no. I was just looking at your backyard. It's nice."

Nice? He viewed the yard suspiciously. Why was it she kept mentioning his backyard? And now that he thought about it, what was the real reason she had been lying under the barbecue grill that day two weeks ago?

"Yeah, thanks. Yours is nice, too." Actually, both yards were well kept and unusually attractive. Why was she so hung up on his? She seemed like such a nice girl, yet he was beginning to wonder if she was just a little eccentric—or just downright weird.

"Have you ever seen anything strange in it?" she ventured hesitantly.

"Strange?" He looked over his shoulder cautiously. "No. What do you mean, strange?"

"You've never noticed anything . . . big . . . and sort of glowing?" She wasn't about to mention the saucer, but maybe he had seen one himself and would bring up the subject.

His eyes grew a fraction wider. "Big and glowing?" For courtesy's sake, he pretended to think about it for a moment, but felt like an absolute fool for doing so. Of course he hadn't seen anything big and glowing in his backyard! "No, I haven't. Have you?" he asked reluctantly.

"No!" Her denial shot out like a bullet.

He looked at her oddly. "Then why do you ask?"

"Oh, no reason." As quickly as she had brought it up, she suddenly seemed to lose all interest in the subject, and she stepped lithely over the hedge and turned around to smile at him. "Hope you beat the socks off your opponent today."

"Uh—yeah, thanks."

A moment later, she had disappeared around the corner of her house, leaving him wondering what in the world she had been babbling about.

Bananas. That's what she had to be!

Saturday tennis had turned into dinner, and dinner into another late night, Toni thought sourly a couple of days later, and here it was Monday with no letup in sight for His Honor.

She sighed enviously as she proceeded to get ready for bed after another long and exceedingly dull evening. She'd sure like to know what vitamins Zackery took.

Around five, she had heard Zack's car roar up the drive, and he had disappeared into the house for thirty minutes. She had been eating her dinner when she saw him reappear, dressed in a white dinner jacket and black tie. He looked exceptionally handsome. Not that he didn't look that way most of the time. She had no trouble understanding why he seemed to have his choice of female companionship.

The evening had dragged on for her, so by the time the ten o'clock news had come on television, she was ready to call it a night.

For a brief moment she let herself play a harmless little game of what if, as she sat in the window seat and brushed her hair the perfunctory hundred strokes.

What if tonight she were the one out with the

48

Honorable Judge Zackery Elsworth Tremayne, and they were enjoying a lovely dinner together? He would sit and gaze with adoration into her sultry eyes, while she totally captivated him with her magnetic charm. Then they would dance the night away, their steps lighter than the brush of a butterfly's wing on a delicate rose. He would be attentive, devastatingly virile, and totally absorbed in her loveliness. She would laugh and be so utterly fascinating that by the end of the evening, he would be left wondering how he had ever lived until she had come into his life. And when it came time to part, his sensuous, smoldering gaze would tell her that their time was not over yet—there was more to come, if she wanted it to. . . .

The phone interrupted her meandering thoughts. Still in a dreamy state, she picked up the receiver by her bedside. "Hello."

"Hi! Toni?"

Toni's pulse did a queer little flip-flop at the unexpected sound of his voice. "Yes—Zack?"

"Yeah, hey, I hate to bother you, but I was wondering if you could do me a little favor?"

She sat up a little straighter. "Sure, what is it?"

"You're going to have to speak up a little," he pleaded. The loud background music at the country club made it difficult for him to hear.

"Yes, I'd be glad to do you a favor. What is it?" she repeated loudly.

"I think I forgot to turn my oven off before I left," he confessed. "And it just occurred to me, I'll probably be getting home rather late, and I hate to leave it on all that time. Would you mind running over and turning it off for me?"

Turn off his oven? Her overinflated ego wilted rapidly. Well, turning off his oven was sure a far cry from dancing with him on butterfly wings all night, she thought wistfully, but of course she would be happy to help him. "Sure, Zack. I'll be glad to."

"You're a honey. Thanks a lot." After a hurried explanation of where he kept the extra key, the resounding click of the phone assured her that he was going back to whatever he had been doing with an unburdened mind.

Grumbling under her breath about the unfairness of life, she slipped on her robe and slippers and padded across the living-room floor.

She was sure there had to be a better way to spend an evening than tending to one's neighbor's oven while he was off, gosh knows where, whoop-dee-doing it up!

It was a clear, balmy night as she stepped out onto the side porch and fastened the tie of her robe. The Big Dipper and the Milky Way were strung brightly across the sky as she glanced upward. An occasional light glowed softly in her neighbors' windows, but other than the sound of a dog barking somewhere in the distance, the neighborhood had a sleepy, peaceful air about it.

Stepping down the concrete steps, she headed for the hedge, and in a few moments she was rounding the corner of Zack's house.

Then she came to a sudden, screeching halt.

Her hand shot up to stifle a scream that was

threatening to fill the air as she hurriedly retreated to the safety of the shadow of the house.

It was there again.

Moving so silently that not a leaf on the trees fluttered was a glowing object floating slowly across the housetops, approaching Zack's backyard.

She felt her heart race up to her throat and threaten to cut off her supply of air; she forced herself to take a deep breath and try to gain control of her senses.

Be calm, Toni. This is only another illusion.

Granted, she was more relaxed and rested than when she had thought she had seen it the first time, but maybe her mind was still trying to play tricks on her. That was it. She wasn't seeing a flying saucer at all. She only *thought* she was. Taking another deep breath, she edged over a fraction and cautiously poked one eye around the corner.

Oh, drizzlin's! It was not an illusion! It was there! Only this time, it was a much larger craft than the one she had seen earlier.

At first glance it seemed to be looking for a place to touch down as it crept soundlessly across the treetops and power lines. The lights on the ship were all pointing downward—brilliant yellows and oranges and reds, as if in search of something.

The sheer size of this vessel was overwhelming. It seemed to be well over eighty feet in diameter, and it had a solid, shiny metallic look about it. As she watched, it continued to glide quietly in the darkness like some sort of evil creature that was looking for trouble.

By now it was centered exactly over Zack's backyard, where it suddenly stopped completely. She watched with bated breath as it hovered motionless for a good five minutes, then slowly began to descend to the ground next to the barbecue grill. Toni wasn't sure if it had actually touched the earth, but immediately following its descent, the lights on the craft flickered and dimmed as if a great amount of power had been used.

Still, the glare from the object was so great she couldn't be sure if it actually had landed or not, and if it had, she knew it would nearly be filling the entire area with its presence.

A few moments later, her suspicions were confirmed as the ship settled gently onto the grass and became ominously still.

By now her legs were threatening to buckle under her as she brought her hand up to cover her mouth. The neighborhood had suddenly grown so quiet, she could have heard a pin drop. Even the dogs had ceased their persistent barking.

She *couldn't* be the only one seeing this strange thing this time! It was too big. Someone had to be witnessing it along with her! She prayed that if it were really there, and not some wild figment of her imagination, that would be the case.

For twenty long, agonizing minutes, the craft sat perfectly motionless. Its lights were now lowered to a dim glow. Not only was Toni afraid to move from her hiding place, but the vessel had her rooted to the spot with fascination. During her periodic cautious peeks around the corner, she had seen no movement in or around the object. To her immense relief, no little green men or frightfully ugly one-eyed creatures came out of the craft to attack her.

Just when she was positive she could stand the suspense no longer, a hatch on the bottom of the ship suddenly opened, and a strange armlike object emerged. The arm had a bright green ball on the end of it, and to her surprise it went immediately to the barbecue grill and began exploring it. Running over every square inch of the grill, it lingered at times, then moved on. She couldn't be sure, but the ball looked as if it had an eye on the bottom of it.

After ten minutes of intense, close scrutiny of the grill, the ball retracted slowly back into the hatch, and it closed.

Another few minutes passed; then the object began to rise. As it came off the ground, Toni could see three massive legs with lights on them; she assumed they were the landing gear that she had been unable to detect earlier. She watched as the vessel reached a height of approximately three hundred and fifty feet; then the legs retracted inside the ship, and it shot upward in a horizontal position and began to pick up speed.

Within seconds, it had disappeared totally from her sight, swallowed up in the starry heavens.

Still unable to move, her gaze continued to span the sky as she followed its path, reluctant for some strange reason to let it go.

Dew had begun to gather on the newly mowed grass, and it was getting cooler now. She felt herself begin to tremble violently as she drew her flimsy housecoat up closer to her neck.

Its speed had been awesome.

As if in a daze, she felt her feet begin to move, taking her in the direction of her house as she continued to cast wondering glances over her shoulder.

Not more than thirty-five minutes had passed since it all began, but it seemed much longer.

How she got there, she couldn't remember, but an hour later she was sitting on her side porch staring up at the sky. The Big Dipper was still there, bright and beautiful, and the Milky Way looked exactly the same as it had earlier. But she felt different somehow: strange and unsettled.

What was out there?

Another planet with a race so advanced in technology that it could silently invade the earth with vessels unbelievable in size and never leave a trace? Or were they, as some people believed, not spaceships from other planets but vessels of terrestrial origin that came from a subterranean race dwelling within the center of the earth itself?

Her gaze remained riveted upward. Who were they, and what in heaven's name did they want with Zack's barbecue grill?

She let out a long, weary sigh. Even more disturbing, what would Zack say when he came home and found his oven still on?

CHAPTER FOUR

By the time Zack's car turned down Fallow Lane, it was close to midnight. Toni was still rooted to her spot on the porch, waiting for him to get home.

She knew he would never believe her when she told him what she had seen, not once, but twice. But she still felt she had to confide in someone, and Zack was the only one she knew well enough to confess such an oddity.

She could only hope he was alone.

Naturally, he wasn't.

The Mazda pulled into the drive, and even before he turned the motor off, Toni could hear the sound of feminine laughter.

The judge must have said something pretty funny because the woman was still giggling as he walked around to the passenger side of the car and opened her door.

Toni sat in the shadows and watched as they proceeded up the drive and disappeared into the house a few moments later.

She was bursting to tell him her news, and yet she knew she shouldn't interrupt his evening. Not only would that be impolite, it would probably annoy him, and she needed him to be in the best possible mood when she told him about the flying saucer.

Biting her lip thoughtfully, she watched the light in his living room come on and heard the sound of music filtering softly out the open window.

Bach, she thought pleasantly. And one of her favorite pieces, too. She closed her eyes and began to absently hum along with the haunting melody under her breath.

Zack walked over to open the window to let in a little more fresh air when his eyes caught sight of Toni on her porch. He leaned forward and tried to make out what she was doing at that hour of the night sitting in the dark in her nightgown.

Humming along with his music. That's what she was doing. Sitting in the dark, humming.

Strange.

He adjusted the window, then turned his attention back to his guest.

Toni snapped out of her dreamy reverie. Rats! What was she doing? She should be thinking of some way to talk to him in private instead of sitting out here in the dark, humming. She rose slowly to her feet. Somehow, she had to get his attention.

Creeping over to the hedge, she carefully stepped over. Glancing about apprehensively, she edged around the corner of the house and paused at his back door. If she could manage to capture his attention without arousing his date's suspicion, then she could tell him about the flying saucer and get it off her mind. Maybe he would have some logical explanation as to why she had seen what she had.

Crouching down, she tiptoed back around the

house and stopped directly under the open window of his living room. Gradually, she peeked up over the ledge to see what they were doing. She felt like such a sneak, and if anyone saw her she would die, not to mention get arrested for being a peeping Tom, but she couldn't take the chance of interrupting him in the middle of some, heaven forbid, romantic interlude. She instantly felt squeamish at that thought, and she was immensely relieved to see that he was standing next to the fireplace talking, while his date was safely seated across the room on the sofa.

Good. Now, if she could only get his attention without the woman noticing.

Jumping up and down, she energetically waved her arms back and forth, praying he would look up and see her. But he was more interested in the topic of discussion than he was in looking out the window and, after a couple of minutes of frantically gesturing with no results, Toni decided she was going to have to try another tactic.

But what? She couldn't just march up to the door in her nightgown and ask if he could come out in the yard for a few minutes. He would think she was crazy.

She couldn't throw a rock through the open window because that would attract the redhead's attention—redhead!

He was with *her* again. Sheesh! What could he possibly see in her? she wondered irritably. This was the second time this week he had taken her out.

Jerking her thoughts back to her immediate problem, she bit her lower lip thoughtfully once more.

If she were really careful, she could stick her hand in the window and wave it around to get his attention. The redhead's back was to her, so that just might work.

Cautiously, she checked to see if the woman was still on the sofa—she was; then before she lost her nerve, she rammed her hand through the open window and wiggled her fingers briskly, then back and forth rapidly.

Zack was about to make a comment when the fingers shot through the window and began their frenzied movement. For a moment he was so stunned by the unexpected intrusion that he fell into a stunned silence.

"And Daddy said what?" the redhead prompted expectantly.

Zack's eyes flew up to the window, and he saw Toni jumping up and down, waving to him.

"Uh—he said—"

The fingers agitatedly motioned for him to retain his composure.

"He said what, darling?" the woman persisted.

"Uh, he said that it wasn't anything to worry about, and he would take care of it," Zack murmured as he managed to regain his voice.

The woman's gaze fastened on the glass she was holding. "That sounds like Daddy. Isn't he precious?"

"Yes, I think a lot of your father." Zack frowned and cocked an inquisitive brow toward the open window.

"You know, Zack, Daddy is very proud of you.

He even predicts you'll be joining him in the Supreme Court someday."

There was only one finger at the window now, and it was beckoning to him pleadingly.

"That's something to think about," Zack conceded quickly. "Uh—would you excuse me for a moment, Karol?"

"Certainly. If you don't mind, I'll just use your bathroom to freshen up a bit."

"No, go right ahead. I'll only be a moment."

Karol disappeared down the hallway as Zack rushed through the kitchen and cracked the door to his back porch open a fraction.

Toni was standing there, an apologetic smile on her face.

"Yes?" He peeked out at her guardedly.

"Hi—I hope I'm not disturbing anything important."

His puzzled gaze surveyed her standing barefooted before him in her gown and housecoat. "Is something wrong?"

"No, except I didn't turn your oven off."

"I noticed that." He looked a little perturbed at her incompetence.

"Aren't you going to ask me why I didn't?" she prompted, hoping he would give her a reason to tell him about the saucer.

He cast a worried glance over his shoulder. "It doesn't matter now. I'm home." He couldn't help but notice how disappointed she looked that he wasn't more inquisitive, so he decided to chance a few more moments with her. "Okay, why didn't you turn the oven off?"

Well, thank goodness he took the bait. "Uh—do you suppose I could have a few minutes with you?" She peered around him warily. "Alone?"

"Can't it wait?" he asked in a hushed voice, glancing worriedly over his shoulder for the second time.

"No," she whispered urgently. "It's very important that I talk to you right now."

"Well, okay," he conceded, slipping out the back door quietly. "But make it snappy. I have company." He couldn't imagine why she would have been jumping up and down in front of his window in her housecoat at midnight, insisting on talking to him; but then, she hadn't been able to give a satisfactory reason as to why she had been lying under his barbecue grill, either.

He was really beginning to wonder about her.

The screen door banged shut behind him as he stepped out onto the darkened porch. "What's up?"

The hair on the back of her neck was what was up, she wanted to say, but instead she cleared her throat nervously. "The reason I didn't turn off your oven was because I was—distracted by something."

"Oh?"

"Yes."

He nodded agreeably. "As I said, that's all right. I've already taken care of it."

"Don't you want to know what I was distracted by?"

No, actually, he didn't. At the moment all he wanted to do was get back to his company before she found him lurking around the porch with a half-dressed woman. "Whatever it was, I'm sure you had a good reason."

"I sure did. It was big—and glowing," she blurted. She held her breath as she watched his face for signs of reaction to her bewildering confession. She glanced around nervously. "And it was in your backyard."

For a moment his polite smile froze on his lips. "What was?"

She edged a step closer to him for fear they might be inadvertently overheard. "You're not going to believe this, but I think I saw a flying saucer in your backyard tonight," she confessed in a frenzied whisper.

"Right." The smile was still there, but his next words were a little stilted. "A flying saucer? In my backyard."

"Yes!" she said breathlessly. "Can you believe it? And you want to hear something really crazy?"

"As if that isn't?"

"No, of course not. I really saw one!" she insisted, then she lowered her voice even more. "I think it's after your barbecue grill!"

His face now registered the reaction of shock that she had expected. "My barbecue grill!"

Hah! Now she really had his full attention!

"You do believe in flying saucers?" she prompted expectantly. "Don't you?"

"No," he stated emphatically.

Her face fell.

Why he should suddenly feel a surge of tender protectiveness toward her he wasn't sure, but strangely, he did.

She stood before him in the moonlight, shivering like a wet puppy in the cool evening air, pale and frightened, trying to convince him she had seen a flying saucer. Not only that, it was supposedly after his barbecue grill to boot.

There was no longer any doubt in his mind. This woman was having some sort of emotional crisis in her life, and as far as he could tell, she had no close family nearby to help her. In fact, he seriously doubted that she had formed any friendships, other than the impersonal one they shared as neighbors, since she had moved here.

"Toni, look." He reached out and took her by her shoulders, aware for the first time of what a delicate, almost fragile frame she had. His hands seemed unusually large on her slender body as she trembled beneath his firm hold. "I don't know what you saw, but trust me, I don't think it was a flying saucer. Hey, are you sure you're all right?" he asked softly as he felt her trembling increase.

"Yes, I'm fine." There was no point in trying to convince him any further of what she had seen. He wasn't going to believe her anyway. "I'm sorry I bothered you," she apologized.

"You didn't bother me." He reached down and tipped her chin up to meet his concerned gaze. "But I'm beginning to worry about you."

"Me?" Her eyes flew up to meet his. "Why?"

He chose his next words carefully so as not to offend her. "I sense you're having a rough time in your life right now. Would you like to talk to me about it? Sometimes, even though another person can't help, it helps to share your misery," he encouraged. "And I'm a pretty good listener. Maybe together we can come up with a solution to whatever it is that's bothering you."

"You think I'm crazy, don't you?" she accused in a voice so low, he could hardly hear her.

And could she blame him? Her story *did* sound pretty farfetched.

"No, not at all. I just want to help you. Will you let me?"

She shook her head wordlessly, deeply touched by his offer. Skip had never wanted to hear her problems, much less offer to help her solve them, and here was Zack, a complete stranger, worried about her welfare.

"Are you sure there isn't something or someone you wouldn't like to talk to me about?" he prompted.

She shook her head once more.

"Well, the offer is always open," he murmured, giving her shoulders an assuring squeeze before he let her go. "Let me walk you home. You're cold."

"No, you have company," she declined softly.

"Karol would understand."

"No, thank you. I'll just run along." She didn't want Karol's sympathy, too!

"It would be no trouble." But his words were barely out of his mouth before Toni had disappeared from the porch and was stepping back over the hedge.

He shook his head worriedly as he watched her slip back to her house and huddle down on the old swing in the shadows of the porch. She was such a

strange mixture of woman: all soft and sweet smell-
ing—and very confused.

The sound of the chain creaking back and forth
was the only indication that she was there. He stood
for a moment, his mind going back over what she
had just babbled out to him. A flying saucer? He
chuckled softly, then sobered as his gaze sought the
perfectly normal, starry heavens.

His brow furrowed thoughtfully. He had never
personally believed in flying saucers, but he knew of
plenty of people who did.

What had she seen tonight that had made her
believe his barbecue grill was under alien surveillance? A plane? A helicopter? Perhaps a satellite or
a shooting star? He shook his head musingly and
turned back to open the screen door.

Ridiculous. There was nothing strange about his
barbecue grill. Unique, maybe, but strange—never.

But the incident had put a damper on his evening,
and it wasn't long after that that Toni heard his car
back out of his drive. She assumed he was going to
take Karol home.

She had no idea why she found such comfort in
that thought, but somehow she did.

If she's still in the swing when I get back, I'm
going over, Zack promised himself as he deposited
Karol at her front door twenty minutes later and
said a hurried good night. Toni could deny it all she
wanted, but something was upsetting her, and he
was going to get to the bottom of the story before he
went to bed.

The lights of the Mazda washed over her front

porch as he pulled back in the drive around one thirty. The swing was in the corner, well hidden by the old rose trellis, so it was impossible to see if she was still out there, but he sensed she was.

He got out of the car and closed the door softly. "Toni?" he called in a hushed whisper.

"Yes?" Deep within the shadows, the small voice answered quietly.

"Are you still up?"

"Yes." She had been lying down in the swing, thinking. At the sound of his voice, she sat up and straightened her hair.

"You care if I come over for a few minutes?"

"No, come on."

He hopped the hedge, and a few moments later he was sitting down next to her in the swing. "Hi."

"Hi."

"I've been worried about you."

"That's very nice of you, but I'm fine, really."

The chain squeaked as he began to slowly move the swing back and forth. "I thought you'd be in bed by now."

"No, I couldn't sleep."

"It's getting pretty late."

"I know."

"Nice night out."

"Yes, it's beautiful." The roses beside the house were spilling their fragrance into the night air, and she found herself thinking how pleasant it was to sit here beside him and talk. She always felt at ease with him, as if she could just be herself. It had never been that way with Skip. She had forever felt as if she were offending him in some way.

"I like the smell of roses, don't you?" he asked.

"Yes, very much."

They swung in silence for a few moments, each lost in the tranquil, sleepy sounds of the night. The neighborhood was dark and peaceful now.

"What did you do before you moved here, Toni?" Zack finally broke the compatible silence.

"Much the same as I do here. I was a court stenographer in Des Moines too."

"You like your work?"

"Very much."

"And your family?"

"I'm an only child with very middle-class, very typical parents. They worry about me a lot," she said thoughtfully. "But I suppose that's natural."

"Yes, I suppose so. My parents are the same way."

"Do you have brothers and sisters?"

"One younger sister, but she doesn't live here anymore. She got married and moved to Los Angeles last summer." Sighing, he locked his hands behind his head and stared up at the ceiling. "Our home was like something out of *Leave It to Beaver.*"

"Oh, that's nice. Mine was too."

"And what about the men in your life?" he asked lightly, turning his attention back to her.

He had decided that that was what was bothering her—it was the only other explanation he could think of, since she liked her job and apparently welcomed the recent move to Texas.

"I would be ashamed to discuss the scarcity of them in view of your active social life," she complained good-naturedly.

He grinned, and she could see the flash of white teeth in the darkness. "A lot of my social life falls under the heading of business," he defended.

"Well, a lot of my social life falls under the heading of Dullsville, U.S.A." she confessed. "I haven't really met anyone but you and Jim since I moved."

"Well, you've met the cream of the crop," he pointed out jokingly.

"Quality, not quantity, huh?"

He grinned again. "Something like that."

They continued swinging for a few moments without saying anything.

"What about before you moved here?" Zack persisted a few minutes later. "Was there a special man in your life before then?"

Toni had never discussed Skip with another person since the relationship had been dissolved. Many of her friends had encouraged her to open up and let her feelings out, but she had chosen to keep her grief to herself. After all, other than providing them with a juicy new tidbit of gossip to toss about, what could they have done? Not even her mother had been able to break her silence. But suddenly, a complete stranger was asking her about her life before Texas, and she found herself wanting to tell him about it.

"I lived with a man by the name of Skip Harden for two years prior to moving here," she said calmly. "I'm not proud of the fact, but I suppose when it comes right down to it, everyone has someone or something in their past that they would like to have the opportunity to do over again. I thought I loved Skip enough to commit myself to that kind of a relationship. I mistakenly reasoned that love was enough. Two years later, I found out it wasn't when I laid down an ultimatum, and he refused to marry me. It was just one of those unfortunate things that happen, and now it's over."

"I'm sorry. That must have been very hard on you emotionally," Zack consoled gently, not at all surprised to hear that's what had been bothering her.

"Yes, it was. But I'll get over it."

"You still love the guy?"

"I'm not really sure. For two years he was my whole life, and that isn't very easy to forget."

"Was there another woman involved in his decision?"

"No, or at least if there was, I never knew anything about it. Skip was just the sort of person who was terrified of legal commitments," she murmured. "In his own way, he loved me. I just wanted more."

"Where is he now?"

"Still in Des Moines. He has his own business there."

The old swing creaked back and forth soothingly.

"What about you?" she asked a few minutes later.

"What about me?"

"Any old live-in love affairs lurking around in your past?"

Zack chuckled. "Are you serious? I may be thirty-seven years old, but my mother would threaten to whip me if she even suspected I was living with anyone of the opposite sex."

Perhaps he wasn't living with anyone, but he certainly was never lacking for female companionship.

She was the one who had to laugh now. "You mean to tell me you're still afraid of your mother?"

"You bet. She can be hell on wheels when she gets on her moral high horse, and I don't want a lecture every time I go over there," Zack admitted without the slightest hesitation.

They both laughed now because Toni knew exactly what he was talking about. Her mother was the same way.

"Well, then, what about being in love? Surely you've been in love before."

"Now you're going to hear something crazy. No, I haven't," he confessed. "Oh, I've been 'in like' with a couple of women, and there was one whom I really respected and looked up to, but I never loved her."

She found that very hard to believe. "You mean with all these women parading through your life, there hasn't been one special one?"

"Hey." He reached over and pinched the tip of her nose playfully. "I grant you that it *may* seem like I'm the town stud, but I can assure you looks can be deceiving. There are a lot of women around my house, but it isn't always what my nosy neighbors think," he said teasingly.

"You mean a lot of it is actually business?" She knew she had no right to ask such a question, but it had slipped out before she knew it.

"Business, personal friendships, and would you believe some of my younger sister's friends still come to me for advice?"

"No, but I have to admit it sounds good." She

had no idea why she was gullible enough to believe that, but she did.

"Actually, I'm very much a gentleman," he murmured coaxingly.

She looked at him. "Gentleman or not, you're still looking for the right girl."

"No, not necessarily," he denied. "I'm very happy with the way my life is right now. If the right one comes along, fine, but if not, then I'll go on just like I am and be happy."

Toni leaned her head back against the swing and closed her eyes. That didn't surprise her. He was like all men—commitment was a dirty word they shied away from. "Well"—she yawned and sat up a few moments later, fatigue beginning to overtake her now—"I suppose I should be going inside. We both have to go to work tomorrow."

"Yeah, I have to be there early, but I wanted to make sure you were all right before I went in."

"That was very nice of you, but I'm fine, really."

He reached over and tipped her face up to meet his. "Are you sure?"

"Positive. I should have never mentioned the flying saucer to you in the first place."

"No, I'm glad you did, but I think after you get a good night's rest, you'll look back on the incident and realize what you saw was only a plane or something of that sort," he said comfortingly. "From what you tell me, you've been under a great deal of stress lately, and sometimes that makes our minds play funny little tricks on us."

"Yes, I know." Even in the dark, his eyes were beautiful, she thought absently. Sexy, bedroom eyes.

"Then you agree?"

"That I didn't see a flying saucer?"

"Yes."

She sighed and pulled her head away from his hand. "No, I'm almost positive that's what it was, but if you don't want to believe it, I understand."

"Toni!" Just when he had begun to think he was reaching her. "Come on. You didn't see a flying saucer! You saw a plane."

"No, it wasn't a plane. I think it was a flying saucer," she insisted. "But I could be wrong."

"Good—at least you admit you could be wrong."

"But I have to tell you, it wasn't the first time I saw it. Whatever it was, there was another one almost like it in your backyard two week ago." She might as well tell it all and get it over with. "That's when it first noticed your barbecue grill."

"Good Lord." He groaned and buried his hands in his hair. They were back to the barbecue grill again! *"If* there was something unusual in my backyard—and I'm not about to admit that I think there really was, except for the sake of argument—why in the world would it want my barbecue grill?"

"I don't know. Maybe because it's so funny looking," she hazarded a careful guess.

He bristled like an old porcupine at the suggestion. "Funny looking! What's funny looking about it?"

"Nothing, really. It's just not your normal, run-of-the-mill grill." She hedged for fear of hurting his feelings.

"I should say not." He sat up straighter and fidgeted with the cuffs on his shirt irritably. "It may not be a Weber, but I think it's pretty darn nice."

"I do, too," she agreed eagerly. "It's really nice; I didn't mean that. I only meant, you don't see one like it in every yard."

"I know. That's what I like about it." He ran his fingers through his hair once more. He couldn't believe he was sitting here actually defending his barbecue grill against an invasion from outer space.

"I know this is all hard to believe. I thought I had dreamed it myself, but when it came back tonight, I was almost certain it was real," she tried to justify her claim and apologize all at the same time.

He shook his head wordlessly. What could he say to a woman who had *obviously* popped her cork?

Deciding that he, too, had had more than he could take in one night, she stood up and prompted him to his feet. She knew how unnerving all this could be, and she couldn't blame him for being confused. "I know this is all very hard to absorb, but after you get a good night's sleep, you'll feel better," she said soothingly as she took his hand and led him to the hedge.

"But—"

"No buts. Just forget I said anything about it. I'm sure whatever it was has satisfied its curiosity, and it probably won't ever return. Although, come to think of it, it wasn't the same flying saucer that was here last time. This one was much bigger."

He looked at her vacantly. "Bigger?"

"Yes." She nodded solemnly. "Nearly twice the size."

"Oh, Lord."

"But don't worry about it," she said again. "I'm sure we'll probably never see it again."

"But—" Forget there was a flying saucer trying to steal his barbecue grill? She must be kidding. He cast a pitiful glance at his grill sitting tranquilly in his backyard. "But—"

"And, Zack, thanks for being such a good neighbor. I really appreciate it." She stood on tiptoe and kissed him lightly on the mouth. Gosh, he tasted even better than he looked.

She wasn't sure how it happened, but suddenly the kiss that had started out as an affectionate peck swiftly changed course on her.

Their mouths touched briefly, then all of a sudden they were kissing—really kissing. Her head grew light as her arms wound around his neck, and with a low groan he pulled her up closer to him.

The kiss continued to deepen until her knees grew weak. It was several long, incredibly spine-tingling moments before either one of them could summon up the courage to break the torrid embrace.

"Uh . . ." Zack's voice was shaky when they finally parted a few moments later. "I think you'd better go in before I make myself out to be a liar." The kiss had left him shaken and wondering what had hit him.

"About being a gentleman?"

"That's right—about being a gentleman." He leaned down and touched his lips to hers again gently. "Good night, my funny little neighbor."

"Good night, Zackery." She backed toward her house, reluctant to leave his company.

"Uh, Toni?"

"Yes?"

"Do you really think you saw a flying saucer?" he prompted. "I mean—are you positive?"

She nodded her head slowly up and down. She hated to upset him further, but after all, he had asked, and she wasn't about to lie to him. "Yes, I'm sure that's what it was, all right."

He was still standing at the hedge, stunned, as she slipped inside her house.

A flying saucer! His eyes searched the darkness helplessly. She had seen a flying saucer?

And it was after *his* grill?

CHAPTER FIVE

Yes, the more she thought about it, the more sure she was that what she had seen last night in Zack's backyard had indeed been a flying saucer.

But like thousands of others, she was going to have a hard time trying to convince anyone else of it.

She sat in the public library the following evening eagerly thumbing through articles on actual public sightings of unidentified flying objects. Book after book had been written on the puzzling subject, and she sat spellbound as she read them, one by one.

There were those who contended that the unexplained phenomena had been seen even as early as biblical days. Another report suggested it all actually began around 1947, when a businessman from Boise, Idaho, was flying his private plane, he encountered nine disk-shaped objects estimated to be traveling seventeen hundred miles per hour speeding by his window. The objects reportedly weaved in and out of the mountain peaks with great mobility and then disappeared.

According to the records, there reportedly have been significant UFO sightings over every major

American and European city and every major military installation around the world, including the American Strategic Command and various nuclear installations since that fateful day in June 1947. Consequently, the Air Technical Intelligence Center of the Air Force set up Project Bluebook, a program designed for high-priority, high-security investigation of reported flying saucers. Since then, literally thousands of people have reportedly witnessed the strange occurrences in the sky.

Something was up there, but exactly what?

Toni closed the last book slowly and sighed. Whatever these UFO's were, she had seen one of them, and even though he was going to think she was crazy, she had to go back over to Zack's this evening and talk to him. It wasn't the ideal solution to this sticky problem, but since she knew no one else in town who would listen to her, she would just have to take the chance that he would lend her his ear once more.

She thought about reporting the sightings to the proper authorities but quickly discarded that. She wasn't quite ready to face what would undoubtedly be a condescending attitude toward her. Zack might not believe her, but so far he had been kind about it.

She drummed her fingers thoughtfully on the table. Then again, he would probably strangle her if she showed up on his doorstep again. She had interrupted him and what's-her-name last night, and although he had been polite about her intrusion, he might not be as considerate if she did it again.

Actually, there was even a minuscule chance he wouldn't be doing anything this evening.

Minuscule, but not totally impossible.

Oh, well, she had to take the chance.

Scooping up the armful of books, she took them to the counter and applied for a library card.

Ten minutes later, she had the card plus the ammunition she needed to convince Zack she wasn't completely off her rocker. She dumped the books into the back seat of her car and started home.

It was a little after nine when she pulled into her drive and glanced hopefully in the direction of his house. Wonders of wonders, the Mazda was sitting in the drive. Of course, that didn't necessarily mean that he was home or alone, but it looked favorable.

She got out of the car and gathered up the books, still keeping a watchful eye on the residence next door. There was a soft light burning in the living room, but the window was closed. Since the weather had turned hot and sultry, he had probably turned the air conditioner on, she reasoned. Still, she wished the window were open so she could hear if he had company.

But surely he didn't. Even Superman had to rest occasionally.

A moment later, she found herself on his back porch trying to balance the cumbersome load of books and find a free hand with which to knock on the door.

The best way to handle this was with sheer finesse, she decided as she briskly rapped on the frame of the screen. When he opened the door, she wouldn't wait to be invited in. She couldn't take the chance that he would try to find an excuse to dismiss her and send her on her way before she had talked this baffling situation out with him.

No, she would simply breeze by him as if she were expected, and hope for the best.

She knocked again.

Maybe he wasn't home after all. Maybe ol' redhead what's-her-face had come by and picked him up this evening, and they had gone out together again. That idea annoyed her and she hammered louder. What he could possibly see in that woman was beyond her.

The sound of footsteps coming across the kitchen floor a few moments later laid to rest her fear that he wasn't home. Seconds later, the back door was cautiously opened a fraction.

"Yes?"

"Hi."

Recognizing his neighbor as the untimely intruder, Zack worriedly eyed the stack of books she was carrying as he opened the door a little farther. "Hi."

"Boy, I'm glad to see that you're home," Toni said with a sigh of relief as she hurriedly pushed her way by him and entered the kitchen. "For a minute there, I thought you had gone out again."

"No, I'm home, but—"

"Now, don't worry," she assured him as he shut the door and began to trail helplessly behind her. "I won't stay but a minute, but I stopped by the library on the way home from work this afternoon and picked up some books on the subject of—" She paused, debating whether to call them flying saucers in his presence. Last night he had made it clear he didn't believe in their existence. "You know what," she improvised quickly, "and I knew you would be interested in what I've learned."

"Toni, I—"

"Honest, I'll only take a few minutes of your time, Zack," she pleaded. "I just need someone to talk to. This whole thing has me unnerved—" Her voice broke off as she burst into the living room. "Oh, dear, I'm sorry. I didn't think you had company tonight."

The redhead was seated at a small table set for two, complete with fresh flowers and candles burning low in elegant crystal holders, sipping a glass of white wine.

Toni felt her heart sink and her face flood with color. Obviously, they were just about to have dinner, and she had interrupted them again.

Zack's guest glanced up in surprise at their hasty entrance and set her glass quickly down on the table. There was an appalling silence for a few moments as the three of them each waited for the other to speak. It was Zack who found his voice first.

"Uh, Karol, this is my next-door neighbor, Toni Cameron. Toni, Karol Massenburg."

Toni shifted the books around to one arm and smiled guiltily as she stepped over to take Karol's hand. "Hello, Karol. I'm sorry to disturb you. I didn't realize Zack had company."

Karol smiled politely. "It's quite all right."

"Well, I'll just be running along." Toni backed toward the safety of the doorway, still trying to juggle the mound of books she was holding.

Zack stepped forward just as they were all about

to tumble to the floor and quickly helped her redistribute her load.

"Thanks." She smiled up at him gratefully.

"Was there something important you needed to talk to me about?" he asked.

It was clear to Toni that he was only being polite, and she wouldn't dream of interfering with his evening. "No, nothing that can't wait."

As she backed toward the doorway once again, one of the books toppled off the stack and slid across the room in front of Karol's stylish alligator pumps.

Karol reached over and picked up the book and read the title with interest. *"Flying Saucers?"* She looked at Toni. "Are you interested in UFOs?"

Before she could assure her she most certainly was, Zack hurriedly intervened. "Uh, Toni's an amazing lady. She has a little bit of interest in all subjects." He shot Toni a warning look that said, *Don't start in on the flying saucers again!* "Let me help you to the door with those books."

It was plain he didn't want her discussing with Karol what she thought she had seen in his backyard. "Well, I find the subject interesting," Toni admitted, sending a resentful glare back in his direction.

"You know, it's strange, but I do, too," Karol confessed. "Once when I was in college, I did a paper on flying saucers. It was interesting and thought-provoking. Tell me, do you believe they actually exist, or do you think that they are experimental aircraft belonging to our government?"

"You know, I've thought a lot about that lately."

Toni maneuvered around a scowling Zack and sat down in the chair across from Karol. She peered at Karol anxiously. Maybe she had misjudged this woman completely; she might have a brain under all those flaming tresses after all! "But I really don't know. What do you think?"

"Now, Toni," Zack protested lamely, "Karol and I were about to have dinner—"

"I honestly don't know, either," Karol admitted, totally ignoring Zack's grumbling. "Zack, dear, where are your manners? Maybe Toni would like to join us in a glass of wine?"

"No, she wouldn't," Zack said quickly. "She has to be running along."

Toni looked at him sharply. "No, I don't. I mean, I could join you—if Karol doesn't mind." She *had* misjudged her. Here was a highly intelligent woman wanting to discuss something that was very close to Toni's heart at the moment.

"I don't mind at all," Karol assured her as she picked up the remaining books and began to thumb through them. "I find the subject of flying saucers simply fascinating, don't you, Zackery?"

"No, I don't believe in them myself," he grumbled as he poured a tulip-shaped goblet of Chablis and handed it to Toni.

She smiled at him sweetly and accepted the glass. She knew he wasn't overjoyed about her staying, but if Karol wanted to discuss UFO's with her, then she wanted to hear what she had to say.

"You know, I read an interesting theory about the big blackout along the whole eastern seaboard in the sixties," Karol mused. "You remember when the lights went out in New York City?"

Toni nodded. "Sure."

"They were never able to come up with a satisfactory reason as to why that blackout occurred, but there was supposedly a formation of flying saucers sighted over the city that night."

"No kidding?" Toni's eyes widened. "That was a horrible blackout. People were stuck in elevators and subways for hours."

"Yes, it was a frightening situation for many."

"It wasn't all that bad. A lot of babies were born nine months later," Zack quipped, slowly coming around to the fact that Toni was going to stay for a while.

"Zackery!" Karol gave him a reprimanding look, then went on with her observations. "Flying saucers are supposed to produce electromagnetic interferences of various kinds. They've reportedly been known to interrupt ignition systems, automobile lights, and radios, and to even turn off car engines. When the saucer has passed over, or shut off whatever directional power they have applied, the engines have restarted by themselves."

"But could they cause such a massive power outage as the one that occurred in New York?" Toni asked incredulously.

"Certainly not," Zack scoffed. "Ladies, I'm not saying there isn't something up there, but it has to be something our government doesn't want known, and if that's the case, then it has to be for defense purposes, and people ought to let the defense department do their job."

"But, Zack," Toni protested, "the sightings are being recorded in all climates and countries."

"The government gets around in strange places, Toni."

Karol shrugged. "Of course, it's only a theory concerning that particular blackout along the eastern seaboard, but who knows? In my research, I've read fascinating stories of people who say they have actually been abducted by the alien visitors and used for experimental purposes before they were released. And what about all those people every year who simply disappear off the face of the earth and are never heard from or seen again? What happens to those people?"

Toni shuddered at the thought. She had read those same stories. There were even people who had radiation burns and other horrifying side affects to substantiate their claims of having had close encounters. But still the public was skeptical.

"Some people disappear and are never heard from or seen again because that's the way they want it," Zack contended, "not because some flying saucer has come down and carried them away."

"Then you think that people who say they have seen a UFO are crazy?" Toni asked worriedly.

Zack's eyes softened. "No, I didn't mean that. I only meant that what they saw must have a reasonable explanation."

"Such as?"

"Optical illusions, weather balloons, experimental aircraft, conventional aircraft, atmospheric conditions, emotional stress—I could go on and on."

Emotional stress. There it was again. He thought

she was under some sort of emotional stress and was seeing things.

"Hey, look. We could sit here and debate the question all night and never come up with an answer that would suit all of us," he pleaded. "It's nearly ten o'clock, and we still haven't eaten yet. I'm hungry."

The night was not exactly going as planned, and he was tired of hearing two women chatter about the pros and cons of flying saucers.

Toni immediately jumped up from her place at the table, painfully aware that she had overstayed her welcome. "Oh, of course. How inconsiderate of me."

"Now, wait," Karol protested. "Don't go yet." She glanced at Zack expectantly. "Why, I'll bet Toni hasn't eaten yet, either, have you?"

"No, but I wouldn't dream of interfering with your evening." Toni shot a smile at her neighbor, knowing full well that Karol was going to insist she stay. "I'll just be running along."

"You wouldn't be interfering," Karol denied. "Would she, Zackery darling?"

Zack shrugged, resigned to the fact that no matter what he thought, he was probably going to be overruled anyway. "No, not at all. We would be happy to have you join us, Toni."

Well, as long as it was put that way, she saw no reason to decline the offer. And besides, she *was* getting hungry.

"That's very nice of you," she accepted gratefully. "But I insist on helping."

"There's no need—"

"No, really. I insist." She grinned at him. "What's on the menu?"

"Steaks."

"Is the grill ready?"

"Yes, *if* some little green men haven't come down and stolen it," he remarked dryly.

"Then I insist you let me cook them." She ignored the not-so-funny joke. She was aware that she had a perfectly sympathetic ear in Karol Massenburg, but for some reason she wasn't quite ready to let anyone other than Zack know about her own personal experience—at least, not yet.

"There is no need for that. I am perfectly capable of cooking our steaks."

But Toni wouldn't hear of it. "No, you've been so nice about me spoiling your evening, I insist on fixing our dinner. You and Karol just sit in here and enjoy yourselves while I grill the steaks." She turned to Karol. "How do you like yours cooked?"

"Rare."

"And yours?" She looked at Zack.

He shrugged. "Done."

"One rare and one done, coming right up!"

Toni scurried out to the kitchen, her mind still lingering on flying saucers. It was a stroke of luck to find someone as knowledgeable about the subject as Karol was, and she hoped during dinner that they could pursue the subject further. By then she might even be ready to confide in Karol about her own strange encounter.

An hour later, Toni and Karol were still chattering over their steaks while Zack sat quietly and ate his dinner. Toni noticed that he had barely said a word during the meal, and she became concerned.

"Is your steak all right?" she inquired pleasantly.

"It's fine," he said curtly.

She absently went back to the discussion of a well-publicized case several years ago concerning a couple who had reportedly had their car blocked on a road by a strange craft in September 1961, at which point they claimed to have lost control over their own volition. She opened one of the books she had brought over and began to read aloud. "The couple contended that five occupants of the craft had taken them into the alleged spacecraft, where they were given a complete medical examination and then released. They were able to clearly recall all but the two or so hours they had spent in the craft itself. That part of their story was incomplete, and it was not until two years later, when they both agreed to undergo hypnosis, that they learned what had occurred during that time."

"I remember the case well," Karol said enthusiastically. "They didn't tell anyone but close friends and relatives what had happened to them, but when the man began to experience health problems after the alleged incident, he decided to see if there was any emotional basis for the ulcer he was experiencing. He was referred to a psychiatrist, and only then did the true story about their encounter begin to unfold."

"How terrible for those people," Toni murmured. "It says here that the craft was disk-shaped with red lights and a double row of windows—and oh my gosh. Inside the windows they could see the silhouette of human-type figures . . . and later on they describe the occupants as being short, and all dressed alike with very large eyes and almost no nose and grayish skin."

Zack cleared his throat impatiently and pushed away from the table; half of his meal remained on the plate. "If you ladies will excuse me."

Karol glanced up at him. "Where are you going?"

"If you two insist on carrying on this discussion, I have some briefs to work on," he replied curtly.

Now Toni did feel bad. Not only had she barged in on him and completely ruined his evening with Karol, but she had dominated the entire meal with tales of flying saucers, which he clearly did not believe in.

She closed the book she had been reading from and immediately rose. She smiled her apology at Karol. "That won't be necessary, Zackery." She decided that from now on she would use his full name when addressing him, the same way Karol did. It sounded so much classier. "I really must be going now."

"Must you?" Zack nearly jumped across the table to assist in her departure.

She shot him a dirty look. "Sorry, but I really must."

"I wish you wouldn't. If Zackery's going to work on his stuffy old papers, you might as well stay. We can have coffee in the living room," Karol invited.

Well, there was one thing she was sure of. Zackery would not be working on his stuffy old papers if she cleared out of here. "No, I really must be going." She began to hurriedly gather up the books that were now scattered about the table.

"Do you need some help with those?" Zack offered, still obviously eager to see her go.

"No, thank you. I'll make it just fine." She said a hurried good night to Karol and started for the back door. Zack followed and courteously held the door open for her.

"You sure you don't need any help?"

"No. But Zack—" She paused and turned to look up at him. He was at least five inches taller than she was and definitely a very handsome man. For a moment she felt an unexplained wave of affection for him. Maybe it was because he was the only one she knew in town, or maybe it was just because he had been so nice to her. Whatever it was, she felt greatly indebted to him at that moment. "I'm really sorry about spoiling your evening. You should have just told me to go home."

"I wouldn't do that, and you didn't spoil my evening," he insisted, but she couldn't help but notice the look of genuine concern he was giving her. "I just hope you don't let this flying saucer thing get you down."

"I won't, and I'm sorry again if I bothered you."

He chuckled softly and reached out to tweak her nose, a habit that was beginning to become a ritual with him. "You're no bother. How many times do I have to tell you that?"

She grinned back at him and sighed. "Thanks. I don't want to be." For just a tiny moment, she forgot that Karol was in there waiting for him, but then she remembered her manners. "Karol's very nice."

"Yeah, she is. Maybe we can all do it again sometime." She knew he was teasing her now, but she didn't care. "Only next time, leave the flying saucer books at home and bring along a date."

"Okay. Will do." She winked at him playfully.

"Try and get a good night's sleep."

"I will." She turned and started down the steps, then turned once more to face him. "Oh, Zackery?"

"Yeah?"

"Now, don't get mad," she warned, "but to be on the safe side, I really think you should put your barbecue grill in the garage."

"Thanks, I'll think about it."

"Good night."

"Good night."

CHAPTER SIX

Well, why not take him up on his offer, even though she knew full well he had only been teasing her when he had suggested they get together again?

He hadn't exactly meant that *they* get together, but what the heck. Somehow she just knew that if she waited for Zackery Tremayne to ask her out, she might have a long wait.

Toni was still flirting with the idea of seizing the initiative and asking him out herself as she dawdled over coffee in the cafeteria the following morning; she saw him come in with two other men and take a seat across the room from her. It would be highly uncharacteristic of her to do such a brazen thing, but lately she hadn't been herself at all.

Her mother's favorite proverb suddenly popped to mind. "Nothing ventured, nothing gained."

If that were true, what would she have to lose?

It was all she could do to keep her eyes on the morning news and off the handsome picture he presented as he fell into a deep conversation with his colleagues. He was dressed in a pair of dark trousers, a pale green shirt, and a charcoal-gray sweater vest. The color of his shirt made his eyes look like two sparkling gems beneath his heavy brows as he talked and gestured with his hands about some point he was trying to make.

To be honest, it was all she could do to keep from outright staring at him.

For just a brief moment she tried to imagine what his eyes would be like if they were gazing into hers over candlelight and soft music—or passionately after just having made love to her. She felt a tiny knot in her stomach tighten. She could well imagine that a woman would be powerless if he decided to turn on his charm. She took another sip from her cup as her eyes peeked discreetly over the rim.

Yes, green was definitely his color.

"Ya through with that sugar, lady?" A burly arm reached in front of her and latched on to the container sitting before her.

"Yes, sure." She moved back as the arm zipped back under her nose and disappeared.

But then again, he looked great in blue, too. She absently went back to her daydreaming. Day before yesterday, he had worn a three-piece blue suit that had looked like a million dollars on him. And last week, he had worn a shade of brown that looked good enough to eat.

Would he think she was overstepping her bounds if she did suggest that they go out for dinner some night?

She sighed and let her gaze drop away reluctantly.

Probably. Zack didn't seem the type who would appreciate a woman asking him out. Oh, he would be polite, but he would make all kinds of excuses as to why he couldn't go. She knew the type well.

Now Skip, on the other hand, would not only have been elated at such an occurrence, but he would be bragging all over town about the fact that a woman had tried to put the make on him.

She laughed mirthlessly under her breath and reached for her purse to leave. But then, Skip was about as different in nature from Zackery as black was from white.

Zack left his table at about the same time Toni decided to step out into the aisle, and they collided with each other rather soundly.

"Oh, I'm sorry," she apologized.

"Oh, pardon me, Toni. Hey, how're you doing?" Zack steadied her with two large hands and grinned down at her. "You're about to get run over, lady."

"Yeah." She grinned back at him. "I didn't see your headlights."

They fell in step with each other as they walked toward the register, still chatting away.

"How are you this morning?"

"Fine, thank you."

"Didn't see any flying saucers out your window last night?"

"None at all," she returned good-naturedly, realizing he was only teasing her again. "Your grill still in your backyard?"

"It was the last time I looked."

"Lucky you."

"I'd say," he bantered back, winking. "I'm pretty attached to my barbecue grill, and I'd sure hate to lose it."

"I can't blame you. It is one of a kind."

Then, before she could object, he reached over and took her check out of her hand and laid it down with his. She immediately rummaged around in her billfold and extracted a dollar to give to him, but he only brushed her hand away and kept on talking. "My pleasure. Nice day out, isn't it?"

"I thought it was raining."

"It is, but I love rainy days," he confessed.

When the bill was taken care of, he held the door open for her, and they exited out into the corridor of the courthouse.

"Do you have court this morning?" she asked conversationally as she sought to keep up with his long strides down the polished hallway.

"Not until this afternoon. How about you?"

"Yeah, nine o'clock." She glanced at her watch and quickened her pace in the direction of the three elevators in the main lobby.

"You coming?" She stepped in the elevator and turned to face him expectantly.

"No, I have business out of the courthouse this morning." He smiled at her unexpectedly as he stepped halfway into the car and reached out with one hand to prevent the door from closing.

Suddenly she felt almost bashful as he continued to appraise her more closely. His eyes were running over her in a most peculiar way, almost as if he were really noticing her for the first time. "I like that dress," he complimented. "You look good in red."

And she did. Darn good, he thought silently. Funny, but she was one of the prettiest ladies he knew. She always looked the same when he saw her, neat and fresh, and her clothes always fit her just the right way—not too tight, not too loose—just right.

"Thank you. I was just thinking how nice you look in that particular shade of green, myself," she returned shyly.

"Thank you." His smile was so sexy, it nearly took her breath away.

Well, at least his noticing her dress was encouraging. Maybe he had come to think of her as more than a neighbor and would ask her out now. But a few moments later he dashed that small hope. Apparently the dress was the only thing that had caught his attention, because he merely winked at her again and let his hand fall away from the door. "Well, you'd better get up there. It's almost nine."

Like a streak of lightning, her hand shot out to prevent the door from closing as she hurriedly gathered up all the confidence she could muster. By golly, she was going to take the bull by the horns and ask him out. He might refuse, but that was the worst he could do. He couldn't burn her at the stake. All he could do was say no, and she was fully prepared for that, so she might as well take the plunge and ask him on the slim hope that he didn't already have other plans made for the evening.

"Say, Zack?"

His eyes traveled discreetly but with definite male appreciation over the way her dress was now stretched tightly over her breasts as she endeavored to keep the door from closing in his face. "Yes?"

She swallowed uneasily and plunged on before

94

she lost her nerve completely. "How would you like to have dinner with me tonight?"

"I'd like to," he accepted without a moment's hesitation. He had been wanting a chance to talk to her in private. This flying saucer business was beginning to worry him, and he wanted to encourage her to get to the root of whatever was bothering her and causing her to see things that weren't there.

"Well, that's all right," she hurriedly rushed on, "I knew you would probably already have plans made and—" She paused in midsentence, his words belatedly sinking in. "You'd like to?" She was almost gaping at him now. He had actually said yes!

"Yes, but—"

Oh. For a minute, she had actually thought he was going to accept! "But?" She wasn't a fool. He was going to be polite and say he'd love too but—

"I was just going to say I'll probably be in court until around seven, but I'm free after that if you are."

She was so floored by his easy acceptance of her proposal, she could barely believe her luck. "Uh—well, sure, seven would be fine with me."

"Good. You want me to come by for you?"

"No, I thought we might go out for Chinese food —that is, if you like Chinese food."

Since she had never asked a man out for a date before, she was rather unsure of the procedure, but he seemed to think she was doing okay. At least he hadn't turned around and run yet.

"I'll eat anything that won't eat me first," he admitted with a boyish grin. "Chinese food sounds great."

"Then I'll pick you up outside a little after seven," she rushed on before he could change his mind.

Then her conscience started nagging her. It really wasn't very nice of her to exclude Karol, especially since she wasn't exactly sure what the relationship between the two of them actually was.

No, if she was going to do this, she would do it fairly and include the redhead in the invitation.

But she wouldn't be held accountable if Zack happened to be more attracted to her than Karol.

"Do you think we should ask Karol, too?"

"Karol?" He looked at her blankly. "No, I don't think so. I think we're old enough to be on our own, don't you?"

"Yes!" And she knew instantly she had said that too quickly. "I mean, yes, I just thought she might enjoy coming along," she said more serenely.

"She'd appreciate the thought, but I think she has other plans tonight, anyway." He grinned at her knowingly.

Naturally, or why else would he have agreed to come to dinner with her?

"Well, whatever you think." Who was she to argue? If he didn't want Karol along, he didn't want her along.

With a brief wave of his hand, he stepped aside to let a newly arrived couple enter the elevator, and seconds later the door closed and the car began its ascent to the third floor.

Slumping against the elevator wall, Toni let the tension slowly drain out of her, delighted that she had found the nerve to ask him out. And for the first time in a very long time, she had the urge to laugh out loud for no reason at all.

Ever since childhood, she had always had an annoying habit of giggling when she was nervous about something. She supposed that's why she was feeling that way now; she *had* been extremely nervous about asking Zack out. She had fought hard all her adult life to control that strange habit, inwardly cringing whenever she thought about how people had reacted to her odd behavior. They would always look at her as if she were crazy when she would dissolve in a fit of giggles during a crisis, and who could blame them? After all, if a person is upset about something, isn't it the normal procedure to wring their hands or cry or stomp their foot in exasperation? But not for Toni. She would stand and giggle!

The man standing in front of her had his hat on at a jaunty, almost cocky, angle and for some reason that struck her as unusually funny. She was fighting back a chuckle when the smell of the lady's perfume standing with him settled over the small car and nearly sent her into fits. It was heavy perfume, stifling actually, and somehow, even though the pair wasn't the least bit unusual, they made a funny-looking sight to her.

Before she could stop herself, a horrifyingly loud laugh escaped her lips.

The man turned sideways and looked at her oddly. She steadfastly ignored his stare and turned her eyes upward, praying she could keep a firm grip on her wavering composure.

But a few seconds later, she guffawed again before she could get herself under control.

As the couple left the elevator, they were still looking at her as if she needed a padded cell, and she was still giggling.

Brother! she thought miserably, her whole body still vibrating with ill-concealed merriment.

If the mere thought of one casual date with Zack Tremayne was going to affect her like this, she would hate to think of what an entire evening alone with him would do to her!

"Are you about ready to strangle me?" Zack hurriedly ducked into the car to avoid the rain a little after seven thirty that evening. "I'm really sorry. I got tied up and couldn't get away."

The drops peppered down onto the windshield as Toni pulled away from the curb and eased her car into the ongoing traffic.

"I figured that's what happened, but don't worry about it. I had a book to read while I waited."

"It's really coming down." Zack looked uneasy as he unbuttoned his raincoat and glanced over at her. "I'd be happy to drive if you want me to."

Toni grinned. "Do woman drivers make you nervous?"

"No, you're doing a great job," he assured. "I'm just used to driving on dates."

They made small talk as they drove to the restaurant, which was about ten minutes away from the courthouse. Toni had called earlier and made reservations, so when they arrived they were shown directly to their table and seated.

"Hey, this is great," Zack said. "I've never been out with a woman before."

"Oh? What have you dated? Ducks?"

"No, you know what I mean. I've never been taken out. I think I'm going to like it."

"Good. I think I'm going to like taking you out," she said, then hurriedly picked up her menu and buried her flaming face in it.

"What sounds good?" Zack had to chuckle at her candor as he picked up his menu. They mulled it over together. "Chow Mein, Egg Foo Yong, Green Pepper Steak, Chicken Livers with Fried Rice . . ."

She wrinkled her nose in distaste, and he laughed. "You hate liver, too?"

"That's putting it mildly." Resuming her study of the menu, she found herself squinting as she tried to make out the small print in the dim light of the restaurant. "I guess I'm going to have to give up and start wearing my glasses again," she complained.

"The old eyesight going on you?"

"It seems that way. I've been thinking about contact lenses."

After much discussion, they finally settled on Cashew Chicken and Fried Rice with a pot of hot tea.

"We're not very adventurous," Zack said teasingly. "I think I would have loved the Barbecued Mandarin Duck with Cherry Sauce."

It was amazing to her just how comfortable she felt in his presence. Granted, they were far from strangers, yet they had never been in the position of

99

actually being out with each other, and she was surprised at how relaxed and natural she felt with him.

And strangely enough, he seemed to feel the same way.

Before they knew it, the dinner had been consumed, and two hours later they were still lingering over yet another pot of tea.

The conversation ranged from politics to their childhoods and even to old love affairs. Since Zack already knew about Skip, Toni found herself relating some of the good times that had occurred during that time of her life. Zack listened with interest, wondering just how much in love she still was with Skip Harden. She talked as if the affair were over and forgotten, yet there was a wistful, almost sad light shining in her eyes when she said his name.

The man had hurt her, there was no doubt about that, but was she really over him? Somehow, Zack felt she wasn't, and for some reason that bothered him.

"He really did a job on you, didn't he?" he sympathized when Toni went into more detail of her recent breakup.

"I guess so, but I'll survive."

"I know you will, but have you ever considered talking to someone about the breakup? Sometimes it can really help a person to get it all out in the open."

She was afraid he would think she was talking too much about her problem. "I have. I'm talking to you," she reasoned.

"No, I mean someone professional."

There was a small, almost imperceptible movement on her part as she tensed involuntarily with resentment. "Are you suggesting I should see a doctor?" she asked coolly.

Now this was really too much. She liked him, a lot, but she felt he might be overstepping his bounds just a little. She could understand his not believing about the flying saucer, and he had caught her in some pretty compromising situations since they had met, but to suggest that there was something actually wrong with her? No way.

"Well, I don't know. I just thought maybe all this upheaval in your life has been too much of an emotional stress on you," he hedged. "That's certainly nothing to be ashamed of. Life has a way of hitting us in the gut when we least suspect it, and it's only reasonable to ask for help at those times."

"Have I done something to suggest to you that I'm not able to handle my stress?" she prodded in the same glacial tone as before.

"No. I mean, yes. Take the flying saucer, for instance."

"I saw it."

"Yes, I know you thought you did."

"I did."

"I thought you admitted yourself that you weren't sure that's what it was," he shot back.

"I wasn't at first, but the more I think about it, the more certain I am of what I saw. You may not believe in flying saucers, but don't try to tell me I didn't see one."

"Okay, okay, so you did. Maybe. But I still don't think it would hurt for you to talk to someone. Now, I have a good friend—"

"Just exactly what are you trying to say, Zack? That I'm a real flake and should be locked up somewhere?"

"No, you're not a flake." He said the words as if he were trying to convince himself, not her, that she was perfectly sane. "Maybe you're just confused right now and *thought* you saw something . . . unusual," he suggested patiently. "That's not surprising for a person who has suffered a traumatic experience such as you have. That's why I think you should seek some professional help before it goes any further."

"Look, don't worry about me, okay? I appreciate your concern, but we obviously don't see eye to eye about the existence of flying saucers." Toni decided to change the subject before they ended up in a big argument. Besides, she felt as if she had been dominating the floor all evening with the boring details of her problems, and she really wanted to know more about him. "What about you, Mr. Sane and completely normal Tremayne? Any lost loves you're mourning over?" She knew he had told her once before there wasn't, but she was just testing.

Zack gave up trying to talk any sense into her and pitched his napkin up on the table in defeat. Obviously she was not open to any suggestions about the improvement of her mental state at the moment. "None at all."

"That figures, but it's disgusting just the same," Toni grumbled. "Everyone should have their heart ripped out once just so they can be accused of being nuts and seeing flying saucers." She grinned quickly to show she was only teasing. "Right?"

"Having my heart ripped out is one thing I've tried to avoid," Zack grumbled, still a little put out at her because she wouldn't let him help.

"You've never been in love before?"

"Only once, and she was an older woman."

"Aha! You told me once you had never been in love with another woman. Remember? The night we were sitting in my swing and—"

"I know, I know, but I had forgotten about Miss Margarite Perriwrinkle. She was my kind of woman: tall, leggy, hair the color of corn silk, and the prettiest blue eyes I've ever seen." He sighed. "But, she was convinced that there was too much difference in our age and the love affair would never work."

"How sad. How many years' difference was it?"

"Forty. She was my second-grade teacher."

"Oh, poor Zackery. That must have been crushing," Toni sympathized with a contrived but appropriately woeful expression on her face. "Some women just have no heart whatsoever."

"I know, and it was crushing. It took me almost a week to pull out of my depression and ask Patty Wilcox to carry the bats outside for me at recess again."

"And no doubt she did?"

"Oh, sure. I was unusually charming for a man of seven, and she couldn't resist. She even offered to be third base for me."

"You mean she offered to play third base for you?"

"No." He sighed heavily again. "She wanted to

103

be third base. I'm telling you, I had it back then, and it was hard to ignore."

She eyed him warily. He had it *now,* and he knew it. "I'll bet; but what about Karol?"

"What about her?"

"Well, I mean, living right next door to you, I can't help but notice you seemed to, shall I say, favor Ms. Massenburg's company more than the rest of your entourage."

"Tsk tsk, Ms. Cameron." He lifted his brow distastefully. "Could I perchance have yet another nosy neighbor?"

"No, I'm not nosy," she denied. "But you have to admit that your social calendar is never lacking for attention, and your front door is usually flapping like a broken shutter in a high wind from the women running in and out of your house."

He shrugged dramatically. "I guess I haven't changed that much from when I was seven." He had to duck quickly to keep from getting hit as she pitched her napkin at him in exasperation.

"Okay, Ms. Busybody. Karol Massenburg and I are just friends. That's all."

"That's not what I hear." Toni couldn't resist in a singsong voice.

"I'm aware of the rumors at the courthouse concerning my intentions toward Karol, but until they are confirmed by me, don't believe a word you hear." His tone suddenly turned very serious as he picked up his teacup and took another sip.

"I wouldn't dream of it."

"And stop watching my front door"—he winked at her solemnly—"and I'll stop watching yours."

"If you're watching mine, you'll die of boredom," she warned, yet she couldn't help but feel an unexpected thrill shoot through her at his admission that he had been taking note of what she was doing, too.

"Yeah, well, I had noticed you were not exactly a social butterfly."

"Believe me, I'm not even a gregarious moth," she murmured glumly.

The hour was growing late as they finally finished their last pot of tea and left the restaurant. Toni insisted on paying the bill, and even though she could tell it annoyed Zack, he permitted it.

"After all, I was the one who invited you," she shouted as they ran to her car in the midst of another downpour.

"Maybe so, but you're the first woman in my life whom I have ever let take me out," he shouted back as they reached the car and he held the passenger side door open for her.

"Don't you want me to drive?"

"No!" He closed the door and raced around the side of her car and got in. "From now on, me man and you woman. Got it?"

"Do your women not drive cars?"

"Not when they're with me. It's an old custom that started with my grandfather. Okay?"

"Okay."

The drive home was pleasant, with the wipers slapping gently in a hypnotic rhythm across the rain-covered windshield. They both hummed along softly with a popular ballad that was playing on the radio.

All too soon, Zack was turning onto her driveway, and she found herself wishing the evening had been longer.

"Okay." Zack killed the engine and turned to face her with an exaggerated sigh. "What's next?"

"What do you mean, what's next?"

"Well, like I said earlier, I've never had a woman take me out, so I don't know what to expect."

"What do *you* think happens next?"

"I'm afraid it's decision time," he said in mock frustration. "Undoubtedly, you're going to want to kiss me and I'll have to ask myself, 'Do I take the chance on letting her kiss me good night on our first date and hope she won't think I'm easy, or do I hold out until we get to know each other better?' "

"Decisions, decisions. Always decisions," she agreed with a hopeless sigh herself. "And then there *is* always the risk I'll think you're loose."

"Yeah, then there's always the risk I'll reveal how loose I really am." He looked at her and wiggled his brows playfully.

"You *said* you were a gentleman."

"I said that?" he asked incredulously.

"That's right."

"A momentary lapse of—something or other, I can assure you."

"Then perhaps I should just play it safe and give you a very sisterly kiss and make a quick departure."

"Good idea. I think we'll be safe that way." He reached over and gently pulled her to him. "Now, don't scare me," he warned. "I'm not very experienced."

She nearly choked on that one.

"I can see that. I'll try to be gentle." Reaching up to wind her arms around his neck, she pulled their faces close together, and the scent of his aftershave made her tingle with longing. The kiss they had shared on the swing had left her weak in the knees, so why was she deliberately walking into this one? She was playing with fire tonight, and she knew it. Already the desire that she had been pushing aside for the past few weeks was coming achingly alive, and warning bells were going off in her head as he drew her nearer.

Careful, Toni. This is only a harmless little kiss, one he will take much more lightly than you will.

She closed her eyes for a moment and savored his wonderful scent as he drew her flush against him. He felt warm and very comforting to her.

"Go ahead, Ms. Cameron," he teased in a husky tone, "Make my day."

Their mouths closed over one another's—gently at first, then with growing enthusiasm. At first he seemed a little surprised at the intensity with which she threw herself into the embrace, but moments later he found himself drowning in the warmth of her womanly softness.

Toni hated to admit how much she had missed this part of her life, and she was terribly afraid he would arrive at the wrong conclusion if she continued to clasp on to him like a love-starved animal the way she was; but as the kiss deepened and grew hungry, almost frantic, she felt herself throwing caution to the wind and kissing him back with a fervor that surely astounded him.

Shifting around in the seat with a muffled groan,

Zack took the initiative this time, and he kissed her with mastery that left her weak with desire. One kiss turned into two, two into three, and suddenly she found herself clinging to him helplessly as their mouths met time and time again. White-hot fire shot through her veins, and she couldn't believe she was responding to him as she was. Even at the height of passion, she had never reacted to Skip's kisses in the way she was to Zack's.

And it wasn't only Toni who had unexpectedly lost control of her emotions. Strangely, Zack seemed to have lost control of his, also.

Within a few moments they were both breathless with desire.

"Toni . . . honey. I don't know about this," Zack groaned again as she brought his mouth back to meet hers in a searing kiss.

She had no idea what had gotten into her, but suddenly she wanted—and needed—him desperately.

Somehow, Zack had the wisdom to realize what was happening.

An average man would have quickly taken advantage of the situation and whispered a sexy invitation to her to adjourn to the bedroom.

Her hunger was a tangible thing, and he knew she wanted him in this dramatic flare of passion as badly as he wanted her. It would be so easy to take her, to hold her in his arms and make love to her and completely forget the fact that she had been deeply hurt by another man who had once felt the same mind-boggling desire for her but had no thoughts for what their relationship would be in the light of morning when the fire had finally died down.

Yes, so very, very easy—she was soft and sweet and all woman. But he couldn't do that to her.

Instead, he very gently broke away from her, realizing that what she was feeling was the culmination of long-denied sexual tension, and that if he lightly took from her what she in her momentary confusion would give, he would later regret this night. Maybe with someone else he would have, but not with her. And he was powerless to understand why.

"You're a very tempting lady," he murmured as he placed gentle, featherlike kisses along the side of her face. "But I think we'd better break this up."

For just a moment, Toni was hurt by his rejection; then the impact of his words hit home. She had once more almost let her emotions overrule her common sense.

What she was feeling was the natural reaction of a woman who had once enjoyed a very fulfilling sex life and was now without one, and wisely Zack had sensed that. Her feelings had nothing to do with him, and even if they did, it was plain that he was not interested in starting a relationship with her.

She should have known that. His type didn't want permanence, and she knew that in the long run she would never again settle for anything less.

To her mortification, a burst of tension-relieving giggles broke out as she scooted guiltily away from him. "Yes, you're right," she snickered, then swiftly clapped her hand over her mouth in mortification. Oh, please, she couldn't start giggling now!

He edged away a fraction and looked at her oddly.

"I'm sorry. When I get nervous, I—" she snickered, then buried her face in her hands helplessly.

What must he think of her sitting here laughing like an idiot when he had just refused to make love to her!

"Are you all right?"

"Yes."

Well, it was plain to see that she wasn't all right, but he had no idea what to do about it.

"What's so funny?" he frowned worriedly. Good Lord, he wished he could figure her out. She seemed perfectly sane most of the time, but then she had *these* times.

"Nothing." As quickly as the giggles had started, they rapidly disappeared, and she straightened herself up and dabbed at her watery eyes. She was really going to have to do something about this annoying affliction.

He waited for a moment while she pulled herself together; then he gently reached out and tipped her face up to meet his. "Are you sure you're all right?"

"Yes, I'm fine—really." Another burst of laughter escaped before she quickly put a lid on it. "Well, I guess I'll go in. It's getting late," she announced in a perfectly normal voice.

Reaching for the handle on the door, she was about to open it when he stopped her. "Toni, at least think about what we discussed earlier."

"Seeing a doctor?" Of course, he *would* think she was a little touched after the display she had just put on, but she knew she was as normal as sunshine. "I don't think so, Zack."

She had no intention of seeing a doctor. She was perfectly all right, except for this minor little annoyance.

"Hey, are you mad at me?" He raised her face back to meet his. He couldn't tell if he had offended her or not, but he certainly hadn't meant to. It was as hard on him to break off their lovemaking as it had been for her.

She decided then not to keep beating around the bush and to let him know she was getting a little tired of him implying there was something mentally wrong with her. "Yes, I *am* mad, Zackery. I *do* giggle when I get nervous, I *may* do a few odd things on occasion, and I *did* see the flying saucer in your backyard, but I'm *not* nuts!"

"Toni, honey. I don't know what to do when you get like this!"

She opened the car door and quickly slid out. "Don't worry, Zack. I won't start foaming at the mouth." She slammed the door loudly and marched up her walk in the rain.

The rat fink! He not only didn't want to get involved with her, he thought she was a mental case!

Well, fine! She didn't like him either!

And even if she did, never again would she let herself become emotionally dependent upon a man, and tonight had served as a good warning to her. No matter how attractive Zackery Tremayne happened to be, he definitely wasn't the man she was looking for in her life.

In fact, she was beginning to think he was nothing but a Skip clone, and that made her stomach more than a little queasy.

Men. Who needed them, anyway?

CHAPTER SEVEN

Well, Zack may think she was a little off, but there was one thing she was absolutely sure of.

That pesky goat was in her yard again.

Toni stood at her window the following weekend and watched the uninvited guest reach up with its mouth and jerk a pair of her newest panties off the clothesline and proceed to munch away on them.

She had no idea how the goat had gotten over the fence again, but it had been nothing but a nuisance to her for the last week.

Throwing the door open, she shouted at the animal to stop its assault on her wardrobe, but by now the panties were a mangled mess.

The goat looked up from his position on the lawn and seemed to decide that although there was a lot of commotion going on, he actually was in no immediate danger. He reached up and jerked her new bra off the line and proceeded to devour it, too.

That was the limit. She had just bought those new underthings, and he was calmly standing there chewing up thirty dollars of her hard-earned money without so much as blinking an eye!

Rushing down the back steps, she waved her

hands wildly and demanded again that he stop it this minute!

Zack was standing in his kitchen, and at the sound of her high-pitched voice, his head snapped up expectantly. Toni was rushing out her back door waving her arms wildly in the air and yelling at the top of her lungs for someone to stop something. He stood on tiptoe and tried to see what she was upset about, but he could find nothing unusual taking place. The goat was well hidden behind the wooden fence, so he had no idea what she was after. He shook his head and calmly went back to mixing up his homemade spaghetti sauce.

That woman had a problem.

The goat jumped and backed away as Toni flew out the door at him; he realized that he had pushed his luck too far.

It was plain to see, even for a goat, that she was in a real snit this time.

The animal bolted and tried to jump the fence that he had come over a few minutes earlier, but he quickly decided that the woman was quicker than she used to be.

Before he knew what was happening to him, she had nabbed him by the tail and was hanging on for dear life while he nearly choked on the bits of bra still hanging out of his mouth.

"I have had it with you!" she screeched angrily. *"This* time, I'm going to call your owners and demand restitution for your despicable lack of manners!"

Ordinarily, she would have been a little more patient in a case like this, but this was not the goat's first offense.

Oh, no. Not by a long shot.

Twice before, she had caught him pillaging her laundry, but at that time she had had no idea who he belonged to. Since then, she had made it her business to find out who owned the little crumbsnatcher, and this time he wasn't going to get away with it.

Dragging the goat by the collar, she manhandled him up the steps and into her kitchen. She wasn't about to give him the opportunity to break away from her. She would bring him into the house with her where she could keep a close eye on him while she phoned the owners.

The goat put up a pretty fair fight, but in the end he realized that she had overpowered him, so he settled down docilely as she slipped a rope through his collar and tied him to the oven door handle.

"There. See if you can chew your way out of that," she challenged smugly.

The goat looked extremely guilty and studiously tried to avoid her eyes. She could almost have felt sorry for him if it were not for the fact that he still had remnants of lace from her bra clinging to his beard.

Snapping open a drawer, she withdrew the phone directory and began to search for the number of the animal's owner, Morgan Dooley on Willow Drive, still mumbling heatedly under her breath about people who didn't take care of their pets.

As she turned her back and began to punch out the digits, the goat managed to get the cabinet door open and pull out a box of cornflakes.

"I'd like to speak to Mr. Morgan Dooley, please!" she demanded as a voice came on the line.

Two sharp raps sounded on the back door, and Toni recognized Zack's knock. She waited for Mr. Dooley to come to the phone.

"Come in!" He probably wanted to borrow something again, she thought as she glanced over irritably at the goat, who was crunching loudly on the box of cold cereal.

That's right! Make yourself right at home! She seethed and proceeded to shoot murderous glares in the animal's direction.

"Hi." Zack stuck his head around the door. "I'm right in the middle of making spaghetti sauce, and I just discovered I'm out of tomato sauce. . . ." His voice trailed off lamely as his eyes fastened on the goat.

"Second cabinet on the left," Toni muttered, then quickly returned her attention to her call. "Yes, I can wait."

Mr. Dooley was apparently out cutting his lawn instead of minding his goat, as he was supposed to be doing.

Well, he would soon be getting his goat, or she would be getting his! She turned and faced the window, her eyes grimly surveying what little of her wash was still flapping on the line.

Stepping hesitantly into the kitchen, Zack cautiously tiptoed around the goat, who looked him over carefully but didn't let his unexpected appearance interrupt his snack. He dipped into the box for another huge bite and munched away.

Zack opened the cabinet door and fumbled

around, quickly locating a can of tomato sauce, all the while keeping a close eye on the animal tied to the kitchen stove. When he found what he had come for, he edged back slowly to the door.

"Find what you needed?" Toni called over her shoulder.

"Yeah, thanks."

"No problem."

Moments later, Zack stepped across the hedge, then stopped and glanced back over his shoulder suspiciously.

Was there actually a goat in her kitchen eating cornflakes?

He frowned. Nah. No way.

He was getting to be as crazy as she was.

Later, after seeing Morgan Dooley and his recalcitrant goat out, Toni closed the door and her attention was drawn to the light burning in Zack's kitchen.

He and Karol were probably eating by now, she thought with a whimsical sigh. That is, she assumed it was Karol he was entertaining again tonight.

Well, he wouldn't have to worry about her butting in on them as she had last time. It was clear that Zackery Tremayne didn't care for lowly stenographers who imagined they saw flying saucers, specifically, flying saucers that were trying to steal his barbecue grill. He clearly preferred the more intellectual type like Karol, even though *she* believed in their existence, too, and he didn't think she was cuckoo.

Since meeting Karol Massenburg, Toni had found

out through the grapevine at work that not only was she a judge herself, but her father was a very influential and prominent pillar of the community.

It was rumored that Karol had her sights set for Zackery Tremayne, and her father, Judge Theodore Massenburg, had big plans for his future, so she guessed that that sort of ruled out any new romantic interests on Zack's part.

And even if Karol weren't in the picture, Toni had to admit that she herself had not always presented her best side in Zack's presence. It seemed he was forever catching her doing crazy things.

Take the other night, for instance. She had hurried home from work, utterly miserable from a kink she had endured all day in her shoulder and neck. The only thing she could figure out was that she had slept on her arm wrong the night before, so that when she had awakened that morning, it was stiff and sore.

She had managed to work all day, but when she arrived home, she had hurriedly stripped off her jacket and begun to try to work the pain out of her sore joints. In her haste for relief, she had left the front door standing wide open, and she was just in the process of swinging her arm around and around in big, wide circles, groaning with agony, when she glanced up. And who should she see standing there watching her with a puzzled expression on his face, but Zack Tremayne!

She had grinned at him weakly as she felt her heart sink to the floor.

But instead of simply explaining about her arm, she was too embarrassed about her seemingly questionable behavior, so like an idiot she decided to not say anything, hoping that perhaps he hadn't noticed.

Instead, she had quickly thanked him for bringing her evening paper to her and hurriedly slammed the door in his face.

And to top that off, only a few days later, he had come over to return the hose he had borrowed, and he had caught her talking and laughing to herself in the kitchen like a blubbering imbecile.

She had been scraping carrots to cook for dinner when a funny incident that had happened at work that day had popped in her mind. Before she knew it, she was reliving the incident, chuckling out loud and saying ridiculous things like "I couldn't believe it!" and "Poor Rita!"

Since she had been living alone, she had found herself talking out loud more than once. She had tried to break the habit, always reasoning that one of these days someone was going to overhear her and think she was completely nuts!

Well, that day had arrived, and she was embarrassed to tears that *he* had been the one to catch her. But again, she decided to ignore what she had been doing in the faint hope that she wasn't losing her mind and he hadn't actually heard her giggling like a deranged hyena.

After all, her mother had talked to herself for years, and she wasn't crazy.

And now, of all the rotten luck, he had caught her with a goat in her kitchen, and he still hadn't said a word.

Could she even dare to hope that he had missed that, too?

Of course not. Granted, he was extremely nice, but he wasn't blind.

And then, of course, there had been the incident the other night when she had made a complete fool of herself by laughing in his face when he had called a halt to their heated necking.

If he had left it up to her, she shuddered to think what might have happened.

The thought of his kisses sent her blood racing once more, and she had to admit that although he was a pain sometimes, he was certainly all man at others.

At times, she worried that she was growing closer to him than was wise. Although they were good friends, she knew that Zack would probably be the last man alive, with the exception of Skip, who wanted any sort of permanent commitment. Yet there wasn't a day that went by that he didn't stop by her house, or she his.

Last night she had been sitting out in her swing when he came home around eleven. There had been a brief thunder shower earlier in the evening, and the smell of the freshly dampened earth was pleasantly in the air.

Zack got out of his car and glanced over at her house, as he usually did.

"Hi!" she called softly.

"Hi. You still up?"

"Uh-huh. You're in early tonight."

He stepped over the hedge and walked over to prop his hands on the porch railing behind the swing. "Yeah, Mom, you can go to bed now." He grinned.

"I wasn't waiting up for you," she denied, but she had been. She always slept better when she knew he was safely tucked away in his own bed.

"What did you do tonight?" He slipped around the porch and took his place on the swing next to her.

For a moment she felt a little embarrassed that he had caught her in her nightgown again. "Not much. Washed my hair and gave myself a manicure."

Zack lifted up one of her hands to admire her handiwork. "They look good."

"Thank you. I'm glad you approve."

Their eyes met and lingered for a moment before she asked in a conspiratorial whisper, "And what exciting thing did you do tonight, Mr. Tremayne?"

"Sat in a stuffy old meeting with six other judges until I thought I was going to nod off on them." She noticed that he was still holding her hand, and she made no effort to retrieve it. "I was glad when it finally broke up."

In a gesture so natural that neither one noticed, Zack's arm went around her, and she laid her head on his shoulder. They sat in silence for a few moments, swinging back and forth, content to share the peaceful time together.

Even though there was a faint trace of cigarette smoke lingering on his clothes, she could still smell his aftershave, and it caused her pulse to race a little faster.

"I like your aftershave," she admitted.

He glanced down at her, grinning. "You do?"

121

"Yeah, it's nice."

"Want to taste it?" he bantered. "I think there may be a trace still left along in through here." He pointed to a spot just at the corner of his mouth.

"Are you sure you wouldn't mind?" she bantered back. "If it tastes as good as it smells, I may go buy a bottle just to snack on."

"No need to do that," he discouraged her, easing her closer to his descending mouth. "You can borrow mine any time you want." And once again they were kissing.

At first they were light, playful pecks; then she settled into his arms, and his mouth hungrily took hers. They exchanged kiss after smoldering kiss, and before long they were both aroused past the point of clear thinking.

"I don't know about you," Zack murmured against her mouth as their tongues teased one another's. She was beginning to worry him. With her he felt something totally different from what he felt with other women. She could send his blood boiling by a mere flick of those blue eyes in his direction. And yet he was reluctant to start anything with her. Somehow he felt that if he did make love to her, he would want more—and he wasn't at all sure he was ready for that sort of commitment in his life yet.

"You know more about me than most people do," she said as she kissed his eyes and then his nose and then, with a soft sigh, went back to his mouth.

"Maybe. But you confuse me."

It would have been the proper time to explore his strange statement, but her heart told her there were more important things to do.

122

Zack was here in her arms, and for the moment everything was right in her world.

Yet Zack continued to keep his distance, even though she had carefully refrained from bringing up the subject of flying saucers in his presence again.

That touchy subject, coupled with the incriminating circumstances he had caught her in recently, made her wonder if he didn't really think she was a little bit bonkers.

Still, she couldn't help but wonder why, in all the weeks she had lived next door to him, he had never once shown any sign of recognizing the fact that she was not only his neighbor but a single woman, completely devoid of male companionship at the moment, *perfectly* capable of accepting a real date with him if he should ever care to ask. But no, *she* had been the one to ask him for the one and only official date they had ever had, and that date had turned out to be less than satisfactory.

She would have thought that, considering his humming social life, just *once* he would be curious enough to invite her out for an evening, but so far he hadn't.

She could only assume it was because of his relationship with Karol. And yet he didn't seem the type to go out with a woman, then return home to steal a kiss from his neighbor.

Yes, she had to admit, Zackery was truly becoming a puzzle to her.

She supposed that most women coming out of the situation she had just come out of would be turned off by men for a while. But strangely enough, she wasn't.

What she and Skip had had together could have been really wonderful if they had entered into marriage to begin with instead of a live-in relationship. True, a legal document did not necessarily assure a happy future, but it seemed to her that there would be more of a commitment, more of a serious binding of two souls, when it was done that way and vows were exchanged.

Yes, she knew there could be joy in the right relationship with the right man, and she was even willing to risk the chance of being hurt again if it meant finding that one right person.

She glanced at the house next door and sighed again. Wouldn't it be something if that right person was living right next door to her?

She quickly cast away the winsome thought. He didn't seem to know she existed other than as his eccentric neighbor.

And by golly, she would rather give up her styling mousse—forever!—before she asked him out again!

"Are you trying to say you think she's a fruitcake?" Jim Howerton glanced up from behind his desk and grinned devilishly at Zack.

"Not a fruitcake—necessarily. I'm just a little worried about her." Zack rose from the chair he had been sitting in and went to look out the window behind Jim's massive oak desk. He could see almost the entire city from where he stood, and he studied the buildings scattered below him thoughtfully.

"You know, I've known her for weeks now, and we've become good friends."

"Now, come on, Zack. Don't try to kid an ol' kidder," Jim teased as he leaned back in his chair and propped his feet up on his desk. "Just friends?"

"That's right, just friends," he stated firmly. "There's nothing going on between us. I just feel sort of responsible for her, that's all."

That wasn't entirely true. She had been in his thoughts lately more than he cared to admit. He supposed this uncharacteristic protectiveness he felt for her was due to the fact that he knew she didn't have anyone else to look after her. At times, he had to wonder if she could take care of herself.

No, that wasn't true, either. In all fairness, she did a pretty good job of taking care of herself, especially since, until recently, she had had someone to help her share her life and solve her problems. He guessed she had the right to act a little screwy after what she had been through with Skip Harden.

The guy must be an idiot to have given her up, he thought, surprised that he should feel a little envious of Toni's previous boyfriend.

No, when it came right down to it, Toni Cameron was a survivor. She would make it on her own, and he had to admit that he admired her spirit to overcome her disappointments and get on with life.

Not to mention her legs. She still had the best set of legs that he had ever seen.

And he had to admit, each time he had been with her lately had left him pretty shaken. Yet there were also times when he had caught her acting weird, and that was what had brought him here today.

"You're sure you're just friends? She's a foxy-lookin' chick," Jim pursued with a mischievous grin.

"I'm positive." But she was sharp, he couldn't deny that, he added silently.

"How's Karol?" Jim abruptly changed the subject as he reached for a piece of peppermint candy that he kept in a dish on his desk.

"Karol's fine."

Popping the candy into his mouth, Jim contemplated Zack thoughtfully. "I figured you two would be engaged by now."

Zack laughed. "Well, you along with all the other busybodies figured wrong."

"Now wait a minute," Jim protested. "You have to admit, you've been seeing her pretty steadily lately, and the fact that her father could set you up on easy street should make you stop and think about the possibilities there. You could do a whole lot worse."

"I don't choose a woman by what she can do for me, any more than you do," Zack replied. "Karol is a lovely lady, and it isn't any secret that I have the utmost respect for Ted Massenburg, but as far as marriage between Karol and me is concerned, that's out of the question. In fact, we had a long talk last night, and we decided we aren't going to see each other as regularly as we have been. I'm just not ready for that sort of commitment to her right now, and I think she understands that."

Jim's dubious "harrumph" annoyed Zack. "What's the 'harrumph' for?"

"Nothing, it was just a harmless little 'harrumph.'"

"Well, stuff your 'harrumphs,' and do me a little favor."

"Name it, ol' buddy, and it's yours."

"Ask Toni out on a date."

"I already have, twice. She won't go out with me." Jim had an irritating smirk on his face as Zack turned around slowly to look at him.

"You've already asked her out?" The swift stab of jealousy that immediately shot through him at Jim's announcement took him totally by surprise. He couldn't remember ever feeling so resentful of another man where a woman was concerned. "When?"

"Oh, just couple of times," he replied evasively. "Why?"

"No reason. I'm just a little surprised, that's all." His eyes turned darkly suspicious.

"I don't know why that would surprise you," Jim reasoned uneasily, aware of the tension that had suddenly cropped up between them. "You just said you weren't interested in her."

"No—no I'm not." Zack managed to pull himself together and turn his gaze back to the window. "I just didn't think about you asking her out."

"Well, it doesn't matter. I've asked her, and she always has some sort of excuse why she can't go out with me," Jim said with a defeated sigh.

"Then we're going to have to think of a way to make her accept."

It was Jim who looked suspicious now. "I had the distinct impression that you weren't too happy about the idea of her going out with me." In his opinion, Zack was not making an ounce of sense. First he wanted him to ask Toni out, then he acted resentful when he told him he already had.

"Nonsense. I don't care whether she goes out with you or not," he lied. "In fact, I want her to, so you can question her and see if you think her problems are getting too serious for her to handle. When I try to suggest she might need a little help, she gets mad at me."

Jim let out a low whistle. "You really think she's gone bonkers?"

"No, I don't think she's bonkers, but then, I'm not the doctor. You are."

"Yeah, maybe so, but what makes you think she'll talk to me?"

"Because as far as I know, she doesn't realize you're a psychiatrist, does she?"

"I haven't mentioned it."

"Good. Then you can question her without raising her suspicions."

"About what?"

Zack began to pace the floor agitatedly. "Well, for starters, ask her about the flying saucers she's seen in my backyard, about the goat in her kitchen, about the way I catch her talking to herself and swinging her arms around in the air, not to mention the way she runs out her back door occasionally screaming at the top of her lungs; and *if* she manages to come up with a satisfactory answer to those questions, then you might find out why she sits and giggles like an idiot for no apparent reason at all when a man has refused to let things . . . get out of hand."

"Oh no! Nothing going on between the two of you, huh?" Jim quickly seized upon Zack's slip of the tongue.

"No, there isn't! It was just a friendly kiss—or at least it started off that way, and when it started getting out of hand, I decided we were neither one ready for that sort of thing yet, so I called a halt, and you know what she did?"

He paused and looked at Jim irritably.

"No, what?" Jim absently crunched down on his mint as he became caught up in the conversation.

"She laughed in my face!"

"No kidding." He let out a low whistle.

"She did. And she swears she's seen a flying saucer in my backyard, and when I suggest that she get some professional help, she gets all bent out of shape."

"What makes you think she didn't see one?"

Zack groaned in exasperation. "Don't tell me *you* believe those cock-and-bull stories about flying saucers, too!"

"Well, I don't know if I do or not. I've heard some pretty fascinating tales on the subject. Who knows? There might be something out there that we don't know about."

"Well, that isn't the case here. Toni just happens to have come out of a relationship that hurt her very much, and I think her mind's just playing tricks on her. That's why I want you to talk to her."

"You don't think she would let me help her if she knew that I'm a doctor?"

"If she finds out you're a doctor, we're both in hot water," Zack warned. "So be careful, Howerton, and don't blow it. Just talk to her, and then tell me what you think I should do to help her."

"I don't think it will ever work, and I'm highly opposed to such unethical and underhanded methods."

"But I've done you a lot of favors, so you'll swallow your morality and help me this time, won't you?" Zack finished for him.

Jim sighed defeatedly. "I will, but I'm against it."

"Thanks. I'll owe you one."

"No thanks needed. I'll collect from Toni—personally," he quipped with a knowing wiggle of his brows. Going out with Toni Cameron was not exactly his idea of punishment.

The scowl on Zack's face told him he didn't find his remark funny.

"Only kidding."

"Just see that you keep your hands to yourself while you're with her."

As old college buddies, Zack knew Jim could come on pretty strong when it came to women, and he was beginning to doubt the wisdom of asking him to take Toni out. Maybe he should have arranged their meeting when *he* could be there to see what went on.

"Yes, Daddy. I'll be good," Jim said mockingly.

"I mean it, Jim."

"Okay, okay. I'll be a real saint."

Zack's grin widened. "You'd better be."

"If you're that worried about my behavior, then maybe we should make it a double date."

"No, I don't think that would be a good idea. I want you to take Toni somewhere where you can talk to her in private, but I just don't want you getting out of line with her. Understand?"

"Yes, sir. I can tell you're not interested in her in the least."

"I'm not—at least not like you're thinking. I'm just not going to throw her to a wolf." Zack grinned.

"Well, whatever you say. But listen, if you're free tonight, why don't I drop by and you can fix me one of your terrific steaks for all the trouble I'm going to for you?"

"I can't fix you a steak."

"Why not?"

"Because"—Zack cleared his throat nervously and glanced back out the window—"somebody stole my grill."

"Stole it?"

"Yes, stole it!" Zack's expression became defensive. "One of those neighborhood hoodlums I see running around must have taken it."

But he really didn't know *who* had taken the grill. It had simply been gone one morning this week when he had walked out to get in his car to go to work. Needless to say, he wasn't about to tell Jim where Toni would insist it had gone. He would think they were both nuts.

"Too bad. Did you report it to the police?"

"Of course I did, but I haven't heard anything yet."

"Well, you'll probably get it back. It's a pretty

distinct-looking piece of property," Jim said comfortingly.

"Yeah." Zack glanced cautiously up at the sky. "I sure hope so."

CHAPTER EIGHT

She knew it! She knew she should have gotten the soft contact lenses instead of the hard ones, but it was too late now. She would just have to suffer through these until she could get used to them. She blinked hard and tried to see through the stream of tears as she sat in Poocie's, one of the nicer restaurants in town, and waited for Jim Howerton to join her.

When he called last night and invited her to have dinner with him, her first inclination had been to make up some excuse why she couldn't, but she quickly discarded the tempting thought.

She had done that twice already, and she didn't want to hurt his feelings. It wasn't that she didn't like him; it was just that he held no particular appeal to her. And she *had* been busy.

She blinked hard again and dabbed miserably at her tears with a handkerchief. It felt as if she had a giant prickly cactus in her eyes.

Her vision was so bad, she wasn't even aware that Jim had arrived until she heard the voice of the waiter seating him at her table.

Squinting her eyes to try to make out his features, she smiled and blinked hard again. "Hi there!"

"Hello. Sorry I'm running a little late, but I got tied up at work."

Jim smiled back at her uncertainly as she blinked forcefully and widened her eyes in an attempt to clear her eyesight.

"Oh, that's all right. I haven't been here very long myself."

He cleared his throat nervously, then glanced down at the menu, trying to ignore her rather strange behavior. It would be too much to hope that she was trying to flirt with him and botching the attempt. No, Zack may be right. She may need his services even more than he had thought.

The waiter returned and took their drink order. When he left, Jim turned his attention back to her. "Well, well. So how have you been?"

Apparently not so hot. Her eyes were red and weepy, and she looked downright miserable.

"Really good, thank you. And you?"

"Fine, fine."

They grinned self-consciously at each other and she blinked three times in rapid succession. She knew he had to be wondering what her problem was, so she decided to fill him in. "My eyes have been bothering me a little."

"Yes, I can see that. Have you had them checked lately?" Jim inquired in a concerned voice.

She sighed. "Yes, but the doctor said I'd just have to get used to them."

Jim looked blank for a moment. Get used to what? Her eyes? "Yes. Well . . ." He snapped the menu back open and pretended to study the entrees while he planned his strategy. Zack was definitely right. She had some problems. "What looks good?"

She tried to make out the small print blurring before her and couldn't. "I'm afraid I can't read," she apologized. She primly folded up the menu and laid it back on the table. "I'll just have what you have."

He lowered his menu a fraction. Was she illiterate, too? "Uh, well, sure. I've heard the prime rib is excellent here."

"That sounds lovely. I like mine medium-well."

When the waiter returned, Jim ordered for both of them as Toni fumbled around in her purse to retrieve a small bottle of solution. While his attention was diverted, she swiftly scrunched down behind the tablecloth and put a drop in her left eye.

Jim finished the order and glanced down at her. "Are you all right?"

She grinned at him sheepishly as she quickly slid back up in her chair. "Fine, thank you."

They sat in silence for a moment, glancing idly around the crowded room. Toni frantically searched her mind for a topic of conversation but could think of nothing.

"So." Jim folded his hands on the table and smiled at her. "Have you seen Zack lately?"

She sat up straighter, relieved that he had found something to talk about.

"Oh, I see him going in and out every day, but I haven't talked to him recently."

"I understand you two work together on occasion."

"Yes, occasionally."

"What do you do?"

"I'm a stenographer."

An illiterate stenographer! How strange.

For the next few minutes, Jim chatted amiably about this and that until he sensed that she was beginning to feel at ease with him. Then, very smoothly, he began to bring up various subjects that she found very strange that he would want to discuss on a first date.

"What about your childhood? Did you have a happy one?"

"Well, it wasn't unhappy," she replied. "I guess you could say it was a very normal one."

"Do you have brothers and sisters?"

"No, I'm an only child. Do you?"

"Uh, yes. I have a brother."

"That's nice. Was your childhood a happy one?"

"Not really."

"Oh, what a shame. Was it due to your parents?"

Jim's face grew resentful. "No, my parents were fine. It was my brother who caused all the problems. We were always competing with each other."

His voice had suddenly turned a little sulky, she thought.

"Oh, sibling rivalry." Toni nodded her head sympathetically. "That can be tough. Would you like to talk about it?" She knew it helped sometimes to have someone to open up to, and Jim looked absolutely miserable at the mention of his brother.

"Well, actually . . ." Before he knew what he was doing, Jim was confiding in Toni about his feelings of insecurity while growing up. For the next

half hour, he droned on and on about the injustices
—imaginary or real, Toni couldn't quite decide—
that he had suffered because of his brother, until she
was almost sorry she had offered a sympathetic ear.

But Jim was delighted to find someone who listened so attentively to *his* problems for a change. He
found Toni to be a good listener and surprisingly
astute about how he should deal with his problem.
This was a woman he could really relate to. Too bad
Zack and he were such good friends. . . .

An hour later, he found himself discussing his
present life with her and having a great time. But
that wasn't what he had come for, and he felt a little
tug of guilt every now and then at the way the conversation had turned the tables on him. He should
be the one doing the questioning. But she was such
a good listener.

"Would you like to discuss Millie?" Toni asked
pleasantly as she tried to stifle a bored yawn, referring to his most recent tragic relationship with a
woman who worked in a local massage parlor. "I
know how unpleasant breaking up with someone
you really care for can be."

"No, I don't think so," he replied guiltily, finally
realizing he was going to have to turn the conversation around to her. "I'd like to talk about you now,
if you don't mind."

"Me?" She laughed. "I'm afraid my life hasn't
been nearly as exciting as yours."

"Oh, I wouldn't say that. Zack told me you just
came out of a bad relationship yourself," he said
encouragingly, hoping she would open up.

"He did?" For a moment she was annoyed. Why

in the world would Zack be telling Jim about her personal life? He knew she didn't like to discuss her recent breakup with just anyone. But as long as he had already told Jim about Skip, she supposed it wouldn't hurt to answer his question. "Yes, as a matter of fact, I did."

"Mmmm." Jim picked up the basket of rolls and extended it to her. "Was it pretty rough on you?"

She shrugged and accepted a piece of the hot bread. "I suppose so."

"Do you talk to yourself out loud sometimes, Toni?" he shot back unexpectedly.

Now, it was odd that he should ask that. "Yes, sometimes."

"Why?" he volleyed back so quickly, it made her nearly drop the roll she had taken.

She quickly recovered the bread and took a bite, chewing thoughtfully for a moment while she pondered his strange question. "Well, it's just sort of a bad habit I've gotten myself into, Jim. How—how did you know I did that?"

"I didn't. I was just making conversation." He smiled politely as he lavishly buttered his roll.

Sheesh! This guy was even stranger than Zack thought *she* was!

"Do you ever talk to yourself?" she turned the tables on him again.

He looked rather uneasy as he picked up his water glass and took a sip out of it. "Occasionally. I suppose everyone does at one time or another."

"Do you ever answer yourself?" she asked teasingly.

"Never."

"Good, that's when they say you're in big trouble."

Reaching for the salt and pepper, Jim sprinkled his salad as he inquired casually, "Zack tells me you saw a flying saucer in his backyard."

This time his question took her by complete surprise. She had thought Zack preferred to keep those little incidents quiet, since he had all but threatened her bodily harm if she didn't keep still about what she had seen. But here he was running around telling all his friends about it.

He was turning out to be a big rat with an even bigger mouth.

She scooted to the edge of her chair and glanced around uneasily. Well, all right. If Jim was asking her if she had actually seen a flying saucer, then she was going to tell him. "Did Zack tell you about the saucer?" she asked in a hushed whisper.

"Yes. Would you like to tell me more about it?"

Her eyes darted around the room frantically, not by choice but because it suddenly felt like one of the lenses had slipped.

With the edge of her fingertip, she made sure the offending object was still in place before she continued. "Well, there isn't much to tell. Actually, I've seen the saucer twice."

"Really?" Jim lifted his brows in interest. "Recently?"

"No, not recently," she had to admit. "The sightings were about two weeks apart."

"Hmmm, how interesting. Did you see these objects in different locations each time?"

"No, both times they were in Zack's backyard," she confessed. "And I only saw two."

"Two, huh? Were you under any particular strain at the time? I mean, other than the one you've been experiencing since your breakup with—with—"

"Skip Harden."

"Yes, Skip. Were these sightings directly after your breakup with Skip?" he inquired pleasantly as he reached for another roll.

She glanced at him warily. Why in the world was he being so nosy? "No, it was a few weeks later," she answered hesitantly. "Why?"

"Oh, no particular reason. Were the saucers doing any thing in particular?" he pursued.

"No, just the normal hovering and glowing that saucers reportedly do." Warming to the subject, she edged closer to him and whispered in an excited voice, "They were big, though. Big with a lot of lights and funny-looking legs for landing gear."

"Really?"

"Yes, really." She couldn't decide if he was really interested in what she had seen or was merely trying to determine if she was just another fruitcake who had only imagined she had witnessed a visit from outer space. "The speed at which they travel, why, you would hardly believe anything could go that fast. One minute I was standing there looking at it, and the next minute it was gone. Poof! Just like that. Up and gone. You wouldn't have believed it unless you were there." She paused again and eyed him suspiciously.

He was looking at her awfully strangely now, almost as if he were studying each word she said. "You *do* believe in flying saucers, don't you?"

"I certainly think the subject is open for discussion," he replied easily.

"Oh. Well, good. Zack doesn't."

"Oh?"

"No, he thinks I'm seeing things."

"Why would he think that?"

"I don't know." She bit into a forkful of her salad thoughtfully. "I think he thinks I'm some sort of screwball."

"And what do you think?"

She put another forkful of salad into her mouth. "I think I saw a flying saucer."

"No, I mean, why would Zack think you're under some sort of strain?" he persisted.

Once more she glanced at him skeptically. "What makes you think Zack thinks I'm under a strain?"

"Oh, he just happened to mention he thought you might be more upset by your breakup with Skip than you think. You know, it goes back to what we were discussing earlier."

My, my. He and Zack *must* have had a long conversation about her. What were the two of them up to?

She placed her fork by her plate carefully. "Well, I appreciate Zackery's concern, but I'm really doing fine, thank you, so you can tell him he can rest assured that I'm not having an emotional breakdown or anything like that, if that's what he's worried about." She looked at him pointedly. "And you can also relay the message that I *did* see the saucer in his backyard whether he cares to believe me or not."

"Oh, yeah. If the subject happens to come up, I'll tell him," Jim said, trying to keep his voice deliberately casual. Boy, if she ever found out what he was doing, he and Zack would both be in big trouble. "So you have been under an emotional strain—you admit that."

She bit the corners of her mouth and turned her gaze impatiently toward the ceiling. Apparently Jim was playing amateur psychologist for his friend, and she was getting a little tired of it. "Yes, I have. But I haven't gone off the deep end, if that's what you mean."

"No, no, I didn't mean that at all."

It certainly sounded to her as if that's what he meant.

"Tell me, Toni, why do you think the saucer appeared twice in Zack's backyard?"

She picked up another hot roll and buttered it irritably. "Because it wants his barbecue grill."

"His grill!"

"That's what I think." That ought to blow his mind, she thought gleefully as she bit into the roll and chewed it smugly. "Crazy, isn't it? But that's what I think it wants."

"What makes you think it wants his grill?" Jim asked incredulously.

She looked at him innocently. "Because that's the only thing it seemed interested in. The last ship, which was much larger than the first one, had this funny-looking telescope that had this strange little eye on it. The scope shot out the bottom of the craft and ran over every square inch of Zack's grill. I think it was computing data back to the mother ship, but then I really can't be sure of that. What sort of desserts do they have here?"

He blinked in disbelief. "Uh, gee, I don't know." He absently signaled for the waiter to bring a dessert menu. "A telescope, you say?"

"Yeah. That's what it looked like to me."

"Did you call the authorities?"

"I checked around with a couple of local television stations and called the newspaper and the police department. No one had received any reports of a sighting."

"You didn't report what you had seen?"

"No, at first I wasn't sure myself if that's what it had been. It was the first night I arrived in town, you remember? When you and Zack moved my refrigerator and sofa into the house for me? Well, I was awfully tired from my trip, and I thought perhaps that maybe I didn't see anything after all."

"What made you decide that you had actually seen it?"

"When it came back the second time."

"And you don't find it strange that you're the only one who saw this, uh—unusual occurrence?"

"I'm not the only one who's seen a flying saucer," she denied. "You wouldn't believe the people who've seen them and can't get anyone to believe their stories."

"Why, Dr. Howerton! How nice to see you!" An older couple paused beside their table as Jim nearly choked on a piece of beef that he had just put in his mouth.

He shot a worried glance in Toni's direction and

immediately rose to his feet and shook hands with the gentleman.

"How are you, Frank?"

"Much better, thank you, doctor."

"Toni, I'd like for you to meet Frank and Meredith O'Reilly."

Toni smiled at the newcomers pleasantly. "Hello."

She watched with growing interest as the couple exchanged a few minutes of small talk with Jim before they walked on to their table. Then her face turned sullen as a tiny light popped on in her head. A *doctor!* For Zachery's sake, she sure hoped that his friend was a veterinarian.

"Doctor?" She looked up at Jim as he reseated himself and tried to avoid her accusing gaze. It was all becoming quite clear to her what Zack was up to, and she didn't care for it one little bit.

"Uh, yes. Didn't I mention it? How careless of me. Now, let's see. You asked about dessert." He tried to change the subject as fast as he could.

She quietly put her napkin back on the table.

Why that low-down, conniving *ingrate,* she seethed. He had sicced a psychiatrist on her!

"You're a doctor," she said sweetly. "How interesting. Zack never mentioned that to me."

He shrugged guiltily. "Well, you know Zack. He doesn't say a whole lot."

"No, that little devil, he doesn't, does he? Tell me, Jim, what kind of a doctor are you?"

As if she had to ask. She would bet her last dime that he was a psychiatrist, but she was going to make him squirm before she dragged it out of him.

144

"Uh, how about the crepes suzettes? They say they're really delicious," he hedged, trying to figure a way out of this sticky situation.

"Crepes. They're nice, but I've suddenly lost my appetite. What kind of a doctor did you say you are, Jim?"

"They have apple pie, too," he suggested weakly. Oh, brother. She had caught on.

"What *kind,* Jim?" Her eyes were still red and weepy, but they had bolts of fire shooting out of them now.

"A psychiatrist," he barely mumbled.

"I should have guessed!" She angrily slapped her hands down on the table and shot to her feet. The force of her blow rattled the dishes and coffee cups on the table, and the diners' heads all whirled around abruptly to see what was going on. "Of all the nerve! You should be ashamed of yourself, Jim Howerton! And so should your friend! Two grown men acting like juvenile delinquents. I'm ashamed of both of you!"

Never one to accept blame when he could avoid it, he quickly defended himself. "It wasn't my idea! It was Zack's!"

"Isn't this just a little unethical for a man in your profession?" she demanded.

"A little." He spoke so low, she could barely hear him. "Sit down, Toni, and I'll explain."

"I don't think you have to explain. I think I know exactly what's going on here, and I don't appreciate it in the least!"

"Zack was only concerned about you—"

"Well, you tell Mr. Tremayne, I'll thank him to stay out of my business!" she nearly shouted.

"Shhh!" He tried helplessly to quiet her, thinking about two of his patients dining at a table close by. What would they think? "He was worried about you."

"Stick it in your ear, Dr. Howerton. There is nothing wrong with me!"

"I know—I know. Shhh." He glanced at the O'Reillys and grinned lamely.

She was so mad, all she could think about was revenge. The very nerve of these two men trying to imply that she was ready to be committed! Well, she may not be able to do anything about one of them at the moment, but she sure could embarrass the pants off the other one!

"You think I'm nuts? Well, I certainly don't want to disappoint you. Watch this, and relay it on to your friend!"

Before Jim could stop her, she whirled around and stuck her thumbs in her ears, screwed up her face, and wiggled her hands frantically in the direction of the O'Reillys. "Yoo-hoo! Frankie and Meredith? I'm nuts, and Jimmy's helping me!" she yelled at the top of her lungs. "I'm seeing flying saucers and little green men, and I'm talking to myself, and—"

Jim lunged for her and smiled weakly at the other diners. "She's a little upset," he apologized as he began to hurriedly drag her out of the room.

Toni knew what she was doing was childish and immature, but it was also just what he deserved.

She was only sorry that the Honorable Judge

Zachery Elsworth Tremayne couldn't be here to get his dose of the medicine, too!

Jim continued to drag her away from the table as the remaining diners gaped in disbelief. Never, as long as he lived, Jim fumed as he hauled her past the frowning headwaiter, would he ever do another friend a favor!

The following morning, Zack was sitting in his chambers going over some papers when the door to his office flew open.

He had been expecting—and dreading—this little visit. Jim had called the night before and had let him know what had happened at the restaurant. He still couldn't believe she had made such a scene!

"Toni! I thought you might drop by—"

Before he could finish the sentence, she marched to his desk and dumped his half-filled coffee cup onto the floor, along with a container of pencils and all the papers that had been on his desk.

Then, picking up the small vase of fresh flowers that remained, she poured it over his head.

Reaching into his back pocket for a clean handkerchief, he calmly mopped at the stream of water dripping in rivulets down his face. "I know you would rather die than let me know it, but you're upset about something, aren't you?"

"You know perfectly well what I'm upset about, you dirty rat!"

"Now, hold on a minute. Jim called me last night and told me what happened, and I want to apologize to you—"

"Save your breath. I don't appreciate you implying to your friends that I'm a loony-tune, Mr. Tremayne. So just stop it!"

"I was only trying to help—"

"Don't even talk to me. Not *ever* again!" She whirled around and headed for the door, then stopped to turn back around and point an accusing finger in his direction. "And not only do I hope that saucer comes back and steals your barbecue grill, but I hope it snatches the pants right off you in the process, you—you—ratfink!"

She went out the door, then slammed it with a resounding bang.

Sighing, Zack reached up and gingerly pulled a daisy out of his hair.

Leaning back in his chair, a slow grin spread across his face and he methodically began to pluck the petals off the flower, one by one. "She loves me, she loves me not . . ."

When the last petal was pulled off and it ended on "she loves me not," he experienced a sharp pang of disappointment at the verdict.

He frowned.

Now, why in the world had he been hoping it would turn out the other way?

CHAPTER NINE

Not that it was any of his business, but he would sure like to know *who* in the hell she had staying over there with her!

Zack was pacing the floor in his living room a few days later and shooting occasional sulking glances out the window.

That just goes to prove that you never really know a person, he grumbled under his breath. His pacing increased in tempo. He would never have believed that Toni Cameron would bring some stray man home, one whom he was sure she barely knew, to stay with her.

But there it was, plain as day.

Some guy had moved in with her over the weekend, and Zack was at a loss to understand who he was or why he was there with her.

Hadn't she just gotten herself out of a mess like that?

If she were still speaking to him, he'd go over there and ask her outright what was going on, but she wasn't. She was still ticked off about Jim, and she had made a point of coldly ignoring him for the past few days. .

His gaze resentfully surveyed the man again.

It was a puzzle to him where he came from. As far as he knew, she hadn't even been dating anyone. At least, he hadn't seen anyone coming in and out of her place.

Well, if she were that loose, he had been right not to get involved with her. He shook his head disgustedly. He had thought she was vulnerable, that she wasn't ready for another relationship so soon after breaking up with that Harden guy, and he hadn't wanted to push her.

And he wasn't all that sure he even *wanted* a relationship with her.

Maybe he didn't. He stuck his hands back into his pockets smugly. Then his face fell as he thought about how much he had missed talking to her this week. Maybe he did. . . .

With a sinking feeling in the pit of his stomach, he suddenly realized that that was exactly what he wanted from her.

Sure, there had been other women in his life, but Toni had been different from the very beginning. For the life of him, he couldn't put his finger on the reason why she was different, but she was.

His brow furrowed into another worried frown. Exactly what did he feel for this childlike woman? Protectiveness and friendship—or did it go deeper than that? No, not love—surely not.

The frown deepened to a downright sulk as he slumped down on the sofa and crossed his arms behind his head. He stared up at the ceiling morosely.

Please, Lord, not love. The woman had undoubtedly gone off the deep end. What was he supposed to do with a raving idiot who saw flying saucers in his backyard?

No, he decided firmly, it was only a brother-sister-type feeling he had for her. He loved her and wanted to protect her—he grimaced painfully as he realized that he had used the word *love* again.

No, he argued, Toni Cameron was nothing to him but a friend. Now that she had pulled this little trick of bringing a total stranger home with her, he was going to wash his hands of being her protector once and for all. She was nothing to him, he repeated again, out loud so the statement would have more credibility.

Good Lord. She even had him talking to himself now!

He rose and went back to the window and carefully lifted the corner of the curtain. His eyes ran critically over the man who was busy washing a red Porsche in the drive next door.

At least he had good taste in cars. And he supposed some women would be turned on by his physical type. But he personally found him disgusting.

He had had plenty of time to reach his conclusion. He had watched the man like a hawk ever since his arrival Friday night.

The precision-cut, rust-colored hair was carefully blown dry and sprayed. The expensive sport shirt and tennis shorts he was wearing were designed to show off the fact that he was a health club nut. His biceps flexed proudly in the hot afternoon sun as the man energetically scrubbed at the car, and the muscles of his sturdy, sun-bronzed legs were stretched taut. No doubt this man was a pretty impressive sight to *her,* but to Zack he looked a little questionable.

A pretty boy was what he appeared to be to Zack —that is, if he had to pick a nice word to describe him.

Letting the curtain drop back into place, Zack ambled over to his desk and tried to divert his mind from what was going on next door.

Personally, he didn't care what was going on.

But she sure had fooled him.

An hour later, he gave up all pretense of being indifferent and fixed himself a glass of iced tea. He had no idea how it had happened, but whether he liked it or not, his feelings for Toni Cameron had grown far beyond being friendly neighbors, and he might as well face it.

Picking up the glass, he went out to the backyard to try to get his mind off his troubles.

He slumped down in a chaise longue and took a sip of his tea, staring glumly at the spot his barbecue grill used to inhabit.

Where in the devil had it disappeared to?

The sound of Toni's voice echoed loudly in his ear. "The saucer took it . . . the saucer took it . . . the saucer took it."

He groaned out loud.

Ever since she had moved to town, things had just not gone well for him at all.

As if she hadn't already had more than her share of bad luck, Skip had to show up on her front doorstep.

Toni was out hoeing in her small garden, trying to

work off some nervous energy and get her mind off her problems. You could have knocked her over with a feather when she had opened the door late Friday evening and seen her old boyfriend standing there.

She reached up to wipe the perspiration from her brow as she remembered that unnerving incident.

"Hi, doll," he had said, just as if nothing at all had changed between them.

"Skip! What in the world are you doing here?" She was sure she looked every bit as stunned as she felt. What *was* he doing here?

"Is that any way to greet an old friend?" He stepped inside the door, and before she could prevent it, he had scooped her up in his arms and was kissing her in an exuberant hello.

A thrill of excitement shot through her as his familiar scent and touch enveloped her. No matter what their problems, they had always been highly attracted to each other, and she guessed she hadn't succeeded in getting over that physical feeling for him as easily as she had gotten over the emotions.

She hated herself, but she found herself kissing him back, forgetting for the time being that this was Skip, the man who had caused her nothing but trouble.

"Now, that's my dollface," he chuckled wickedly as their mouths finally parted long minutes later. He rubbed his nose against hers. "I knew you'd be glad to see me."

He was the same old Skip, she thought resentfully. Cocksure and needing to be taken down about five notches. Well, she had her whittling knife all ready.

Backing away from him before he tried to kiss her again, she closed the door and walked a safe distance across the floor before she turned to face him. "How did you find me?"

"I have connections." He glanced around the small apartment nonchalantly. "Nice. But it's a little small, isn't it?"

"Not for me. I like it."

"Well"—he grinned and took a few cautious steps closer to her—"that's all that counts." When he was within reaching distance, his arm snaked out with lightning speed and captured her once more. He kissed her again, but this time she managed to break it off and move away from him before she found herself responding.

Noting her coolness, he shrugged and dropped his arms reluctantly to his side. "Hey, the apartment's nice, and I suppose we can get by on a little less room," he murmured cajolingly.

She shot him a withering look. "What are you doing here, Skip?" she demanded again.

He smiled at her patiently. "A little of this, a little of that."

"What's that supposed to mean?" He had always had an infuriating way of beating around the bush.

"Oh, I thought I'd come down here and look things over and see you. Find out how you're doing."

"I'm doing fine. And I intend to keep it that way," she said with a distinct note of warning in her voice.

The million-dollar smile that had been so winning a few moments before dulled somewhat as he realized that his charms were not affecting her the way they usually did. "You're still mad, and I don't blame you. I acted pretty rotten, but I was hoping you were ready to let bygones be bygones." He sighed. "I've missed you, doll."

"Well, you can forget about letting bygones be bygones. Yes, you were rotten, and yes, I'm still mad, and think again if you think we can make due with less room." She had not failed to notice his earlier reference concerning the apartment. "I don't know what you're up to, Skip, but count me out of your plans." Her tone immediately softened as she saw hurt cross his face. "Look, I'm sorry. Okay? I don't want to hurt you, but what we had is over, Skip, and I don't ever want to get in a situation like that again."

Once again the smile brightened as he threw his hands up in complete innocence. "Hey, baby, I'm not trying to push in on you. I just thought you might put me up for a few days while I look around. I know you need a little more time to get your priorities straightened out."

"I'm not the local Howard Johnson's, Skip, and I've had two years to think about my priorities," she snapped. "Can't you rent a motel room like anyone else?"

"Well, I'm a little short of funds at the moment," he confessed. "You know, ever since we broke up, I've had a lot of financial problems."

She laughed ironically. "Life hasn't exactly been

a bed of roses for me, either. What happened to your part of the savings?"

Even with Skip's tendency to overspend, she had managed to save quite a nice little nest egg for the two of them while they had been together.

"Oh, that." She took heart as she saw that he at least had the decency to look shamefaced while confessing what he had done with his part of the money. "I was so torn up after you left that I went completely crazy. In an effort to get my mind off you, I went out and bought that Porsche I had been talking about." He shrugged sheepishly. "I'm afraid I spent every penny."

That didn't surprise her a bit. He had wanted a Porsche ever since she had met him, and somehow, someway, he had always managed to get what he wanted.

But it still irritated her that he was managing to make it sound as if it were all her fault that he was broke.

"I hope that useless squandering helped salve your conscience," she returned coolly.

"No, it didn't, baby. I've been miserable without you," he confessed.

She was totally unimpressed by the whipped-dog act he had decided to hand her now. Skip Harden should have been an actor. He would have surely won an Academy Award for this performance.

"So you spent all your money. You still have your business, don't you?"

"I sold it. The buyer took me to the cleaners, but I wanted out." He stepped forward again, and Toni cautiously took another step backward. "Don't be afraid of me, doll." His expression suddenly grew very childlike. "I've missed you, Toni. I'm no good without you. I was hoping you'd missed me, too, and that maybe we could start all over. I'm ready for marriage now," he admitted. "You set the date, and I'll be waiting at the altar to meet you."

It was so uncharacteristic of Skip to make such a statement that she had no choice but to believe that he was sincere in his proposal.

"Thank you for the offer, but I'm afraid it's too late for marriage now," she refused gently.

"Oh, come on, baby."

"Don't start with me," she warned. She knew his sneaky tactics by heart. Soften her up, make her feel sorry for him, and he would soon have her eating out of his hand.

It had always worked well for him in the past, and she had to admit that once or twice she had felt her resolve waver. After all, she had loved him very dearly at one time.

But this time his pleas fell on deaf ears.

"If you spent your money on a car, then that's your fault, not mine. And I have no intention of picking up where we left off. I'm very happy with the way my life is right now. I'm sorry, Skip, but I don't love you anymore."

"Is there another man?" he asked quietly. This wasn't his Toni at all. She had changed, matured.

"No." She thought of Zack and wished she could say there was. "No, I guess I've just fallen out of love. I'm sorry."

She was stubborn when she wanted to be, and Skip knew her every bit as well as she knew him.

"Okay, okay," he returned in a placating tone. "Just let me stay with you until I can check out the job situation here in town."

He could work on changing her mind later on. He was going to need some time to update his tactics for this new woman.

As much as she would have preferred to tell him to get along little dogie, she supposed that he had just as much right to live in this town as she did.

"Just a few days," he pleaded. "I won't get in your way, and when I get back on my feet, I'll pay you back for letting me stay here."

"You bet you will," she agreed firmly. His line of credit was now defunct with her. "With interest."

Her attention was diverted back to her work when a rabbit scurried past her feet and darted through the pole beans.

"Get!" She shooed the pesky animal off with the tip of her hoe and went back to work. She had to suppress a smile when she thought of how Zack had been peeking out his window all weekend. He was a fool if he thought she hadn't seen him gawking behind the curtain like one of those nosy neighbors he was always talking about. He had to be wondering who was staying with her, but she'd be darned if she was going to call and let him know it was Skip. He would start in on her about going back to her former lover, and that was the last thing she needed right now—especially since she had come to the sickening conclusion that she had fallen in love with her neighbor.

She stopped again and pushed her damp hair up

off her forehead. It was too hot to be hoeing, but she had to work off her frustrations.

A few moments later the top of a man's head popped up on the other side of the fence, then quickly disappeared again.

Toni had caught the movement out of the corner of her eye, but she decided to ignore it.

It was probably him spying on her again, and she was still not speaking to the traitor.

She supposed that he was hoping to catch her foaming at the mouth or something.

The dark blond head bobbed up and down again twice more in quick succession before she decided to call a halt to his less-than-discreet surveillance.

"Do you want something in particular, Zackery?" she demanded, leaning on her hoe and eyeing the fence with hostility.

It took a moment, but he soon realized that he was trapped. Slowly his face reemerged over the boards, wearing a sheepish grin. "Hi there."

"Hi there," she returned, none too nicely. It was hot and miserable, and she was in no mood to confront him. She turned her back on him and went back to weeding the garden.

"Hot out here today, isn't it?" He propped his arms on the fence and peeked over at her hopefully.

She grunted and kept on working.

"You still mad at me?" Funny how she seemed to grow prettier every day. His eyes lingered hungrily on her shapely outline.

"Yes, I am."

"I thought so."

There was a few moments of silence while she worked and he thought.

"Who's the guy?"

"None of your business." She wasn't about to ease the curiosity that apparently was about to kill him.

He gazed up in the sky and vowed to keep his patience with her. "You seen anything of my barbecue grill?"

Her hoe paused, and she glanced up at him irritably. "No, why? Is it gone?"

"Yeah. I figure some neighborhood kid took it."

Her mouth dropped open at this unexpected news, and a thrill of elation shot through her. So the saucer *did* come back and get the grill! But she'd be willing to bet her last dime that he wouldn't believe her, and she certainly wasn't in any mood to try and convince him again, so she merely dropped her eyes back to the ground again and viciously uprooted a clump of weeds. "Hah."

"What's that supposed to mean?"

"It means, hah! I could tell you in a minute where your barbecue grill went, but you would only accuse me of being crazy—again!" she added in a snappish afterthought.

He sighed tolerantly. "No, I wouldn't. Whether you want to believe it or not, I don't think you're crazy. I'm concerned about you. That's all."

She kept her eyes on her work and tried to ignore him.

"Okay. Where do you think my barbecue grill is?" he asked a few moments later, knowing exactly what she was going to say.

She leaned on her hoe and jabbed her finger up-ward in exasperation. "Guess!"

He grinned. "Those thievin' little monsters. Do you suppose they're having a party up there and forgot to ask us?"

"Very funny."

In an effort to appease her, he wiggled his brows at her affectionately. "I'd take you, if the little green devils would ask us."

"I'd sooner go out with a goat," she informed him.

He chuckled, then watched her in silence for a few moments. "So you really think it was the flying saucer that came back and snatched my grill?"

"It's gone, isn't it?"

"Yes."

"I assume you've reported it to the police, and they have been unable to locate it?"

"Yeah."

"*You* haven't been able to find it anywhere?"

"No."

"I saw a flying saucer looking it over very carefully." She narrowed her eyes, daring him to dispute her next words. "Didn't I?"

He grinned and shrugged his shoulders agreeably; he wanted to get back in her good graces. "So you say."

"I rest my case."

He sighed again. She might have a point. Stranger things had been known to happen, and the darn thing had disappeared awfully suddenly.

"All right. In the name of peace, let's say I accept that theory for the time being. I'm tired of this cold war, and I'm sorry I made you mad," he apologized. "But I had nothing but the best intentions when I asked Jim to talk to you." He leaned over the fence and put a restraining hand on her hoe as his eyes pleaded silently with hers for forgiveness. "Let's kiss and make up."

There was something about Zack Tremayne that made it terribly hard for her to stay mad at him—or else she was just a born sucker. Her hoe paused in midair as she took his apology into consideration.

She might accept it, but she had to know one thing first.

"What did Jim say about my state of mental health?" she asked hesitantly.

"He told me you are mean as the devil, *never* to take you to Poochie's again, and that you are without a doubt as sane as I am."

She glanced up and grinned impishly. "And that's supposed to make me feel better?"

"It should."

"And Jim doesn't think I'm crazy?"

"No, not at all." Zack paused, debating whether to tell her everything Jim had said. The words would be hard to say, but he loved her enough—yes, loved.

It was painfully clear to him now. He was crazy in love with her. He had stopped fighting that fact the moment he had seen her again today. But he loved her enough to want her happiness at any cost, and if that meant her going back to that bum she had been living with, well, he would just have to face it. "He said he felt you had been under a strain, as anyone would be after a breakup with someone they loved, and he thought that you might want to consider going back to Skip and trying to work out your differences, if that would make you happy. These things have a way of working themselves out if two people love each other."

She knew it! He was back to that again.

"Well, tell Jim I appreciate his advice, and you two can stop worrying about me. I'll be fine," she said coolly, then turned her attention back to her work.

She could have told him she wasn't going back to Skip, that that was the last thing on earth that would make her happy, but she declined. It hurt to think that he was so blind, he couldn't see it was him that she wanted, not Skip Harden.

Reaching out to tweak her nose, he smiled at her tenderly. "I'm trying to quit worrying, but you've become very special to me, Toni."

"You've become special to me, too, Zack."

"Then is my humble apology accepted, or do I have to get down on the ground and eat dirt to get back in your good graces?"

His touch made her weak with longing, and she felt her anger melting away. "That might be fun to watch, but you don't have to go to those lengths. Apology accepted."

She held out her hand in friendship, but instead of shaking it as she expected, he pulled her up to the fence and proceeded to kiss her—lightly at first, then with hunger that stunned her.

If he thought she would protest, he was in for the shock of his life. On the contrary, her arms went around his neck, and they kissed deeply for a few minutes.

"I think I'd like to discuss this further," he murmured between snatches of heated kisses. Seconds later, he had jumped the fence, and when he took her in his arms, they kissed until she was fairly breathless.

"I've missed you, funnyface," he murmured with a low groan. "Really missed you."

She closed her eyes and savored the feel of him pressed tightly against her.

"Now, before I go nuts, will you please tell me who this guy is?" he pleaded in a husky voice. His hands caressed the sides of her bare arms, and then he brought her back into another nearly bone-crunching embrace. It was as if he wanted to pull her inside of him and make them one.

"It's Skip," she confessed.

For some reason, that was not what he had expected to hear. At the mention of her former boyfriend's name, Zack's face clouded with anger.

"Skip? The Skip—the guy you used to live with?"

"Yeah, that's the only Skip I know," she confirmed hesitantly, sensing his sudden change of attitude.

"What's he doing at your house?" Zack suddenly backed away from her, a cold, sickening stab of jealousy slicing through his middle.

"He's just here to visit for a few days," she explained.

"Visit?"

"Yes. He's looking for a job."

"He's going to *live* here?" The jealousy was now

164

an acute, agonizing pain in the middle of his stomach. Granted, he had been encouraging her to try to reconcile with Skip—but if she actually should, he didn't know if he could take it or not, no matter what he had previously thought.

"Yeah, I think so." She was confused by the look on Zack's face. He looked upset, almost sick, and yet she had thought he would be elated to hear that Skip was back.

"And he's staying with you?" he asked, a certain coolness invading his tone.

"Yes," she said honestly, "but—"

"How cozy." Zack's arms dropped to his side limply. "I'm sure that makes you feel better."

"It doesn't mean anything," Toni found herself defending quickly. She didn't want him to get the wrong impression.

The thought of Toni in some other man's arms sleeping right next door to him made him literally sick to his stomach. "Yeah, I'm sure. Well, hey. I have to go."

"Zack." Before she knew what she was doing, she had reached out and drawn him back to her, savoring the feel of him for one more moment. She knew Zack Tremayne would never view her as anything but a good friend, but that didn't keep her from loving him. "I'm honestly not mad at you anymore," she consoled. "And I do appreciate your concern."

He knew she was another man's woman, but at that moment she was his Toni, and her soft, pink lips were too much of a temptation for him. His arms came back around her slender waist, and their mouths met again . . . and again . . . and again.

When he finally set her aside, they both ached with desire and a deep sense of hopelessness.

"I'll be seeing you," Zack murmured.

"Yeah."

They kissed once more, lingeringly, then he was back over the fence and out of sight, leaving Toni choking back the gathering tears.

The saucer might have stolen his grill, but he had gotten what he deserved, she sniffed, leaning forlornly on her hoe.

Because Zackery Tremayne had stolen her heart, and that was much more valuable than any darned old grill.

CHAPTER TEN

"Yes, Mother. I know he's a louse and will never amount to anything." Toni sighed and shifted around uncomfortably in her seat.

Unfortunately, Skip had answered the phone this afternoon while Toni was at work, and it had been her mother calling.

Needless to say, the phone had been ringing off the hook when she'd arrived home that evening.

"No, Mother. It isn't all starting up again. I told you. He's merely staying here while he looks for a job."

She tapped her hands impatiently on the table and rolled her eyes upward. "Because he didn't have anywhere else to stay. Believe me, I don't want him here any more than you do."

She got up and poked the tip of her finger into the wilted philodendron plant on the windowsill, then dumped a glass of water onto it. "As soon as he's found a job. . . . I don't know. He's looking every day, that's all I know."

Her eyes wandered wistfully over to Zack's backyard, where he was just hauling a trash bag out the back door.

It had been almost a week since he had talked to her at the fence, and the memory of his kisses still sent white heat searing through her.

Zack glanced over in her direction, a habit that was painfully familiar to her, and she leaned over and pecked on the window to gain his attention.

"I'm just pecking on the window, Mother."

Zack grinned and winked at her, and her pulse raced feverishly. He looked absolutely delectable in an old pair of faded jeans and ragged sweat shirt, and she longed to run out and throw herself in his arms.

"Just my neighbor. He's taking his trash out."

She grinned back at Zack and waved.

He returned the wave, then disappeared around the side of his house, dragging the trash bag behind him.

"No, Mother. There isn't anything funny going on between me and him," she said irritably, and turned her attention back to the wilted plant. "Good grief, I don't hop into bed with every man I meet."

Not that she wouldn't have given it some serious thought in Zackery's case, but—

"Well, I'm sorry, but I don't think that was very nice of you to say that, either."

She sighed again. "I don't know. Thirty-seven or thirty-eight. . . . Very nice looking. . . . No, he isn't married. . . . I don't know. I see a few women going in and out over there. I'm sure he's a perfectly healthy male and has all the female companionship he wants."

Brother, was that an understatement! But if she

had told her mother how many women actually went in and out of Zack's on a weekly basis, her mother would be on the next bus to save her daughter from the evil clutches of the dirty old man next door.

But he seemed to be changing. She had not noticed one single woman around his doorstep this past week.

"Mother! How should I know if he's a Methodist? I don't keep track of his religious preferences. I just live next to the man. . . . Okay. If he happens to ask me to marry him while he's taking his trash out some morning, I'll make sure he's not a heathen. Does that relieve your mind?"

Toni loved her mother as much as anyone loved a parent, but there were times . . .

"Oh, look, don't be upset. I'm sorry, okay? I'm just a little testy lately, and I say things I shouldn't," she apologized, and plopped back into the chair.

She had been more than testy. This week had been miserable, with Skip hanging around and Zack keeping his distance. She really didn't know how much more she was going to be able to take.

"Yes, I'm eating right. . . . I feel fine, really. . . . Well, I can't help it if I sound like I'm not feeling fine. I am—you'll just have to take my word for it. . . . At least eight hours every night."

She groaned silently. "Yes, I eat lots of fruit and whole wheat bread to keep me regular. How's Dad? . . . He shouldn't be doing that. The doctor told him to take it easy. . . . Okay. I'll talk to you in a few days. . . . No, I promise. I'll call. . . . Okay, if I don't, you can call me. . . . Do you want me to take an oath in blood? I swear on Grandmother Plachie's grave, I won't drop off the face of the earth. I'll call you next week, Mom. . . . Okay. I love you. . . . Give Dad my love and tell him not to overdo it. . . . Yes, one day next week. I promise. . . . Okay. 'Bye."

Toni hung up the receiver and threw her head back in the chair to stare morosely up at the ceiling.

The things a daughter had to do to keep peace!

If Toni's week had been bad, Zack's had been even worse.

He had a crick in his neck from straining behind the curtain to keep a close watch of what went on next door, and his jealousy gnawed away at him every day.

The bum was still over there, so undoubtably they had reconciled. The mere thought of that man holding Toni in his arms and making love to her made his blood run cold.

He should be the one doing that, not Skip Harden.

Friday morning, he stepped out of the shower and toweled himself dry irritably. Another sleepless night had passed, and he felt tired and grouchy and out of sorts with the whole world.

Squirting a gob of shaving cream into his hand, he slapped it onto his face carelessly and stared back at his reflection in the mirror.

If he were any man at all, he would go over there and give that Harden a run for his money. After all,

Toni might be living with him again, but she wasn't married to him.

He frowned as he brought the razor up to his face. At least, he hoped she wasn't.

Surely he hadn't rushed her off to the altar. Zack had watched her house diligently, and there had been no sign of anything like that happening.

Toni had gone to work every morning and come back home at about the same time every night.

In fact, he hadn't seen her go out at all in the evening since Harden had arrived.

He let out a low curse as he nicked himself. Why couldn't the man leave well enough alone? he fumed and reached for the styptic stick. Given time, Toni would have gotten over him completely. Zack would have personally seen to that.

As he dressed, his irritability grew. Why was he sitting over here mooning over her like a sick calf? Why wasn't he in there vying for her attention just as Harden was?

He was just as capable of marrying her as Skip was. . . .

His hand paused as he angrily jerked a tight knot in his tie. Funny, here he was seriously thinking about marriage to a woman he had only officially been out with one time in his life. But living right next door to her, he felt he knew her habits and her one-of-a-kind personality about as well as anyone. Besides, even though he officially hadn't dated her, he had spent a lot of time with her, had had many long talks . . . exchanged many a long kiss.

A wry chuckle escaped him as he thought about

171

the words he had just used in describing Toni Cameron.

One of a kind. Well, that she was, but that's why he loved her.

And was there anything seriously wrong with her state of mind? He stared into the mirror pensively. No, not really. She had just been a little unsettled for a while after the breakup, but now that Skip was back in her life, she seemed to be fine.

He had no idea what it was that she had seen in his backyard, but other than those incidents and the little odd quirks almost everyone had, she seemed to be sound.

After all, the human race was a pretty strange breed, when you got right down to it, and everyone had a few little idiosyncrasies that could be misinterpreted as loony if the person were caught unawares.

His eyes automatically sought to catch a brief glance of her as he walked to his car ten minutes later.

She wasn't standing in the window as she usually was, and he felt a sharp stab of disappointment before he realized that she probably wasn't even up yet. Because of an early-morning meeting in his chambers, he was leaving much earlier today than he usually did.

It was the beginning of a beautiful day, he noted with little enthusiasm as he turned the key in the ignition. The sun was just breaking over the crest of the old trees behind her house, spreading its warm rays over the earth. The pleasant smell of newly mown grass, kissed by dew, filled the air.

Her bedroom windows faced the east, and he thought how nice it would be to lie in bed with her in his arms on a glorious morning such as this and watch the sun come up together.

In fact, he thought it might be nice to start every day with her in his arms . . . or making love to her while she was still soft and warm and drowsy from sleep. . . .

By the time he pulled his car into his parking place at the courthouse, he was aching with desire for the woman who lived next door. If he didn't think she was happy with Skip back in her life, he would be tempted to go to her this morning and tell her how he felt.

These feelings were new and puzzling, yet oddly exciting. No woman had ever affected him this way before, and yet now he was going to be denied the chance to tell her of his love.

The day dragged on sluggishly. At midmorning, Zack threw his pencil onto his desk and stood up to stretch. He hadn't been able to keep his mind on his work.

He had called his secretary "Toni" twice already, and since her name was Wanda, she had looked at him rather strangely.

He wandered out into the hall toward the coffee machine, and his spirits lifted when he saw Toni emerge from one of the courtrooms.

It was hard to tell whose smile was brighter as they hurried toward each other.

"Hi!"

"Hi." Her eyes eagerly surveyed him standing before her, and her smile widened. "I was worried about you."

"Me? Why?"

"I didn't see you leave for work this morning, and I thought perhaps you might not be feeling well."

"Oh, no. I feel great. I just had an early-morning meeting in my chambers," he explained. "I left about an hour earlier than I usually do."

"Well, that explains it."

"I knew you weren't up when I didn't see you standing at the window the way you usually do."

"No, I probably wasn't. I'm a lazy-head in the mornings."

The pit of Zack's stomach ached as he thought about her lying in bed with Harden, doing—He didn't even want to think about what they might have been doing. "Yeah, I am too. Coffee?"

"Yes, thanks."

"How's Skip?" he asked politely, really not caring how the man was but trying to get a few more minutes with her.

"Fine. How's Karol?"

"Fine."

"I haven't seen her around much lately," Toni prompted, trying to keep her voice light and casual but dying to know what was going on in his life.

"No, we haven't been seeing a whole lot of each other lately." Zack handed her a paper cup. "We've both been busy."

"Yes, I know what you mean."

She was wearing the red dress he was so fond of, and it made the encounter that much more painful as he tried to keep his gaze from being downright lustful.

They stood and drank their coffee, idly chatting for a few more minutes, before Toni glanced at her watch and groaned. "Oh, gee. I'm going to be late." She handed him her half-full cup and picked up the stack of papers she had left on a nearby chair. "I have to rush. See you later."

He stood watching her go down the hallway with a deep ache in his heart.

Glancing down at the cup in his hand, he smiled as he saw the faint traces of her lipstick on the rim.

Raising the cup, he touched his mouth to the outline of her lips, as his eyes, dark with desire, followed her until she disappeared through a large set of wooden doors at the end of the hall.

When Toni walked to her car late that afternoon, she couldn't believe her eyes when she saw Zack leaning against the hood waiting for her.

It wasn't that she wasn't thrilled to see him; her accelerated heart rate told her that that would be a lie. But in a way she almost wished he hadn't been there.

All afternoon she had forced herself to put him out of her mind and concentrate on her work. But it had been hard.

"Hi. What's up?" She paused in front of him and shaded her eyes against the hot late-afternoon sun.

"Nothing. I thought I'd just hang around and see if you had car trouble or anything."

She looked at the car, then back at him. "Why would I have car trouble?"

"I don't know that you will, but I'd hate for you to be stranded here if you did," he theorized. "It's awfully hot out here, and other people have been having problems with their cars."

She shrugged and walked over and opened the car door. It felt like a blast oven inside as she slid behind the wheel and inserted the key into the ignition. "Thanks a lot, but I think I'll be fine. . . ." Her voice trailed off as the starter ground away loudly.

Pumping the foot pedal, she tried again. She grew more puzzled by the minute. Her car had always been dependable, so why all of a sudden didn't it want to start?

"I don't know how you knew I was going to have car trouble," she confessed as the stifling heat forced her back out of the car. "But the darned thing won't start."

"I'll take you home."

"Would you mind?"

He moved away from his casual position on the hood and took hold of her arm, a suspicious grin on his face now. "Not at all."

His car was farther down in the parking area, and they chatted pleasantly as they walked. Toni had a strange feeling that he had deliberately planned this whole thing, but she couldn't figure out why.

If Zack wanted to see her, all he had to do was ask.

"I suppose you have to get straight home," he remarked as he started the car and flipped on the air conditioner to high.

"No, not particularly. Why?"

He glanced at her expectantly. "Won't Skip be waiting for you?"

She immediately turned her face away and looked out the window. "No, I don't think so."

"You sure?"

"Positive."

Well, he wasn't about to insist she go home to him. Let Harden fight his own battles. He had offered to take her home.

Zack pulled out of the parking lot and merged into the ongoing traffic. "Want to get a bite to eat before we go home?"

"Sure."

"How about Colonel Sanders?"

"Sounds good."

By the time they had eaten and gotten back into the car, the sun had set. The air was beginning to cool down, and it was a pleasant ride home.

As always, they had laughed and found it very easy to talk with each other. There was something indefinably wonderful about the way she felt when she was with him.

It was a comfortable feeling, yet his nearness always set her senses to tingling.

When they pulled up into Zack's drive, she was still laughing over some silly little incident that had happened that day.

He came around to her side and helped her out of the car, and then they both walked over to the hedge together.

"Well, I guess you'll need to be going in." He paused and put both his hands in his pockets so he wouldn't be tempted to take her in his arms.

"Yes, I guess I'd better. It's been a long day."

"It's still early."

"Yeah, I know. Want to come over and sit in the swing with me awhile?" She peered up at him, and he tried to avoid her gaze. She had beautiful eyes, and he sincerely wished she didn't look so damned kissable all the time.

"No, I guess I'd better not. We wouldn't want to get Skip all upset."

Casting her eyes away guiltily, she sighed. "He—he wouldn't get upset. Come on."

They stepped over the hedge and headed for the side porch. "Why wouldn't he be upset? I sure would be if another man were sitting in the swing with you," Zack blurted out before he knew it.

"You would?" Her eyes snapped back up to meet his.

He was powerless to avoid her gaze this time. "Darn it—yes, I would."

She paused on the second step and tilted her head sideways a fraction. "Why?"

"Why? Well—because. If I were Skip, I would figure you were mine, and if you were mine, I wouldn't want any other man near you."

His words sent shivers of delight through her. To be his—what a marvelous thought. She inserted the key into her door, her mind whirling.

Just exactly what was Zack trying to tell her? That he might be interested in her if Skip weren't in the picture?

Surely not. But if by some small miracle he *was* trying to let her know he was interested . . .

And she wasn't being fair with him by letting him

continue to think that she was Skip's, even though it would probably upset him when he found out she hadn't reconciled with him after all.

Maybe she should clear her conscience and test the water at the same time, just to see what he was getting at.

"But I'm not Skip's," she confessed softly, so softly he almost didn't hear her.

"What?"

"I said, I'm not Skip's," she repeated more firmly.

His face suddenly took on a stormy look. "You mean you're just living with the guy again, but you have no plans of marrying him?"

"No, I'm not living with him, and I'm certainly not going to marry him!" she returned sharply. "So you might as well forget about starting in on me again. I don't love Skip Harden, and I'm not about to go back to him just because you and Jim think that's what I ought to do. It's my life, Zack, and I'm not about to live it with someone I don't love just to make you guys happy!"

Zack could hardly believe her words as he slumped weakly against the doorframe. "You don't love him?"

"No. Not anymore."

"But he's staying here—"

"He *was* staying here. He left yesterday."

"And you let him go?"

"Let him? I insisted he leave."

"I don't understand. What am I supposed to think? The guy you lived with two years suddenly shows back up on your doorstep, and he stays for nine days!"

"I thought that would make you happy. Besides, he was here only eight days!"

"It was nine!"

"Oh, you're counting the Friday night he arrived, and that's not fair!"

"Whatever. He was here too darned long!"

"I agree, but he was trying to find a job."

"Oh, brother. I've heard it all now."

"He was," she defended. "But he couldn't find one, so I told him I didn't care where he went, he couldn't stay here any longer."

"And he accepted that?"

"There wasn't anything else he could do."

"Did he try to get you back into his bed?" Zack's eyes narrowed angrily at the thought.

"Well, yes, but I didn't go."

"Are you sure—"

"Oh, for heavens sake!" She threw the door open angrily and marched into the apartment. "No, I didn't go! How could you think that of me?"

"It was easy," he protested as he followed her into the apartment. "You let me. You even encouraged it," he accused.

The fact that Toni was not Skip Harden's was just beginning to sink in on him, and he was weak with relief.

"I did not, and you're beginning to sound just like my mother. Do you really think that I go to bed with just anyone? For your information, Zachery, I view sex as a very binding arrangement. At the time I lived with Skip, I loved him and was committed to him in every way except by marriage. But let me warn you, the next time I go to bed with a man, it will be because of love *and* commitment—on both sides. Got that?"

"Got it." A slow grin spread across his face as he reached out and pulled her up close to him. "And as long as you brought up the subject, how would you feel about going to bed with me?"

Without blinking an eye she looked at him and said, "I thought you'd never ask."

"You mean, you would?"

"I would if I thought you really loved me—as I love you."

His face broke out in a wide grin. "You love me?"

"I know you think I'm crazy about half the time, and I am—about you," she confessed.

"Oh, Toni." His face instantly turned serious. "I love you—you have to believe that."

With a squeal of joy she flew into his arms, and they kissed until they were both breathless with emotion.

"Oh, Zack," she whispered as their mouths were finally able to break apart for a moment. "This is all so wonderful, finding out you actually love me as much as I love you. I can hardly believe it." She kissed him again to make sure he was really there.

She really didn't know how he felt about the subject of marriage. She wasn't going to repeat her past mistake this time, no matter how much she loved him. "Zachery, how do you feel about marriage?"

"I think marriage is a perfectly acceptable institution."

"If you like living in institutions," she finished the old joke wryly.

"I think I'd like living anywhere with you, Ms.

Cameron." His gaze grew incredibly tender as he reached out to touch the tip of her nose. "In fact, I've just been thinking about asking you to marry me. How would you feel about that?"

"I'd feel very good about that," she said softly.

"And do you think you might?"

"It's possible," she teased.

"Well, first"—he scooped her up into his arms—"I think I'd better see what I'm getting myself into."

She frowned at him warningly.

"Hey, look. We're officially engaged now," he protested.

"Yes, but that isn't like being married," she argued, still not at all sure she wasn't being taken in again.

"You're going to have to learn to trust me, funnyface. From this day forward." He knew she had been misled once before in her life, and he wanted her to know that she could always depend on him. "Can I?"

He leaned forward and touched his nose to hers. "By the time I get through with you, you're going to believe everything I say, lady, for the rest of your life."

She grinned at him. "I assume you know where the bedroom is?"

"Yeah, I spotted that a *long* time ago."

The moonlight made pretty, symmetrical shadows across the bed as Zack carried her into the room.

It was time for love and not for reflection about

the past, so Toni put aside all her doubts as he let her slide seductively down the length of his masculine frame. She could feel what her nearness had done to him, and her fingers tightened in his hair as they exchanged a long, welcoming kiss.

The only sounds in the still night were sighs of love as their mouths came together again and as they stood in the middle of the room holding each other.

At first they touched each other gently in a loving exploration of each other; then as their passion grew, so did their eagerness to know one another.

"Did I mention I think you have the best set of legs of any women on earth?" Zack murmured as he began to carefully remove her clothing. The thought of actually being able to feel her next to him without the cumbersome burden of clothing sent his blood racing to a feverish pitch.

"Oh? And just what makes you such an authority on women's legs?" she challenged, then clamped her hand over his mouth for fear he would tell her. "Never mind, I'll accept the compliment."

He chuckled deep in his throat and gently kissed the perfumed softness of her bare skin as he began to unfold her beauty. "You're beautiful, Toni. Not just your legs, but your heart, and that's what makes me love you."

His words were spoken with such sincerity, they brought tears to her eyes. "Thank you, Zackery."

She finally stood before him, vulnerable and naked. His mouth refused to leave hers as he eased out of his own clothes, and then he picked her up and laid her on the bed gently, like a rare and beautiful jewel that had been given to him, his deep, unmistakable love for her radiating from his eyes.

"There will still be a legal ceremony, but I take you, Toni, as my wife, to love, honor, and cherish, for as long as we both shall live," he whispered, and then with agonizing sweetness he began to show her just how right their love was.

Their kisses were searching and feverish as he brought her up to his bare loins. The feel of his body pressing tightly against hers sent a wild surge of joy through her, and she wanted more, much more. But suddenly his mouth jerked away from hers, and he searched deep within her eyes as if a horrible thought had suddenly occurred to him. "I love you, Toni. For me, you are the only woman I have ever said that to. But I have to know—"

"What, darling?" She could see the agony written in his troubled gaze, and she wondered what could have brought it on, especially at this moment.

"Skip," he answered miserably. "I know he's out of your life, but is he out of your heart?"

She laughed and cradled his face in both her hands as she sought to lay his fears to permanent rest. "There isn't even a fraction of an inch left in my heart to harbor love for any man except you, Zackery. Skip was gone long ago, darling. Now and forever, there is only room for you."

"You're sure?"

"I'm very sure. But I could ask you the same of Karol."

"I was never in love with Karol," he stated simply.

"And all the other women?"

184

"I've told you before, there were not that many other women that I was seeing on a personal basis. The few that I did, well"—he kissed her again suggestively—"we were like ships in the night. I wouldn't have thought about tying any one of them up in my harbor."

"But you would me?"

"I would you."

Her sigh of relief was muffled as he took the initiative once again in their lovemaking, and there was no longer any doubt about where their love lay as he claimed her for his own.

Later, when their passion had been spent, they lay exhausted in each other's arms, holding each other tightly.

Toni had never known love could be this way, and she told him so as she snuggled down against his bare body and hugged him closer.

"I love you, Zackery Elsworth."

"I love you, too. Now, aren't you glad I stole the distributor cap off your car today?"

"Is that what you did!"

"Yeah. I couldn't think of any other way to be with you."

"Had you ever thought about just asking me?"

"Sure, but I figured you would turn me down."

"Well, I wouldn't have."

"I didn't know that. I thought you and Skip had reconciled."

"I wanted you to think that so you wouldn't keep nagging me to get professional help. Honestly, Zackery. You were a real pain in the you-know-what."

He grinned at her affectionately and lovingly patted her. "It nearly tore my heart out to suggest that you go back to Skip, but I wanted you to be happy."

"I know, and I love you all the more for it."

"You'd better love me more and more and more. . . ." They kissed again lingeringly; then one kiss led to another, then another, and then the hunger took over again.

They made love once more, with searing intensity, their love for each other overflowing all boundaries.

Later, as she lay drowsily in his arms, she thought about all the parties they would be required to attend and how proud she would be to be his wife. "Umm, Judge Zackery Elsworth Tremayne and his—" She considered the proper way to announce a judge and his wife. "What's the proper way to say that?"

"Say what?" he asked in a sleepy voice.

"Say that Judge Tremayne and his wife have arrived."

"The Honorable Judge Zackery Tremayne and his old broad are here. I think that's it."

"Zack!" She punched him in the ribs.

"Hey!" He rolled over and trapped her arms above her head and kissed her into quiet submission.

"Are you happy?"

"Very, very happy," she whispered.

"I'll try my best to always keep you that way, Toni," he promised solemnly.

As they became lost in each other's kisses once more, a bright, searing flash of light suddenly streaked across the room. It lit up the room, casting red, rosy shadows across the walls.

"What in the—" Zack's head popped up and he looked around the room expectantly.

"Oh, dear. I think it's back," Toni said in a resigned voice.

And for a change, it had perfect timing! Maybe *now* he would believe her.

Zack glanced down at her blankly. "What is?"

"You know—the thing."

His eyes grew round as saucers—not necessarily the flying kind, but very round and very large nevertheless. "You mean, the thing—"

"Yeah."

"Where?" he asked in hushed expectation. His eyes darted around the room nervously.

"Well, if I were to make a guess, I'd say it's in your backyard again."

"Oh, come on, Toni. It can't be!"

Slipping out of bed, she extended her hand encouragingly. "Come on. Don't be afraid. I don't think they're here to hurt anyone. I think they're just inquisitive."

Hesitantly, Zack let her lead him out of bed, and they both tiptoed over to the window.

An eerie red glow lit up the room as Toni carefully pulled the curtain back to reveal to Zack's stunned eyes a bright object, almost eighty feet in diameter, hovering silently over his backyard.

"My Lord," he murmured reverently, "it's . . . there. . . ."

"I told you so," she whispered smugly, and

breathed a sign of relief that he had seen it this time. Now let him try and call her nuts.

"What's it doing?" he asked in a hushed tone.

"I don't know, but you can bet it's up to something," she whispered over his shoulder.

The saucer looked like the same one that she had seen the second time. It was large and impressive, with flashing lights that had dimmed somewhat as it had descended to earth.

"Do you think anyone else is seeing this?" Zack asked excitedly.

"No, I doubt it," Toni said glumly. "It seems that no one but me in this neighborhood ever does."

While they watched, the bottom hatch opened, and an arm shot out and carefully replaced an object on the grass.

With lightning speed, the arm withdrew, the hatch closed, and the object shot upward, then streaked away in the night.

"How nice," Toni said pleasantly. "Look what they brought back, Zack."

"My barbecue grill," he said lamely.

"Yeah, I guess they didn't like outdoor cooking. See, I told you they were only inquisitive." She let the curtain drop back into place. "Let's go back to bed."

"Toni, I—" He didn't know what to say. He knew it was impossible, yet he had seen it himself. "I feel I owe you an apology," he stammered weakly. She had seen the darned thing after all!

"Oh, darling." She wrapped her arms around his neck lovingly. "You don't owe me anything. Just let this be an important lesson to you. From now on, you'd better believe me when I tell you something. I'm not talking just to hear my brain rattle. Okay?"

He glanced back out the window worriedly. "Okay. But don't you think we'd better tell someone about this?"

"Nah." She took his hand and began to drag him back to bed, where she felt their time would be much better spent. She had been through all of this before and knew what the outcome would be.

"Maybe someday they'll reveal why they're coming here, but trust me, Zack." She held up a warning finger. "No one would ever believe us now."

FOREVER AFTER

In loving memory of my parents, John and Josephine Smart. Their time on earth has passed, but somehow I know they're still watching over me.

CHAPTER ONE

From the way the sky looked, the small midwestern town of Meadorville was in for a real storm. The dark, bilious clouds marched angrily across the threatening horizon as Taryn Oliver peered anxiously out the window of her grandfather's parlor. Because of the high heat and humidity the town had experienced all day, Taryn viewed the approaching storm with mixed emotions.

"It looks like it's going to storm, Grandpa," Taryn remarked, a worried frown on her pensive features, as she brushed her red hair away from her face.

The distinguished, elderly white-haired man who had just walked into the room, chuckled softly as he walked over and switched on the lamp next to the comfortable blue and white wing chair Taryn was standing by. "Let 'er rain," he consented merrily. "No one can deny that we need the moisture."

"Yes, I suppose that's true," she mused, "but I certainly hope it isn't going to be a bad storm."

Martin Lassiter smiled, then patted his granddaughter on the arm affectionately. "No need for you to worry. It's just another one of those late summer thunderstorms that come through here periodically. Nothing unusual about that."

Taryn let the curtain drop back in place, his words of comfort doing little to still her mounting apprehension. "I know, Grandpa, but I've always hated—" She paused and listened intently for a moment to the muted sound of a siren in the distance. "Is that what I think it is?"

Martin cocked an ear, a frown crossing his pleasant features. "Sounds like the civil defense sirens."

"Civil defense . . . Oh, goodness, maybe we'd better turn the radio on." Taryn's face had gone pale as she brushed past her grandfather and quickly hurried toward the kitchen. Unless there had been a malfunction, there would be no reason for the sirens to be activated except in case of enemy attack or—a tornado warning! Either thought made her grow weak with fear as she switched on the radio sitting on the kitchen cabinet.

The voice of the local DJ issuing curt, concise instructions filled the room ". . . residents are advised to seek shelter immediately. We repeat. There has been a funnel spotted on the ground twenty miles from Meadorville, moving in a northeasterly direction at approximately thirty miles per hour. All residents are advised to take shelter immediately. . . ."

"Oh, Grandpa." Taryn's face paled as she reached out to grip his hand in fear. "What do we do now?"

"Don't get upset. Just because it's twenty miles

away doesn't necessarily mean it will strike Meadorville," he said calmly. "But we will go down to the basement."

"Basement?" Taryn's mind refused to function properly for a moment. She had been away for over a year and had completely forgotten that there *was* a basement under the large two-story home.

"Taryn." Martin patted her reassuringly on the shoulder as he walked past her, heading for the front door. "Pull yourself together, dear. I'm going to open the front door so that the neighbors can get in. There are several families in the area who don't have a basement, and I'm sure they'll all want to take shelter here. You go on down and start gathering up the candles and the battery-powered radio I keep down there in a box marked 'Emergency.' There should be a couple of flashlights on the shelf beside the box, too."

Taryn's legs felt like rubber as she followed her grandfather through the house listening to the sound of the rising wind. She glanced uneasily out the window and saw the tops of the huge old oaks surrounding the house sway restlessly as the sky turned the bright day into premature darkness.

The sound of loud, insistent pounding filled the house as Martin hurried toward the front door and pulled it open. A small group of frightened people surged inside, babbling nervously about the approaching storm, trying to reassure each other that it would surely miss the town, as it had done so many times in the past.

"I hope you don't mind, Martin," a large heavyset man apologized as he rushed by Taryn carrying a sleeping child in his arms.

"Of course not, Ferris. You know you're always welcome to share my home in times like these," Martin told him. "Everyone just follow Taryn. She was on her way down to set out the supplies."

Taryn suddenly snapped out of her stupor and once more became her usual efficient self. She hurriedly led the group to the basement stairs and within minutes had them comfortably settled, with candles, a radio, and flashlights readily at hand.

Assuring them that she would be back shortly, she raced back up the stairs to see if she could be of assistance to others coming in out of the storm.

An indeterminate number of people were swarming in the front door as she anxiously made her way over to her grandfather. Her greatest fear at the moment was that the storm would hit before Martin would take shelter. Her grandfather's life had been devoted to seeing to other people's needs before his, and she knew today would be no different.

"Come on, Grandpa," she urged, taking his arm and steering him toward the stairway. "Just leave the front door open for any latecomers."

"I will . . . I will. I just want to check on . . . things," he said quietly.

"I'm sure things . . . are fine, Grandpa," she assured him quickly. "No one's going anywhere."

"I know, but I still want to check," he replied stubbornly. "You go on down to the basement and I'll be along in a few minutes."

"Do you promise? The storm sounds like it's getting closer," Taryn pointed out in a voice filled with anxiety.

"I promise. Now run along, worrywart," he chuckled as he disappeared through a set of double wooden doors on his left.

Taryn shook her head. That Grandpa! Always the businessman first!

The front door burst open again as a loud clap of thunder was followed by a jagged streak of lightning that illuminated the room. A man was struggling through the door, his arms full of potted plants, African violets, and a large birdcage. Inside the cage a bright green parrot was talking in a high, shrill pitch, nervously swinging back and forth on its perch. Following the man was a rotund older woman, holding a cat, a goldfish, and a photograph album. She had three dogs on leashes trailing behind her.

"Oh, good afternoon, dearie. Is Martin in?" the woman inquired.

"He's in the other room right now. Did you want to use the basement?" Taryn stepped forward to relieve the woman of some of her pets, her eyes discreetly watching the man standing inside the door. His rich, wavy brown hair was plastered to his head from the downpour that had opened up only minutes before. Although Taryn had been raised in this small midwestern town, the woman and her male companion were unfamiliar to her.

"You must be Taryn." The woman stepped forward and smiled. "Martin's told me a lot about you! I moved here a little over six months ago, and I've gotten to know your grandfather quite well," she chattered as they moved hurriedly toward the stairway. As they descended the stairs, it sounded as if the state zoo were moving into the cramped concrete shelter.

"By the way, my name's Sadie Mullins, and I bought the old Hoskins house," the woman called over her shoulder as they threaded their way down the winding steps.

"Nice to meet you," Taryn responded politely as she tried to still the squirming cat she held in her arms. She noticed the man had still not uttered a word.

The sound of the storm was increasing as it eerily rattled the large old house. Taryn turned to peer over her shoulder at the man following her. "Are you Mrs. Mullins's son?"

"No." He reached down and irritably thumped the cage holding the screaming parrot. "Pipe down, will you, fella?"

Taryn swallowed nervously, hoping that Sadie wasn't one of those women caught up in the current craze of marrying younger men. *Much* younger men!

This man didn't look to be over thirty-five. "Are you her husband?"

A distasteful set of the coldest gray eyes that Taryn had ever seen met her hazel ones. "No. I'm not her husband!" he returned coolly.

"Okay. I give up." Taryn smiled guiltily. "Who are you?" If he wasn't going to introduce himself, she would seize the initiative and ask.

"The name's Reed Montgomery. And I'm no kin to Mrs. Mullins whatsoever. I happened to be passing through when the radio began forecasting the approaching storm. I thought I'd be able to make it to a motel for the night before the storm hit, but time ran out. I left my car out on the street and ran for the nearest ditch. I happened to meet Mrs. Mullins running across the yard—or trying to." He held the birdcage out in front of him and shook it soundly. "Unfortunately, I offered to help her with Motormouth and her potted plants. I said knock it off, bird!" He glared at the parrot sternly.

"Do you live around here?" Taryn grimaced as the bird screeched even louder. They had paused on the steps to let Sadie work her considerable bulk, along with her bundles, down the narrow stairway.

"Just passing through," he grunted, unconsciously banging the birdcage loudly against the wall as they began to make their way once again down the tight enclosure.

Taryn heard him mutter a low curse under his breath as his feet slid down two unexpected steps, sending the parrot into another screaming fit and fern petals flying wildly. By the time they'd reached the bottom of the stairs, Reed seemed to have reached the bottom of his patience as well.

"Oh, Malcolm! You're being such a naughty little boy today," Sadie scolded lovingly as she took the cage out of Reed's hand and shook her finger disapprovingly at her little feathered friend. "You're going to make the nice man think you act like this all the time!" She turned to face Reed, her motherly features beaming. "Isn't he a doll!"

Reed's face definitely disputed that statement, but he replied politely. "Yes, ma'am. He's real cute." His gray eyes turned guiltily toward the ceiling.

"Grandpa!" Taryn felt a tremendous relief a few minutes later when she saw Martin Lassiter come down the basement steps. "Is everything all right?"

"I've tried to secure things as much as possible," he said quietly as he reached for one of the flashlights and checked the batteries. "What's the latest news on the storm, Ferris?"

Ferris was glued to a radio, listening attentively to the continuous coverage of the storm. "The twister is still on the path to Meadorville leaving thousands of dollars' worth of destruction in its path. As of yet they haven't given any estimate on death or personal injuries," Ferris reported in a shaky voice.

Two of the small children whimpered in fright as their mother pulled them closer and whispered consolingly to them.

"Nothing to worry about," Martin assured everyone in a steady voice. "We're good and safe right where we are."

"Unless the building falls in on us, or the gas pipes blow," Reed muttered tensely under his breath.

"You're a real optimist, aren't you?" Taryn uttered irritably, hoping that no one else had heard his thoughtless remark. Everyone was visibly upset, except her grandfather, who had always had nerves of steel.

"I consider myself more of a realist," he said as he sank down on the floor against the concrete wall of the basement to await the outcome of the storm.

Taryn noticed that his clothes were soaking wet. She searched through a pile of folded linen, withdrawing a large white sheet and handing it to him. "Here, you can dry yourself with this. We don't have any men's clothing—at least not down here," she added.

Reed glanced at her in surprise, then took the proffered gift gratefully. "Thanks." With deft, sure strokes he toweled his thick hair dry and mopped ineffectually at his wet clothing. A few minutes later he withdrew a comb from his back pocket and hurriedly worked the thick waves carefully back into place. Taryn was mesmerized by that dark mass of hair. It was extremely attractive, styled in a cut perfect for his rugged masculine features.

Glancing up unexpectedly, he narrowed his eyes

in suspicion as he saw her watching him. "What's wrong?" he confronted her warily.

"Oh . . . nothing." She felt a slow blush staining her cheeks red. How embarrassing that he had caught her staring at him like that!

"Did you say you were just passing through town?" she asked, hoping to divert his attention.

"Yeah, I'm on my way to New Mexico." He placed his comb back in his pocket and looked around him. "Where am I, anyway?"

"You mean, what town are you in?"

"Yeah."

"Meadorville. Population six hundred and forty-two people—No, I take that back. Grandpa said Betsy Merrill had her baby last week, so I guess that makes the population six hundred and forty-three. One of the biggest little towns in the Midwest!" Taryn smiled proudly.

"Never heard of it," he admitted.

"Most people haven't. But it's a lovely town. I've lived here all my life until about a year ago. By the way, my name's Taryn." She sighed and shifted around on the hard concrete floor to get more comfortable. "I've only been back home about a week. I wish now I'd waited another week! Are you a salesman?" The last three sentences had been said all in one breath as Taryn turned to face Reed.

Reed looked at her blankly. "Attorney. A criminal attorney."

"Criminal attorney! How interesting. I once

thought about being a lawyer, but that was a long time ago. I'm afraid I've met some pretty shady lawyers in the last few years. Not that they were all crooked—" She broke off, leaving her sentence hanging in midair after she saw the defensive glare Reed was directing at her. "Anyway, I really haven't decided on what I want to do with my life yet. I used to think I knew exactly what I wanted, but that was before I got married. Now I'm having to rethink my whole future. Grandpa wants me to stay here and work with him again, which wouldn't really be all that bad since I was raised in the business and have helped him ever since my parents died. They died when I was sixteen, you know, leaving me with Grandpa. That was over nine years ago—it's hard to believe—well, anyway, after I married I thought I would probably go into the insurance business with my husband and I would have been happy doing that," she assured with an earnest nod of her head. "I would have been happy doing anything Gary wanted; anything but racing those darn motorcycles that he insisted on racing! I always told him he was going to get himself killed." She paused for a moment, thinking about Gary. She was determined not to get choked up about it again. Especially not now—and not around a stranger. She turned her thoughts back to Reed. "But that's all in the past and everyone tells me I'm young and can make a new life—"

"Excuse me," Reed said curtly.

"Yes?" Taryn looked expectantly at him, unaware

that she had been talking so much. Talking had always been one of her downfalls.

"Do you mind? I'd like to hear the radio." He looked at her as if she were going to start frothing at the mouth any minute.

"Oh . . . I've been talking too much, haven't I?"

"Well—" Reed paused and looked uneasy. "I don't mean to be rude, but I've got a lot of things on my mind. I should have been in Santa Fe hours ago, and the way it looks, I'm not going to make it until this time tomorrow."

"Oh? Do you have pressing business to attend to?" She didn't want to sound pushy; still, they were in such close quarters, it seemed unfriendly of her not to inquire about his destination.

"Pressing business?" His grin was mischievous. "I suppose it's 'pressing.' I'm on my way to a wedding."

"Oh, how nice!" she gushed. "Are you the best man—usher—?"

"Groom."

"Oh—" Her smile died a sudden death. "How nice," she repeated in a tone somehow lacking the enthusiasm of moments earlier. Naturally a man as good-looking as Reed would be either married or spoken for. Not that she would be interested, even if he wasn't. She had just come through a traumatic period in her life and certainly wasn't ready for another relationship yet. Gary had only been dead about a year and his ghost was still very much alive in her heart. Nevertheless, it was with extreme difficulty that she turned her eyes away from Reed's obvious masculine attributes, which were noticeable against his wet clothing.

A streak of longing shot through her as she willed her mind away from the mental picture it had suddenly thrust upon her. This was the first time that she had been so blatantly made aware that sexually appealing men still existed in the world. For longer than she cared to admit, her mind and body had been totally numb, simply living from day to day without any thoughts of the past or future. For a brief moment it angered her to think that her body was going to betray her and start feeling again.

"I wonder what's going on." Reed shifted around restlessly, trying to hear the radio Ferris had glued to his ear. "The storm's sure taking its own sweet time getting here."

"I'm sure it would be terribly upset to think you were anxiously awaiting its arrival and it was late," Taryn observed, still irritated by the feelings he had aroused in her. Why did his pants have to fit so tight! He was undoubtedly one of those crooked lawyers she had referred to earlier. In her opinion, *all* crooked lawyers wore their pants too tight.

"All I'm getting is a bunch of static on the radio now," Ferris called from across the room. "Has anyone else brought a radio with them?"

The occupants of the room all shook their heads no as Ferris sighed and went back to fiddling with the tuner.

"I'm getting tired of sitting here." Reed got to his feet, towering over Taryn like a giant. "I'm going upstairs to check things out. It's probably all blown over by now."

"Oh, gosh, do you think you should?" She was instantly on her feet beside him. "I really don't think it's safe yet—"

"Hey, let me worry about that, okay?" He sounded unnecessarily cranky to her. "This waiting around drives me crazy!" He began to pace the floor fretfully.

"I know it's hard, but we're relatively safe here," Taryn argued. "I'm sure you're right and it will miss us, but I still think we should wait for an all-clear signal from the radio. I've lived with these warnings all my life, and we never have had a tornado hit Meadorville," she finished encouragingly.

Reed continued his pacing for another few minutes before he sank resignedly back down on the floor, burying his hands in the thickness of his hair. "What a hell of a mess!"

Taryn smiled to herself. He was beginning to remind her of her late husband. Gary Oliver had had the same streak of impatience. A shaft of pain coursed through her at the thought of her husband. They had been married such a short time. Only six weeks before his death. And they had only dated a few weeks before they married. Her love affair with Gary had been short, painful, but joyously happy.

208

"Where did you say you lived?" Reed's impatient voice sliced through her thoughts.

"I've been living in Georgia the last year," she answered quietly, trying to overcome the lump that had risen tightly in her throat. The loud crying of one of the children wanting to get off its parent's lap was beginning to grate on her nerves.

They were sitting next to each other again, so it would be close to impossible for Reed to have not noticed the thin film of tears that now misted her eyes.

"Hey," he said softly, reaching over to wipe gently at the wetness slipping down her cheeks, "it's going to be all right. I'm sure the storm will go around. There's nothing to be frightened of. I just get a little antsy when I'm put in a tight spot." His smile was supportive. "I suppose I'm dreading to face Elaine and her mother. Did I mention I was supposed to be in New Mexico tonight by six o'clock?"

Elaine must be the intended bride, Taryn surmised as she hurriedly wiped at her rising tears. "You probably won't be delayed over a few hours. You can call your fiancée from here if you like. I'm sure she'll understand the delay."

"I'm not." He said flatly, "Elaine likes to have things run on schedule."

"When is the wedding?"

"Next Saturday, exactly one week from today, but there's a string of parties we have to attend," he grumbled.

"Well, you might have to miss one or two of the parties, but I'm sure you'll make the wedding."

"Hey"—Reed reached back over and offered her the corner of the large sheet he had used earlier—"everything's going to be okay, I tell you."

"Please forgive me, Mr. Montgomery, but this has nothing to do with the storm," she apologized with a shaky laugh, wiping the corner of her eyes with the huge sheet. "It's just that your impatience reminded me of someone I used to know. . . ."

"From all the waterworks, you must have known him well," Reed observed softly.

"Yes, very well. He was my husband."

"Was?"

"He was killed in a motorcycle accident six weeks after our marriage, didn't I tell you?" The words still brought almost unbelievable pain when they were spoken.

"Yes. It must have been rough for you," Reed murmured uneasily, glancing away.

"Yes, it was," she agreed.

The sudden sound of an explosion filled the small basement as the occupants snapped to attention.

"What was that?" Taryn lurched toward Reed, her body trembling uncontrollably as his two strong arms unexpectedly caught her up against his broad chest.

"If I were a gambling man, I'd say the storm has just arrived," Reed predicted grimly, pulling her closer into the shelter of his arms.

The roar of the wind was deafening as the occupants of the basement cringed in terror, praying the old house would not blow in on them, or any gas line erupt, posing yet another threat to the already growing list. No one spoke above the fury of the storm as they grouped together in a frightened huddle. Except for the handful of small children crying, the room was filled with nothing but the sound of the angry roar of the storm venting its fury on the small town of Meadorville.

CHAPTER TWO

Taryn closed her eyes and buried her face in the comfort of Reed's neck, her arms clasped tightly around him. He smelled so clean—so masculine. The faint aroma of soap and a woodsy aftershave drifted pleasantly up to her. For a second, the feel of a man's body next to hers was a jolt. It had been a long time since she had been held in such strong, capable arms and she had nearly forgotten how comforting it could be. She was instantly ashamed of such intimate thoughts, especially in view of Reed's being another woman's soon-to-be-husband. But as long as he never knew how much she was enjoying the sensation of being in his arms, what harm could there be? Her only concern at the moment was trying to keep his attention diverted from the way her body was automatically responding to being pressed against him. Her breasts unexpectedly felt tight and full, aching for the touch of a man, a man who could ease the longings and sexual frustration that suddenly seemed to be overwhelming her. They both moved closer, their bodies fusing together intimately.

For one crazy instant, Taryn could have sworn he was beginning to respond to *her* soft curves crushed against his rigid thighs.

The storm continued to scream vehemently as Reed and Taryn cowered in each other's tight embrace.

After what seemed an eternity to the occupants of the basement, the wind began to die down and heavy rain began to fall from the angry heavens.

Raising her head, Taryn encountered the cool gray of Reed's eyes looking at her in an oddly disturbing manner. They were still locked tightly in each other's arms, a position Taryn was reluctant to give up.

"Are you all right?" he asked in a voice that wasn't quite steady.

"I think so. Are you?"

He gave a shaky laugh. "I'm not sure."

They both stepped out of their embrace, embarrassedly avoiding each other's gaze.

"Anyone hurt?" Reed called out worriedly.

"No one's hurt, thank God," Ferris called back, gathering a crying child back into his arms. "What about you?"

"We're fine." He looked dazedly around, still trying to pull his senses together.

"Grandpa?" Taryn moved across the room, searching for her grandfather's familiar face. The group of friends and neighbors were beginning to mill around, relief evident in their voices as they relived the past few minutes. "Has anyone seen Grandpa?"

she asked again, pushing her way through the maze of bodies.

"He was here just before the storm hit," Ferris supplied helpfully as he sat the child back down on the floor. "Hey, Martin! Where are you hiding?"

There was no answer as all eyes began to search the room for the missing Martin.

"Maybe he's already gone back upstairs." Reed spoke reassuringly from Taryn's side.

"Oh, no—surely he hasn't. There's not been time," Taryn said in disbelief.

"I'll run up and check," Reed offered, moving swiftly to the bottom of the staircase.

"I'm going with you." Taryn hurried to his side, forgetting for the moment the dangers that could still exist.

"No. You stay here," Reed ordered curtly as he bounded up the stairs. "I'll be right back."

As he reached the top of the stairway, the sound of heavy rain pounding on the roof met his ears. His eyes quickly assessed the destruction of the room, noting with relief that the house seemed to have been spared the brunt of the storm. It was pitch-dark now as he picked his way through, shining his flashlight over the various pieces of debris scattered throughout the house. Broken glass from blown-out windows · littered the floors, slowing down his progress considerably. Reed hadn't noticed how large the old house was when he had hastily entered it an hour ago, but he noticed now that it was indeed huge. A comfortable two-story interior met his dim vision as he moved about, barely able to ascertain the function of each room he passed through. In the front part of the house there was what seemed to be a large parlor, furnished tastefully in French Provincial furniture. What appeared to be an office sat directly across from the parlor. Two large wooden doors were closed and locked immediately to the right of the office, and farther on down the hall were an additional two rooms with their doors closed. Reed couldn't help but wonder what an elderly man and his granddaughter would need with all this space!

Stumbling over a limb that had been blown through the front window, Reed reached out to steady himself on the door handle of a closed room. The door swung open, throwing Reed into the dark interior. He swore silently as he heard the flashlight he had brought up from the basement hit the floor and roll away. Dropping to his knees, he began to feel his way across the floor, looking for it. When the flashlight hit the floor, its beam had gone out, making it virtually impossible for Reed to try to regain his only source of light. Deciding he would have to go back down to the basement for another flashlight, he rose and started blindly to feel his way across the room. Just as he thought he had made it, his foot encountered a solid object lying on the floor close to a window that had been blown out. Kneeling down, he ran his hands over the object in puzzlement. Instantly he jerked back, his heart racing frantically.

Deciding that he surely hadn't felt what he thought he had, he returned his hands to examine the still form once more. This time the fine hair at the base of his neck stood erect. Jerking his hand back once more, he rose swiftly to his feet. Whatever was lying on the floor was cold, and very, very still.

Could Taryn's grandfather have wandered in here and fallen? Reed earnestly hoped not. It seemed to him that the slight, trembling woman he had held in his arms earlier had already been through quite enough in the last year without suffering the additional loss of her grandfather.

If he only had a flashlight! He stood up and stifled a sneeze. Darn! His allergy was acting up. He frowned. That was strange. The only thing he was allergic to was flowers. Edging slowly around the fallen object, he hurriedly made his way back out of the room, fumbling back down the path he had come, trying to shake off the sense of eeriness that assailed him. This whole thing was beginning to give him the creeps! He had never been one to crawl around in dark places. Even as a small boy, he had never indulged in haunted houses, visiting graveyards at the mysterious witching hour of midnight, or in any other strange ideas his friends were always coming up with. Strong, powerful Reed Montgomery had barely acknowledged Halloween, let alone gone running around after things that go bump in the dark! Give him the strong light of day anytime! Not that he was particularly afraid of anything; he considered himself as brave as the next guy, but he preferred to look the enemy straight in the eye, and know exactly what he was up against.

Cautiously rounding the last corner, he let out a yelp of pure terror as a cold hand reached out and rigidly clamped down on his wrist.

"Did you find him?" A female voice drifted impatiently out of the pit of blackness.

Issuing an expletive, Reed sagged weakly against the wall, his heart hammering wildly in his chest.

"Did I frighten you?" Taryn apologized as she stepped over and tried to help support his sagging frame.

"What do you mean by sneaking up on me that way!" he yelled.

Taryn's hand dropped from his shoulder. If he was going to take that attitude, he could stand on his own!

"You don't have to get so testy, Mr. Montgomery," she said in a defensive voice. "I wasn't sneaking up on you!"

"Next time, let someone know when you come slinking up like that," he snapped as he shoved his shirttail back down in his trousers. "You walk like a cat!"

"I'm very sorry! In our business we have been taught to walk and *speak* quietly. Something you've obviously never been taught—"

"Have you got an extra flashlight with you?" he interrupted, making it abundantly clear that he wasn't interested in what she had, or had not, been taught.

"Not an extra one, but I do have mine—"

"Good." He snatched it out of her hand before she could protest. "Stay here."

"I will not! Not in the dark! I'm coming with you." She grabbed hold of his belt and he dragged her along behind him.

"Can't you walk?" he fussed as they picked their way back through the rubble.

"I'm walking. Just slow down! Oh, dear, has the storm destroyed the house completely?" she fretted as they made their way slowly toward the front of the house.

"No, actually I think there will be very little damage when the rubble is cleared away. There're several windows blown out, but that can be easily taken care of." He shook the dimming flashlight irritably, trying to get it to come back on. Finally a faint, weak ray shot out of the cylinder. "These batteries are almost gone."

"I know. Grandpa forgot to rotate them."

"Great! Simply great!" He pointed the weak light toward the center of the room, trying to make out the shape of objects. "Why don't you step outside and take a look around? Maybe your grandfather's decided to do the same thing." He wanted to get her out of the way so he could take a closer look at what he had discovered earlier. "Just be careful. There may be some power lines down," he warned.

"Okay, but I'll need the flashlight," she agreed hesitantly.

"Are there any matches or candles up here?"

"Yes, I think so. Why?"

"Get them for me. I'll need a light to check around. I think it's safe to strike a match. If there were any gas leaks we would have smelled them by now." Taryn took the flashlight he offered. "Meet me back here in a few minutes," he ordered curtly.

The rain was still coming down in sheets as Taryn made her way into the kitchen. She was sure that her grandfather wouldn't have gone out in this kind of downpour, but she had the feeling Reed was in no mood to argue, so she hurried to find the matches and candles.

A low moan met her ears as she searched hurriedly through the bottom cabinet drawer. Feeling her way over to the sound, she turned the weak light back on and gasped when she saw her grandfather's crumpled form lying on the floor.

"Reed!" she shouted, kneeling down next to the still figure and feeling for a pulse. Thankfully, she found a strong steady beat and she breathed a sigh of relief.

"What?" Reed shouted. She could hear him bumping into furniture as he tried to fight his way into the kitchen.

"Come in here. I've found Grandpa!"

Reed hurriedly found his way across the dark room and knelt down beside her. "Is he all right?"

"I think so. He must have fallen and knocked himself out. Here, hold the light while I get a wet cloth." Within minutes she was back, placing a cold compress to her grandfather's forehead.

Martin moaned softly as Taryn leaned over and spoke loudly to him. "Grandpa, can you hear me?"

Another low groan escaped his lips as he reached out and grasped her hand. "I think I've broken my leg."

"Just lie still. We'll get you some help," she consoled, patting his hand gently. She turned to Reed and whispered urgently, "We've got to get an ambulance."

"That's probably close to impossible," he returned quickly. "If there've been many injuries—"

Taryn slapped her head in exasperation. "What am I talking about! There isn't an ambulance service here."

Reed looked at her anxiously. "Now what?"

"I don't know . . . let me think. Foster! Foster Savage and his wife help Grandpa in the business." She bit her lip thoughtfully. "I haven't seen Foster tonight, have you?"

Reed looked at her blankly. "Hell, I wouldn't know Foster if he walked up and spit on me!"

"Go look in the cottage in back of the house. And hurry!" she pleaded as she went to run cold water over the cloth again.

Reed ran out the back door and returned in five minutes, fighting for every breath. "There's no one out there," he wheezed. "I nearly tore the door down and there was no answer." He sagged weakly against the kitchen counter.

"Oh, I just remembered. He was taking his wife to the doctor this afternoon. They must have gotten caught in the storm somewhere. Go down and get Ferris. Tell him to bring one of the cots from downstairs. We'll have to get Grandpa to the clinic by ourselves."

"The house . . . is it gone?" Martin tried to rise from the floor.

"No, just lie back, Grandpa. The house has very little damage to it." Taryn pushed the jacket she had just removed from him under his head for a pillow.

"Martha. Did you check on Martha?"

"Not yet, but I will. You don't need to worry about a thing, Grandpa," she repeated, looking around anxiously for Reed's return. In a few minutes he came bounding back into the room, dragging Ferris and a large cot with him. He was still fighting to draw a normal breath as he helped lift Martin gently up on the cot. "Listen," he gasped between gulps of fresh air, "I think there's someone else hurt up there in that room on the left side of the office."

Taryn paused in draping a light blanket over Martin and thought about the room he was describing. She glanced up sheepishly at Reed and asked, "What do you mean 'hurt'?"

"I mean, while I was up there looking for your grandfather I stumbled over someone lying on the

221

floor. At first I thought it was your grandfather, but apparently it wasn't. Since it was so dark, I don't know if it's a man or woman, but I *am* sure it was a body!"

"Oh, dear. That was probably Martha," Taryn mused worriedly.

"Well, the poor woman needs help! We'd better try to get both of them to the doctor at the same time," he urged adamantly. "She's out cold!"

"Just calm down," Taryn said quietly as she leaned over and kissed her grandfather on the cheek. "Ferris will take you out to the car—"

"No . . . the car has a flat tire. Foster was going to buy a new spare on his way home this afternoon," Martin said weakly.

"Oh." Taryn thought for a moment. "Then I suppose we'll have to use the business car."

"That seems to be our only alternative," Martin agreed.

"Okay, Ferris, you go ahead and get Grandpa loaded in the limousine and Reed and I will take care of Martha." She looked at Reed hopefully. "Or would you rather load Grandpa and let Ferris help me with Mrs. Feagan?"

"Let Ferris load Martin and I'll help you."

"Good!" Ferris heaved a tremendous sigh of relief. "I'd rather see to Martin than have to help with Martha." He hurriedly pushed the stretcher out the back door.

Reed gave Taryn a cocky grin. "What's the matter with Ferris. Don't he and Martha get along?"

"Why, of course he got along with Martha. She's taught school in Meadorville for over fifty years," Taryn scolded. "Everyone loved her."

Reed shrugged his broad shoulders. "Just wondering. He acted mighty relieved that he wasn't going to have to help you with her. I'll go get the other cot."

"I don't think we'll need it," she said evasively as they made their way back through the dark house.

"Yes, we will," he stubbornly persisted. "I'm telling you, the woman's hurt!"

"Trust me. We'll take care of things without a cot," Taryn soothed as she opened the door on the left side of the office. "Here, light this candle and set it on the table in back of you." She handed him a candle and a box of matches.

"She's still out, huh? I told you she was in bad shape." The candle flared into light, casting a weak, wavering shadow across the room. Reed paused and sniffed the air suspiciously. "What's that sickly sweet smell? Smells like flowers." At the mere mention of the word he sneezed explosively.

"*Gesundheit!*"

"Thanks. What do you want me to do?"

"I think we'll just pick her up and lay her on the sofa until I can get . . . things arranged again."

Reed walked over to kneel down beside Taryn. He looked at the woman's face he had touched earlier.

"Gosh, she's pretty old," he said sympathetically. "I hope she hasn't broken anything."

"Yes." Taryn touched the weathered face tenderly. "She is old. For as long as I can remember, Martha Feagan has been such a vital part of Meadorville." Taryn turned to face Reed. "I'll bet she's responsible for over three fourths of the population's education in this town. I wish you could have known her. Here, help me lift her onto the sofa."

The blood vessels in Reed's neck nearly exploded as he grunted strenuously, trying to heave the dead weight onto the couch. "Ho . . . holy cow," he groaned, "Martha is going to have to cut down on the late-night pizzas and seconds on potatoes!"

It was all Taryn could do to lift her end, too, but they both managed, and in seconds they had Martha Feagan resting comfortably. Reed stood staring down at the quiet figure in repose. "Do you think she'll be all right? I suppose the storm made her faint." He clucked his tongue in sympathy. "Poor old thing looks white as a sheet." He sneezed loudly once more.

"Gesundheit!" Taryn repeated.

"Darn it!" he groaned, reaching into his back pocket and dragging out a large white handkerchief. "Are there any flowers around here?"

"Are you serious? There's a whole roomful," Taryn said, confirming his worst fear. "I told you Martha was well loved by this town. Can you come over here for a minute? I want to set the casket back upon the pedestal, then I'll gather up the—Reed?" She turned to check on him, wondering why the room had grown so silent.

Reed had turned back around to look at Taryn, *his* face ghostly white now. "Set the what, where?" he asked.

"I said, can you give me a hand with the casket? This one is very heavy. It must have been one heck of a wind that went through this room. I don't think I can manage it by myself," she mused thoughtfully.

"Cask-et?" he repeated in a hoarse whisper.

Taryn smiled tolerantly. Here we go again! He was going to have the typical reaction all strangers had when she told him what he had accidentally stumbled into while seeking shelter from the storm. "Now, there's nothing to be alarmed about, Reed, all you have to do is help—Reed!" She rushed forward and tried to break his fall, but they both went down, his large frame wilting heavily on top of hers. Powerful, strong Reed Montgomery had fainted clean as a whistle!

Taryn was sure he had broken her arm as she tried to crawl out from beneath him, every bone in her body aching. For the life of her she didn't know why everyone always got so upset about being in a funeral home!

Giving one authoritative shove, she pushed his limp body off her and struggled to her feet. "Reed? Reed!" She gave his face a sharp slap, trying to get a response out of him. "Wake up!"

Reed's six feet plus lay stretched serenely out on the floor, an angelic smile plastered to his face. No amount of pleading brought him back to the present.

With a sigh of disgust she picked up a vase and removed the flowers, then stood back as she dashed the cold water on his face.

With a loud, unpleasant oath he sat straight up and looked around him in bewilderment. His eyes focused on Martha Feagan lying quietly on the sofa.

"Oh, good Lord," he groaned, burying his face in his hands and lying back down. "Tell me it's a bad dream," he pleaded in a muffled voice.

"You are acting very childish," Taryn said sternly, walking around the room to straighten up the damage the storm had done. "I'm not saying you're the first one to act this way, but I certainly think you're old enough to be a little braver about the situation."

Another sneeze ripped forcefully through him. "Get those flowers out from under my nose!" He irritably shoved a bouquet of carnations away from him. "My allergy is killing me. . . ." His eyes flickered toward Martha. "Let me rephrase that . . . my allergy's acting up," he corrected quickly.

"I'm sorry, there's nothing I can do about that. You'll have to simply stay out of this room if you're allergic to flowers."

"*That* you can count on," he moaned. "I want out of here."

"You're free to go any time you choose . . ." she

226

said, patiently rearranging a bouquet of gladiolus and mums.

He was on his feet streaking by her like a bolt of lightning when he felt a firm hand clamp down on the back of his shirt collar. ". . . just as soon as you help me get Martha's casket set back on the pedestal and Grandpa to the hospital," she finished sternly.

"Oh, come on! Give me a break, Taryn!"

"It is not going to hurt you to lend me a hand. After all, this is an emergency," she told him curtly, "and supposedly you're a big boy now and know that the boogie man isn't going to jump out and get you."

"The 'boogie man' wasn't exactly what I had in mind," he grumbled as he backed farther away from the sofa.

"Rubbish! Pure rubbish. Being in the funeral business is one of the most gratifying experiences a person could ever wish to have. Think about it, Reed. I'm privileged to do some of the last things done on this earth for people who have been a part of my life ever since I came into the world. You should have no fear of the dead. Why, if you had been here three days ago, I would have shown you Lila Stewart, a lovely old saint who was my Sunday school teacher all during my teen-age years. They're the same people they always were, Reed. They're moms and dads, grandparents, aunts, uncles, children . . . all of them were loved and cherished," she finished softly.

"Fine! If you like your job, then more power to you, but as far as I'm concerned"—he glanced over at the sofa and shuddered—"this place gives me the willies and I'm cutting out just as soon as I get your grandfather loaded in the car and that"—he shuddered again—"box set back up on the pedestal."

"That's perfectly all right with me," she returned calmly. She could sympathize with his fear, but she honestly didn't understand it.

"You can just get your nose out of the air, lady," he said curtly. "You're talking to a guy who'll drive five miles out of his way to keep from passing a cemetery!"

Ten minutes later they stepped out of the room and securely closed the door. "Now, that wasn't so bad, was it?" Taryn chided as they walked back toward the kitchen.

Reed grimaced and made a face. He had thought he was going to throw up when she made him help her lift Martha back in the . . . The very thought of the casket made him shudder for the fifth time in the last ten minutes.

"Are you cold?"

"No. Let's just get your grandfather to the hospital and then I'm leaving."

"But it's so late!" Taryn protested. "And all the roads will probably be closed due to the storm. You better plan on staying here tonight—"

"Forget it!" he stated bluntly. "If I have to crawl on my hands and knees out of this town, I'm not staying in your *house* tonight!"

"Baby!"

"Ghoul!"

"There's no need for sarcasm," she pointed out resentfully.

"Then get off my back. I'm not staying here all night and that's final!"

They were still grumbling at each other as they walked out the back door. Reed stopped and looked at the car parked in the driveway. "I suppose the 'business car' you were referring to is that hearse!"

"That's right. Now what's wrong?"

"I'll tell you what's wrong! I'm not going to drive that . . . that thing, that's what's wrong!"

"Oh, for heaven's sake. Why not? It's just a car!"

"I said"—he took a deep breath and gritted his teeth stubbornly—"I am *not* going to drive that hearse. You get such a kick out of your job, *you* drive it!"

"I can't," she admitted guiltily.

"Why not?"

"Because I'm a lousy driver and Grandpa told me never to drive the hearse again under any circumstances. Last time I didn't get the door in the back closed properly and when I swung around the corner too fast, it flew open . . ." Her voice trailed off sheepishly.

Reed's face turned a sickly green. "Oh, hell . . . you mean—"

"Oh, no! Not that! Nothing happened, actually, but

it made Grandpa and the minister so nervous that Grandpa forbade me to drive it again."

"Well, if this isn't a fine kettle of fish!" he muttered angrily, his eyes once more going to the long black limousine sitting in the drive. He nervously chewed on his bottom lip. "What about Ferris? Let him drive it. I owe the rat fink one for what he pulled on me earlier! No wonder he was grinning from ear to ear when I offered to help you with Martha!"

"There's no need to bother Ferris again! Besides, his driving is supposed to be very limited."

"I don't believe you," he said brusquely.

"Well, it's the truth! Ferris likes to tip the bottle some and last time he was caught, Pryor, that's our town sheriff, well, he took his license away from him for a few days, and when he returned it he told him he couldn't drive unless he had to help Grandpa take someone to the cemetery! If you don't believe me, go ask Pryor."

"Go ask Pryor, go ask Pryor," he mimicked childishly. "He was probably as juiced up as old Ferris was!"

"He was not!" she returned indignantly. "He doesn't smoke, cuss, chew tobacco, or run around with other women. He's a decent, law-abiding citizen of Meadorville and I won't hear of you bad-mouthing Pryor!"

"All right." Reed held up his hands in surrender. "I take it back. Ol' Pryor isn't a boozer."

"That's better," Taryn replied in a miffed tone.

"He's an idiot."

Taryn glared at him.

"Look, if I'm going to be forced into driving that
. . . thing, I want to get it over with. Let's cut the
small talk and get on the road."

"That sounds perfectly wonderful to me. I can
hardly wait to see your backside fading into the sun-
set," Taryn said regally as she brushed past him and
walked to the back of the hearse. "I prefer to ride
with my grandfather."

"And I prefer not to go at all!"

Taryn climbed into the back of the hearse and
loudly slammed the door. "Oh, sorry, little baby. I bet
you're afraid I'll 'wake the dead,' " she chided as she
slid the back glass panel and leaned over his shoulder
to taunt him.

"Just stop with the sick jokes!" He started the engine and glanced around him in resignation. "Just
wait until I try to explain this to Elaine and her
mother!"

With one final shiver, he put the hearse in gear and
screeched out of the funeral home parking lot with a
loud squeal of tires.

CHAPTER THREE

The town's only clinic was filled to overflowing as the long black hearse pulled up in front and stopped. It seemed to Taryn that most of Meadorville's six hundred and forty-three people must be there, seeking attention for numerous minor injuries.

She stopped several times to offer words of encouragement to a number of people as they brought Martin into the small emergency area that was already overflowing with other cots and stretchers.

Hours later they were still waiting for word on his condition. Taryn leaned tiredly against the wall, trying to mentally block out a child's screams. Reed walked up and handed her a cup of black coffee and suggested they step outside to catch a breath of fresh air.

"I gather you don't like hospitals any more than you do funeral homes," she teased lightly as they sat down on a low brick wall just outside the emergency room.

"You're right. I'm not particularly fond of either one." He took a sip of his coffee and lit a cigarette.

Glancing over in her direction, he belatedly offered the pack to her.

"No, thanks. I don't smoke, and you shouldn't either. They're bad for you," she said, giving him a disapproving frown.

"Is that the truth? I hadn't heard that," he mocked dryly. "Next thing you know, they'll be trying to take artificial sweeteners away from us."

Leaning back against the wall, he took a long drag off his cigarette, then looked up at the clear, starlit sky. "You'd never know there had been a storm earlier this evening, would you?"

"No, it is hard to believe. It sure is a beautiful night now." The low chirping of the tree frogs filled the peaceful night as they sat drinking their coffee and relaxing.

"Did you ever make your call to Elaine?"

Reed took another drag, then flipped his cigarette over the wall. "Yeah. I called her while you were in talking to the doctor."

"The clinic's phones are still working?"

"Yeah, there was a lot of static, but the call went through."

"Good. I hope she understood."

Taryn heard what sounded like a discouraging word come from where Reed was sitting, but he didn't answer her directly.

"It's none of my business, but I think she certainly should understand," Taryn commented. "After all, how could you know that you would be driving

233

through a town and be caught right in the middle of a tornado! That could have happened to Elaine just as easily as it could have happened to you and if she can't see something that simple, then I really don't know what kind of a woman she is," she pointed out quietly. "Probably she's very similar to a friend I once knew. She always wanted things to go her way and when they didn't, she was always looking for an excuse to start an argument, which used to drive me batty because I'm the type of person who would much rather have things go along smoothly than always be in a fight with someone. Wouldn't you? Now, I know that men are different from women, Gary used to always—"

"Excuse me—" he tried to interrupt.

"—laugh and say that of course men were different from women, that's what made it so nice, but I meant that men were different in the sense that they are able to take things in stride a lot easier than women. My grandpa always said that being a woman is like waking up in a whole new world every day, but I don't agree with him. Some people would call him a male chauvinist, but that's not true either. He was raised in a different generation than we were and they viewed a woman's place as being in the home and raising children, which really isn't all that bad. What do you think?"

"Well, I—" he began.

"Personally, I think it would be nice to be able to stay at home and raise my children. Naturally my husband would have to make enough money so that we could all live comfortably on his salary because with the price of groceries alone nowadays—well, it's simply astronomical what it takes to keep a household running! Why, take the price of a roast. Do you have any idea how much an average-size lean rump roast costs today?"

"No, I—"

"Over three dollars a pound, that's what! Unless you're lucky enough to catch it on sale, but that's a horse of a different color. Most of the sales are not really sales. And what about a head of lettuce? You would think you were going to line your shelves with it instead of eat it! Now of course I realize that a lot of women want and need a career and that's all well and good. I don't have any qualms about that, but for me, I think I would—"

"Hey!" Reed let out a loud shrill whistle between his teeth.

Taryn paused, and looked at him in surprise. "Yes?"

"What in the hell are you talking about?"

A rush of color flooded her cheeks. "Oh, dear, have I been rattling on again?"

"Carrying on a conversation with you is like trying to have a discussion with a dot matrix printer," he said tactlessly.

Now that hurt! "Well, excuse me. I was only trying to be friendly," she said in a tone that left him no doubt that she was more than a little put out.

"Do you jabber like this all the time?"

She turned her head away from him haughtily. "*If* I have something to jabber about. You should try it sometime, Mr. Montgomery. You're entirely too quiet. That makes people automatically suspicious of you."

"A man would have to have nerves of iron to live with you," he grunted, turning back to his coffee.

"My husband never complained," she stubbornly pointed out.

Reed's eyes came back to meet hers. "What was he like?"

Taryn's heart skipped a beat. She wasn't at all sure she wanted to discuss Gary with this arrogant stranger. "He was everything a woman could ever want in a man," she replied factually.

"Everything?" His tone was skeptical.

"Everything. And don't try to dispute that. You didn't know him," she pointed out.

"No, I didn't know him, but I can't help wondering if your opinion of him has been colored somewhat by his death. No one's perfect, Ms. Oliver."

"How dare you!" Taryn's eyes bore heatedly into the gray coldness of his. "Our love was perfect! How can you even suggest that what Gary and I had wasn't wonderful."

"If you'll recall, I didn't say a thing about 'what you and Gary had.' I simply suggested that he may not have been 'everything' a woman could desire."

"He was everything I ever wanted," she said stubbornly.

"Then I'm glad to hear it. You two must have been some of the lucky ones," he returned dryly.

"You're getting married in a week, surely you and Elaine are eager for your wedding day to arrive."

Reed gave a dry laugh. "Eager. Hardly. At least I wouldn't describe myself as eager."

Taryn's mouth dropped open. "You're not looking forward to your own wedding?"

Reed indifferently shrugged his broad shoulders.

"Are you in love with Elaine?"

Again the shoulders lifted and fell disinterestedly.

"Well, this is about the craziest thing I've ever heard of! Why would anyone want to get married if they weren't at all sure they were in love with the person? Why, Gary and I knew without a doubt that we were hopelessly in love with each other a week after we met—"

"Hey!" he cut in impatiently. "You're doing it again."

"Doing what?" she snapped.

"Talking a mile a minute!"

They sat for a while in strained silence before Reed finally picked up the conversation again. "I didn't mean that I didn't like Elaine. I probably like her as much as I'll like any woman, but I'm not marrying her for the supreme reason of being head over heels in love with her."

"That makes no sense whatsoever!" Taryn said

tersely. The idea of marriage without overwhelming love for each other was completely foreign to her.

"This may sound cold and calculating to you, but Elaine's and my marriage is in a sense a sound business investment." He shifted around uneasily and reached in his pocket for another cigarette.

"I'm afraid I don't understand," she said. "Are you going to smoke another one of those lung abusers?"

"Well, I sure don't plan on eating it!" He lit another cigarette, defying her scowl.

It was several minutes before he resumed the conversation. "I've known Elaine for several years. We dated off and on all during the time I was going through law school. I got a late start on my profession since my dad died while I was still in high school. I had to support the family until my last sister was through school." He looked at her sharply. "Just so you don't get any wrong idea, I didn't resent that fact in any way."

"I didn't say you did."

"Anyway, Elaine and I have dated for the last four years. Her father has a very lucrative law business in New Mexico, and he's never made any bones about the fact that he would like to take me in as a partner, and Elaine had never made any bones about the fact that she wanted to get married."

"This is getting disgusting," Taryn said crisply. "Are you saying you're going to marry Elaine just so you can step into an established law practice?"

"Something like that," he agreed calmly.

"That stinks."

Reed gave her a solemn look. "Why?"

"Why?" Taryn couldn't believe his gall. "Because it isn't fair to Elaine *or* you," she pointed out.

"What's not fair? I told you, I like Elaine as much as I've ever liked any woman, and since the business is sitting there waiting for me, why not take advantage of it?" He really couldn't see what the problem was.

"Listen to what you're saying, Reed! You *like* Elaine."

"That's right. I like her!"

"You should *love* Elaine!"

"Love." He dismissed the thought with a wave of his hand. "That comes along so very few times in life it isn't even worth discussing. Elaine and I can have a good marriage without . . . all that . . . mush."

"You are unreal." Taryn shook her head in disbelief. "I would hate to think I had to spend my life never knowing the joy of loving someone with all my body, heart, and soul."

"Well, now, apparently that hasn't been your problem, has it? You and your husband were madly in love, to hear you tell it," he said.

"You bet we were!" she stated flatly. "And you are going to be one miserable man if you go through with this farcical marriage."

"Please spare me the sermon. I'm thirty-four years old and should be able to know what I want to do with my life," he replied curtly.

"Yes, you *should*," she agreed tightly.

He threw his cigarette away and chuckled mirthlessly. "You want to know what I really wanted to do with my life?"

"I assumed you wanted to be a criminal lawyer."

"No, not really. That's what Mom and Dad always wanted me to be. No"—he leaned back against the wall and gazed up into the starry sky, his voice taking on a dreamlike quality—"I also wanted to own a chicken ranch."

"A what?"

"A chicken ranch." He looked at her. "Do you like chickens?"

"I like eggs. I love fried chicken, and chicken and dumplings and chicken pot pie—"

"But do you like chickens themselves?" He sat up straighter and stared at her earnestly.

"I guess so . . . I'd never really thought about it."

"I love them. When I was a kid, I used to get to take care of the animals we had on the farm. That was the good life. No worries other than running the farm every day and taking care of my own family."

"Why don't you buy a chicken farm?" she said crossly. "With all the money you'll be making from your 'business arrangement,' you'll have enough to buy enough chickens to be another Colonel Sanders of New Mexico!"

"You think I'd let people eat my chickens!" he gasped in disbelief.

"Sorry," she grumbled, surprised at how upset he was over the mere thought of anyone touching one feather on his precious chickens! "You wouldn't have to sell the chickens."

"I *have* thought seriously about buying a chicken ranch," he confessed, "but Elaine . . . doesn't like chickens." He sounded like a disappointed child.

"That's what can happen when you marry someone for business reasons, instead of love," she said seriously.

"I suppose you want me to hold out until I find someone who loves chicken ranches?" Their gazes met in the moon-drenched evening. "That may take a lifetime."

"Is that so crazy? I'm sure there're a lot of women out there who would be more than happy to live anywhere you wanted."

"You don't say." He reached over and lightly touched her bottom lip with his finger. "Would you be willing to live on a chicken ranch?"

Taryn's insides quivered at the light, playful touch of Reed's finger. "I would live anywhere with the man I loved."

"Gary was lucky." His finger slipped down to gently caress her creamy complexion. "Have you started dating again?"

"No." Her voice came out small and wistful.

"Why?"

"I'm . . . not ready."

"Still grieving? How long has it been. A year?"

"I'll never forget him."

Reed shook his head thoughtfully. "Hard act for

any man to follow. Don't you miss the companion-ship a man and woman can have with one another?" His tone was low and suggestive, leaving no doubt in Taryn's mind about what type of "companionship" he was referring to.

"I haven't yet," she answered honestly.

"The day will come when you will," he predicted, his breath fanning softly against her cheek. "Is the man who takes you to bed going to have to fight the ghost of your husband?"

"No, when that day arrives, he'll be taking just me," she whispered sincerely.

"Whether you realize it or not, you're closer to that day than you think. When I held you in my arms earlier tonight, I could sense your response," he cautioned her huskily.

Her eyes dropped shyly away from his. "I was afraid you would."

"Hey"—he tipped her face back up to meet his—"that's nothing to be ashamed about. We all have our needs."

"I know, but I feel like I'm betraying Gary if I feel those . . . needs."

"I understand that's perfectly natural when some-one loses their mate. But you're a young, beautiful woman. You're not going to be able to deny those needs forever, you know."

Her hazel eyes darkened as she felt desire surge through her like a hot electrical current. "You shouldn't even be talking to me like this. You're about to be married," she scolded halfheartedly as she watched his mouth slowly descend.

As his lips gently met hers, she froze for a moment, the shock of touching anyone other than her beloved Gary rendering her immobile.

"Relax," he urged cautiously, experimentally brushing his mouth across hers.

"I . . . don't think we should—"

"I don't think we should either, but I figure we're going to anyway, so let's enjoy it."

His mouth closed over hers, as he stood up and drew her tightly against him. Their lips moved together hesitantly at first, tasting, touching, and acquainting themselves with the feel of each other.

"Okay?" he murmured against the sweetness of her mouth.

"Okay," she returned breathlessly.

Their mouths came back to hungrily recapture each other's as they stood pressed tightly together. This time there was no mistaking his response to her lush, ripe curves molding suggestively to his. Taryn had forgotten how quickly she could be aroused by the touch of a man, but she soon remembered as his hand moved caressingly down her back, sensuously stroking her as his tongue began to claim hers. No one had ever kissed her this way. In her marriage to Gary their kisses had been . . . normal . . . satisfying, to be sure . . . but nothing like the way this man was kissing her.

When they parted, they did so with reluctance, his

gray eyes clouded with desire. "You could be a dangerous lady," he whispered, brushing his lips across hers one final time before he pushed her gently out of his arms.

"Why?" Her breathing was as uneven as his, and she felt a great sense of disappointment when he moved away from her.

"You could put a kink in a man's plans, and that would be suicide," he said curtly.

"You mean you're afraid you'll actually feel something for a woman, other than 'like,'" she chided.

"No, I'm not worried about that. But my future is well established and I'm not going to do anything to endanger it."

Taryn's arms dropped to her sides in disgust. "You are hopeless!"

"Look, I hope you didn't read anything into that kiss. It was a matter of a pretty woman being available at a weak moment," he said tactlessly.

"Oh, the kiss meant nothing to me, Mr. Montgomery. As I said before, no one will take my husband's place," she said blithely, fighting the urge to knock his teeth down his throat.

"Good, because the last woman in the world I would get involved with would be a"—he stepped back even farther from her and shivered outwardly —"mortician."

"And the last place in the world I would want to live is on a stinking old chicken farm," she assured him readily.

He acknowledged her statement with a polite nod of his head. "Just so we keep the record straight."

Taryn turned on her heel and started back into the clinic. "I'm going to see about Grandpa!"

Reed trailed along behind her as they entered the emergency room. The doctor looked up as the door opened, and smiled. "There you are, Taryn."

"Hi, Doc. Is Grandpa ready to go home?"

"That's what I wanted to talk to you about. I think I'm going to keep him here for a couple of weeks. He took a pretty bad fall, and besides the broken leg, he's complaining of a headache. In view of his age, I want to watch him closely."

"Whatever you think, Doc." Taryn peeked worriedly behind the curtains at her grandfather. "He's asleep?"

"Yes, we gave him a sedative earlier. You go on home and get some rest yourself. It's been a long night for everyone."

Taryn smiled tiredly and gratefully accepted his offer. "Thanks, I think I will."

"Was there much damage over at your place?" Doc Beason asked as he draped his arm around her waist and walked to the door with her.

"Not a lot. Some, though. I'll have to get someone over to fix the broken windows as soon as possible. Martha's services were to be tomorrow afternoon, but I can change it until Monday."

"Well, let me know if I can help. Can you run things for a while without Martin?"

"Oh, sure. That's no problem."

"Good girl. There shouldn't be any problem with your grandfather, either. A few days rest and he'll be as good as new."

Taryn and Reed walked back out to the hearse and got in. "I'll take you home, then be on my way," he said, starting the engine.

"I still think you should wait until morning," she said coolly.

"No, I've wasted enough time as it is," he returned firmly as he backed the big black limousine out of the parking space.

Fifteen minutes later they pulled into the back of the funeral home and he reached down and turned off the key. "I'll wait until I see a light go on. You know, make sure you got in all right."

"The power probably hasn't come back on yet," she reminded him as she reached for her door handle. "But I still have the candles."

"You'll be okay in there . . ."

"I'll be fine. Martha will keep me company." She couldn't resist the jibe.

Reed's large frame shuddered visibly again. "I'm glad it's you and not me."

"Will you please stop that shuddering? You're going to give me the willies!" she scolded.

"I can't help it. If I had to be in that house another five minutes, I'd croak."

"Look at it this way," she said, grinning, "you'd be in good hands if you did!"

He paled significantly at the unwelcome thought, and let out another long, exaggerated shudder.

Taryn laughed and shook her head in disbelief. "Well, good night, little baby." She opened the car door and stepped out as he exited on the driver's side. He came around to stand next to her, handing her the keys to the limousine.

"Good night. It's been . . . nice meeting you," he returned politely.

"Yes, same here." She looked away from his silvery gaze with frosty aloofness.

"Well, guess I'll go get my car. I left it out front somewhere."

"It's still there, I imagine," she returned in a bored tone, wishing he would hurry up and leave and get it over with.

"If you're ever in Santa Fe, look me up."

"Sure . . . I'll do that."

"Well . . . so long."

"So long, Mr. Montgomery."

She swallowed hard as she watched him stride determinedly away from her and disappear around the side of the house. She didn't understand her sudden feeling of loneliness.

With a sigh, she let herself in the dark house and reached for the light switch. She had been right, the power was still off. Reaching for the candle and matches in the kitchen, she lit the wick and walked on through the dark house. She picked up stray litter here and there as she walked, and her arms were soon filled. She nearly tripped over a large white sheet that had fallen off the cot they had put Martin on. Since her arms were full, she giggled and draped it over her head and laughed out loud as she thought of what Reed would say if he could see her now!

She suddenly jumped nervously as a loud pounding erupted at the front door. Reed had her as edgy as he was!

Her white sheet trailing eerily behind her, she walked to the door and held the candle up. "Who's there?"

"Me!"

"Reed?"

"Yeah, open the door."

Taryn reached down and unlocked the door and swung it open.

A loud gasp met her as Reed jumped back, his face turning ashen.

"Reed? What's wrong?"

"What do you think you're doing?" he asked weakly.

Taryn looked at him quizzically, then down at the flickering candle in her hand, and the sheet draped playfully over her head. "Oh"—she reached up and jerked the sheet off—"I was just straightening up a little bit. Did I frighten you?"

"Oh, hell, no. I'm used to ghosts answering the doors at funeral parlors," he scoffed.

"What's the matter? I thought you were leaving,"

Taryn asked as he brushed by her and stepped into the room.

"I was, but there's a twenty-foot tree lying across my car."

"Oh, that's too bad!" Taryn suddenly felt very happy once more. "I guess there's no one to remove it tonight, huh?" She tried very hard to keep the delight out of her voice.

"Not in this one-horse town," he grumbled.

"Well, the offer's still open to sleep here tonight."

"I was thinking that you might run me down to the nearest motel."

Taryn smiled serenely. "The 'nearest' motel is about seventy miles away, Reed. We don't even have a boardinghouse in Meadorville, let alone a Holiday Inn. I heard some people talking at the clinic and they said the full brunt of the storm hit over in the direction of the main highway, so undoubtedly it's impassable. I'm afraid you're stuck."

Reed looked defeated. "Then I guess I haven't any choice."

"You could always sleep in your car if you're afraid something's going to get you," she whispered in a low, ghostly tone of conspiracy.

"You think I haven't already thought of that? My Bronco happens to be packed full or that's exactly where I would be sleeping," he whispered back tersely.

Taryn laughed and supportively put her arm around his waist. "Come on, you big baby, I'll fix you a bed on the sofa. I personally guarantee, barring an act of God, you'll still be safe and sound in the morning."

"Don't put me anywhere near that room . . . Martha's in," he warned in a whine.

"You don't want to be bunkies?"

"Cut the clowning, Taryn!"

"Such a baby," she clucked again, and affectionately squeezed his waist. For the life of her she didn't know why she was so glad to see this arrogant, cold-blooded lawyer, whose secret dream was to become a chicken farmer, back on her doorstep, but she was. That was what really worried her. She was not only glad, she was delighted.

CHAPTER FOUR

"Would you care for another slice of toast?" Taryn turned from the stove where she was frying bacon to confront a very haggard-looking Reed.

"No, thanks. I'll just have another cup of coffee, if you don't mind. Man alive! I don't feel like I've even been to bed," he confessed in a sleepy voice.

"That doesn't surprise me." Taryn's grin was mischievous as she lifted the crisp slices of bacon out on a paper towel to drain. "It couldn't be very relaxing to sleep with one eye open all night," she granted in a solemn voice.

"Both eyes open," he corrected earnestly as he polished off the last of his eggs and bacon.

"You sure you don't want more bacon or toast?" she prompted. She had gotten up early to make him a good breakfast and wanted him to stay as long as possible.

"Nope. As soon as I finish my coffee, I'm going to be on my way." As if to emphasize his words, he drained his cup and hurriedly set it back down on the table.

Taryn filled her plate and sat down at the table

opposite him in the sunny breakfast nook. Buttering her toast liberally, she bit into the crisp bread and idly wondered why the thought of his leaving disturbed her.

"What's the hurry?" she asked in a casual voice, trying to keep her tone impartial.

"I have to see about getting someone to get the tree off my car, and get it fixed as soon as possible. Elaine expects me in Santa Fe as soon as I can get there."

"Oh, yes. Elaine." Taryn forcefully attacked her eggs, trying to ignore the reference to Reed's fiancée. "As soon as I eat, I guess I better get busy myself," she confessed. "I have to see about getting the house put back in shape, then I'll go over and check on Grandpa."

"I hope the old fellow is doing okay," Reed offered.

"Oh, I'm sure he is. There's nothing 'old' about Grandpa," Taryn replied in a positive manner. "He'll bounce back in no time at all." She ate the last slice of bacon on her plate and hurriedly downed her orange juice. "I'd suggest you walk over to Hess's garage and see if Max can help you with your car. Ferris dropped by earlier this morning and told me Foster and his wife have been slightly injured in the storm, so he won't be able to help you."

"Who?"

"Foster. You know, the man who lives in the cottage out in back of the house. He and his wife help Grandpa run the funeral home."

252

"Oh, yeah. Well"—Reed stood up and stretched—"I suppose I should get started."

Taryn eyed with despair his rumpled clothes and the dark stubble on his face. "I'm sorry. I've forgotten my manners this morning. I'm sure you'll want to shower and change clothes before you leave," she proposed tactfully.

Absently rubbing the dark growth of his beard, he smiled self-consciously. "I hate to be a bother, but I do look rather disreputable, don't I?"

"A little," she agreed. "Why don't you go get your suitcase and shower and shave before you tackle the problem of your car," she suggested brightly as she rose from the table and walked over to the sink with their plates. "I'm sure Elaine wouldn't want you showing up in Santa Fe looking like an . . . opprobrious chicken farmer," she encouraged with a teasing grin.

"No, I'm sure she wouldn't want that, whatever that is," he acknowledged wryly.

"Not many women would," Taryn conceded, hating to allot Elaine any points in her favor, but after all, she knew *she* wouldn't want her intended showing up the way he looked right now! "The chicken farmer part wouldn't be so bad," she hastened to add, noting the look of distress on his face, "but I'm sure she would prefer you to look a little more . . ." She searched frantically for a diplomatic description of what she thought Elaine would prefer. ". . . successful . . . maybe."

His laugh was deep and sincere and filled the room pleasantly. "Good try."

Taryn's shoulders lifted apologetically.

"I'll go get my suitcase," he chuckled, "and take you up on your very gracious offer."

"Good. Do you want me to walk you through the front part of the house?" she offered, knowing how uneasy he was in his present surroundings.

"No, thank you, I'm going out the back door."

"It's a lot farther," she reminded him.

"I need the exercise," he said quickly.

"Really? The way you've been racing through the front part of the house this morning, I would think exercise is the last thing you need," she teased him.

He opened the back door and saluted her in a cocky way. "In the words of someone famous: 'I shall return.'"

"In the words of someone not so famous, hurry up. We have a lot to do."

While he was gone, Taryn straightened the kitchen, thankful that this room had sustained the least damage. In fact, the entire living quarters had survived the main onslaught of the storm, with the exception of a few broken windows. Because of the storm, Martha Feagan's services would have to be postponed until the following day. Taryn was worried over the fact that for the next couple of weeks she would have to run the funeral home by herself until her grandfather recovered. Her concern wasn't over whether she could handle the responsibility.

She could, with her eyes closed. Although she had been gone a year, it didn't feel that long to her. It seemed like only yesterday she had left this town as a carefree bride, looking forward to a future filled with love. Little did she know she would be returning a mere twelve months later, alone.

A soft tap at the back door brought her abruptly back to the present as she called out for Reed to enter.

Minutes later she was ushering him to the bath off the main hallway and leaving a clean towel and a washcloth on the vanity. "If you need anything else, just yell," she instructed as she backed out of the small room.

"Thanks. I shouldn't be too long," he acknowledged gratefully.

Oh, dear Lord, *please* let him have a pair of trousers that don't make him look so darn *virile!* she prayed silently as she returned to her work.

She busied herself straightening up the family room and minutes later suddenly found herself softly singing along with the deep baritone voice coming from the shower in the bathroom. When she realized what she was doing, she paused and listened intently to Reed's voice drifting pleasantly through the air. He was unconsciously entertaining her with a popular ballad she had heard many times before, but never in the rich, soul-stirring way he was performing it.

When the bathroom door opened ten minutes

later, she was still marveling at how beautiful his voice was.

"It is amazing what a shower and shave can do for a person's morale," he conceded as he walked into the family room and set his suitcase down. "I actually feel human again."

Taryn's attention was drawn to his slacks, and she heaved an inward sigh of relief that her prayers had been answered. Although he looked stunningly handsome in his khaki slacks and polo shirt, they sufficiently disguised his impressive body.

"You smell good enough to attack," she teased, then caught herself in embarrassment. "I mean . . . you smell nice," she amended quickly.

"Attack, huh?" He hadn't let that unfortunate choice of words go unnoticed.

"You also have a very nice voice," she hurried on, hoping to distract him. "Do you sing professionally?"

"Attack, huh?" His grin was mischievous as he continued to pursue her slip of tongue. "Do you know something? It suddenly occurred to me I have never been attacked by a woman. Now that could prove interesting. I might want to give the idea some serious thought."

"Do you?"

"Yes, I've thought it over very carefully and you have my permission to attack me."

"No! I meant, do you sing professionally," she scolded, her face turning red at his teasing words.

"Do I sing professionally? Good grief, no! Where in the world would you get an idea like that?"

"I was listening to you sing while you were in the shower, and your voice is lovely," she said sincerely.

His face turned a miserable shade of pink now. "Could you hear me?"

Taryn nodded. "Martha and I both enjoyed it."

"Oh, come on. I had almost forgotten about . . . Martha," he groaned, not quite sure how to take her friendly badgering.

"Well, I can't forget Martha. I'm going to have to get busy and get the home back in shape for her services tomorrow. If you're ready, though, I'll walk to your car with you to see the damage myself. And since the phone is still out, I'll have to personally talk to Junior about getting the windows replaced."

"I'm ready," he acknowledged, picking up his suitcase. "I need to find a phone that's working and call Elaine and let her know I'm on my way."

"By all means," Taryn returned coolly. "She'll want to start whipping up her punch."

Forgetting for a moment Reed's aversion to his surroundings, Taryn led them through the front part of the house on the way outside. She noticed that Reed fell unusually silent and his eyes grew noticeably rounder as they passed the double wooden doors that were marked PARLOR A&B. A workman Taryn had visited and recruited earlier that morning was busy cleaning up the debris as she paused to talk to him.

"The man from the phone company said he'd have the phone back in commission by late this morning," the man told her as she stepped into the office and surveyed the progress being made.

"That's good to hear, Ronnie." Even though this was a very small town, a funeral director was on call twenty-four hours a day and a telephone was a necessity. "It looks like you're getting the bulk of things back in shape."

"I'm trying. You were real lucky, you know. The storm barely skimmed over this neighborhood, but the folks over on Wilder Street didn't fare as well."

Taryn frowned. "Was there a great deal of damage over there?"

"Afraid so. Tore down five whole blocks," he confirmed in a grim voice.

Taryn started straightening some papers on the desk. "We can be thankful there weren't any deaths, although I hear one man's injuries are still considered very serious." She glanced up and noticed Reed standing in the background as she chatted with the workman. "I'm sorry, Ronnie. I don't believe you've met Reed Montgomery."

Reed stepped forward and firmly grasped the older man's hand. "Hello, Ronnie. Nice to meet you."

"Reed was just passing through town when he was caught in the storm," Taryn explained. "I was just walking with him to his car."

"Then I won't keep you," Ronnie assured. He

reached for the broom he had been using and quietly went back to his work.

"This place doesn't look so bad in the light of day," Reed remarked casually as Taryn stepped out of the office and they began their journey once more.

"It isn't 'bad,' " she laughed. "Would you like me to show you around?"

"No . . . I don't have time. . . ." he refused swiftly.

"Oh, for heaven's sake. There isn't that much to see, actually." She reached over and took his hand and pulled him along beside her. "Now look. Over here we have the parlor." Pausing at the entrance of the elegantly furnished room, she let him survey the scene before him. "See. It's just a nice, quiet room that our families use for time alone to gather their thoughts," she explained, retracing their steps down the carpeted hallway. "We have four lovely slumber rooms, although we rarely use more than two."

"Slumber rooms?" Reed repeated in a weak voice.

"Yes, slumber rooms. Would you like to see one?" The look he shot her assured her he didn't.

"Martha is in . . . well, you know where Martha is," she said hastily, impatiently tugging at him as his footsteps faltered.

"Yes, I know where 'Martha' is, and it's my heartfelt desire she stay there . . . at least until I can get out of here," he grumbled.

All too soon, in Reed's opinion, they were standing

in front of another doorway, one that he immediately started backing away from.

"And here we have the preparation room," Taryn announced proudly. "Even though we are a very small business, Grandpa has always insisted on the most modern, up-to-date equipment for his home. . . . Reed! Get back here!" she demanded. "I'm not going to take you in there, I only wanted to point out where it was," she chided, firmly holding on to his hand, as if he were a child about to misbehave.

"I appreciate your time and consideration, but I think I've seen enough," he said in a determined voice, jerking his hand from hers almost belligerently. "I have to go."

"But you haven't seen our showroom," she protested in a small, disappointed voice. "There is the most gorgeous casket in there that you simply have to see. It has this yummy light-colored beige silk interior with a real innerspring mattress—"

"Taryn!"

"Yes?" She turned innocently to face him.

"No, I don't want to see a casket with an innerspring mattress!"

"Oh, you don't? Then how about the one with the water bed in it?" she tormented with a devilish glint in her eye.

"No! I don't want to see any of it!"

"Oh." She shrugged her shoulders and trailed along behind him as he stalked back through the hallway muttering something under his breath about getting out of this place before it got to him.

The morning sunlight was warm and exhilarating as Reed and Taryn stepped out the front door of the home and started their walk to his car.

"I love this time of year, don't you?" Taryn enthused, taking a deep, cleansing breath of the rain-washed summer air.

"It's all right," Reed muttered as she hurried along to keep up with his long strides. It was clear his mind was still back at the funeral home.

"Oh, you party pooper! Why are you so serious all the time?" Taryn reprimanded in a bubbly voice. She waved at an attractive, well-dressed, older couple walking on the other side of the street, calling out a friendly greeting to them.

"That's Lester and Elizabeth. They own the local market here in town, and they are two of the nicest people you'd ever want to meet. You want to meet them?" she queried hopefully. She didn't know why she was trying so hard to make him like her town, but she was. "You'd really like them," she promised.

"I haven't got time to meet them," he said firmly but politely. "I'm sure I would be crazy about them, but I have to take care of getting my car fixed and be on my way."

"Oh, well you just might be staying longer than you think and then you could help me . . . you know . . . until we see how Grandpa is going to be. . . ." Why had she opened her big mouth! Why, indeed, would he consider helping a strange woman who operated a business he was literally terrified of? But she plunged on anyway. "You know, you might not be able to get anyone to cut the tree off your car today and you really don't know how badly damaged it is," she warned, hurrying to catch up with him as he started walking again, and at a much faster pace than he had before, she noticed. "Everyone's busier than a long-tailed cat in a roomful of rockers. It took me a while this morning to round up someone to clean the mortuary."

"If I have to chew the tree off my car, I'll do it," he said matter-of-factly. By now they had reached the car, which he grimly surveyed. "Elaine is not the most patient person in the world," he added as an afterthought.

"Well, it's quite possible that she may have to develop that characteristic," Taryn returned, her voice showing annoyance for the first time.

"It's also quite possible that she won't," he pointed out blandly.

"You still have six days before the wedding takes place."

"Six days? Yeah, I guess it is only six days away now." For a moment it sounded like the idea had unexpectedly sneaked up on him. "But that doesn't matter. I have to get there as soon as I can."

Taryn seethed inwardly as he walked around the blue Ford Bronco, quietly assessing his chances of getting an early start out of town this morning.

He sounded as if his precious Elaine had brain-washed him, she thought, simmering irritably. Taryn bade him a cool good-bye and started on down the street, leaving him alone with his troubled car, his misguided forthcoming marriage, and hopeless dreams of a chicken ranch he would never have.

It took most of the morning for her to arrange for the windows to be repaired, and to visit with her grandpa, who was doing remarkably well. Assuring him again that she would have no problem running the business by herself until he could take part once more, she returned home and ate a light lunch, then went upstairs to take a short nap.

As she lay across her bed, she reached for the small photograph on her bedside table of a smiling, blond-haired man with laughing blue eyes. Rolling over on her back, she hugged the picture close to her heart and desperately tried to remember the smell and feel of Gary. She hadn't wanted to forget the smallest detail about him, but it was growing harder every day to recall even the simplest things about him, like what shade of blue his eyes were, or was his hair really blond or just slightly golden? Every night, she would fall asleep staring at his picture trying to renew her memory, but an old photograph was a poor substitute for a pair of strong arms to hold her through the long, lonely nights.

"Oh, Gary," she murmured. "Why did you have to go?" She sighed once more, and propped up on her elbow. A terrible sense of loneliness crept over her.

"Oh, Gary. I wish you were here with me," she whispered in a muffled sob as her eyes drifted shut in weariness. "When will the pain ever stop?"

She couldn't have dozed for more than a few minutes before she heard the peal of the front-door chimes. Trying to overcome the drowsiness that held her captive, she struggled off the bed and stumbled downstairs. Someone must be coming to check about Martha's services, she speculated sleepily. Ronnie had told her there had been a steady stream of people dropping by this morning, while she had been out, to ask about the new arrangements.

When she opened the door and found Reed Montgomery standing there, a thrill of elation shot through her before she quickly covered her delight and made herself comment in a blasé tone, "Why, hello. Are we slumming again?"

" 'We' still have a tree on our car," he lamented in a miserable voice saturated with defeat.

"How heartbreaking! Couldn't you manage to chew it off?" She was trying her darndest to keep the elation out of her voice.

"No, but I tried," he solemnly hastened to add. "But you were right. It looks like I'm going to be stuck here. I've covered every square inch of this town looking for an available man to clear the tree off my car, and there just isn't any. Say," he asked, suddenly coming up with a hopeful solution, "you don't happen to have a chain saw I could use, do you?"

"No." She sighed in mock resignation. "Contrary

to what you've seen in old horror movies, we don't use chain saws in our business anymore."

His face turned a shade paler. "Will you cut that out!"

"Oh, all right," she relented crossly. This guy was something else! "I assume you have chosen to grace my doorstep again for some reason. To what do I owe the honor?"

"Now, look. If you weren't looking at a desperate man, I wouldn't be within two hundred miles of this place right now, but the way I see it, I don't have a whole lot of alternatives. There isn't a room available anywhere, my car isn't going anywhere, not to mention the fact that all of the highways leading out of town are blocked with fallen power lines, so what am I gonna do!"

"So, you're 'gonna' have to stay here again tonight," she stated simply, her pulse racing at the unexpected but highly welcome prospect.

"I suppose I will," he returned glumly. "I don't want to seem ungrateful but—"

"You don't have to sleep downstairs again. You can use Grandpa's room," she offered, trying to make the sleeping arrangements a little more palatable for him. "I don't know why I didn't think of that last night."

A look of pathetic relief invaded his features now. "Thanks, I really would appreciate that."

Reed was about to step through the open door

when Taryn heard a woman's voice breathlessly calling out to him.

Reed turned and watched as Sadie Mullins came scurrying up on the porch, carrying Malcolm in his birdcage.

"Oh, I'm so glad I caught you," she gasped. "Malcolm would have never forgiven me if I had left him with anyone else while I was gone!"

Both Reed and Taryn stared wordlessly at the squawking bird swinging back and forth on his perch. "Are you going somewhere?" Taryn finally asked.

"I have to check into the clinic for a few days," she moaned. "I have a heart condition and with all the excitement I'm afraid it's decided to act up again. I know this is asking an awful lot of you, but Martin always told me to call on him if I needed anything. . . . Oh, I hate to be such a bother, but I don't have anyone to watch Malcolm and then I remembered how firm Mr. Montgomery was with him the night of the storm and I just knew he would be the one to watch him while I was in the clinic. Even though Malcolm acts as if he doesn't like Mr. Montgomery, I'm quite sure he does! I'm afraid Malcolm has become a little unruly since my husband died and he needs a good firm hand!" she admitted candidly.

Reed glanced helplessly at Taryn, silently willing her to get him out of this mess. "Uh . . . oh, boy . . . I'm afraid I'm in a bad position to watch your bird right now, Sadie . . . I've got to—"

Malcolm let out an ear-piercing squawk, followed by a round of violent swinging on his perch as he yelled over and over, "Malcolm is a baaad boy! Malcolm is a baaad boy!"

"No, no dear. The nice man didn't say you were a bad boy!" Sadie crooned, trying to console the frantically swinging bird. She cast an apologetic look in Taryn and Reed's direction. "He's such a sensitive little darling. I shouldn't have said what I did about him getting out of hand since Lonnie died. . . ."

"Squawk! Malcolm wants Poppy!" the bird demanded in a belligerent voice.

"Oh, dear me, now I've got him thinking about Poppy again, that's what he called my husband," she explained with a wail, hovering close to tears herself now.

Taryn hastily took the birdcage out of her hand and thrust it toward Reed. "We'll take care of Malcolm," she promised, ignoring the look of "wait till I get my hands on you!" he had shot her. "Reed may be too busy trying to get his car fixed, but I'll take good care of your bird."

"Oh, would you?" Sadie's tears ceased instantly as she smiled at Reed, who was now tapping on the side of the birdcage, irritably trying to assert his authority over the unruly bird.

"You know, he isn't really a bird," she confessed. "He's more like the child I never had."

Taryn smiled tolerantly. "You go on to the clinic and don't worry about a thing."

"Would you water my plants and feed my other pets while I'm gone?" she asked hopefully. "Malcolm is the only one who needs personal attention at all times."

"Just leave me a key and I'll take care of everything," Taryn promised.

Minutes later, after a round of loud, squawking good-byes from Malcolm, Sadie was on her way, assured that everything she loved would still be intact when she returned home in a few days.

"I can't *believe* you agreed to keep this loudmouth for two days!" Reed groaned, jerking his finger back from the cage moments before Malcolm could take a hunk of skin. "This bird hates me!"

"You're imagining things," Taryn excused, uneasily eyeing the bird from a distance. "Didn't you hear Sadie say he secretly liked you?"

He turned his eyes up toward the heavens in a desperate plea. "What have I done to deserve this?" he beseeched. "Don't you think a redheaded mortician and a psychopathic bird are a little severe?"

"Squawk! Malcolm is a baaad boy! Malcolm is a baaad boy!" the bird shouted.

"He sure *is!* Squawk! He sure *is!*" Reed parroted in disgusted agreement.

The sound of Taryn's laughter followed him as he entered the house and hastily went in search of somewhere to put his new charge.

CHAPTER FIVE

"You look sleepy this morning."

"I *am* sleepy this morning," Reed confirmed in a grouchy voice the next day at breakfast. "That darn bird talked all night."

"About what?"

"Who knows! I'm telling you, Taryn, that bird needs some kind of therapy. He's got the worst inferiority complex I've ever encountered! When he wasn't jabbering about wanting something to eat, he was shouting 'Malcolm is a baaad boy' all night long."

Taryn got up to pour more coffee for them, silently noting that two nights of disrupted sleep was leaving its mark on him. They had had an early supper the evening before and both had retired to their rooms, hoping to catch up on their rest. Apparently, Reed's effort had failed.

"You can put Malcolm in my room tonight," she offered.

"I hope I won't have to," he pointed out. "I've got to call Elaine again," he murmured to himself.

"Instead of promising her you'll be there a certain

day, why don't you simply tell her you'll be there as soon as you can?"

"I've told her that every time I've called."

"Does she know where you are? Where you're staying?"

"She knows I'm stranded in a town named Meadorville, but she doesn't know exactly where I'm staying," he hedged.

"Well, it's all very innocent," Taryn reminded casually. It disturbed her when she thought of his marrying Elaine, especially the reason he was marrying her for. She didn't know why she felt so protective of him, but it just seemed to her he deserved much better in life. A marriage without love would, in Taryn's opinion, be unbearable.

"Are you sure you really want to go through with this marriage?" she asked him gently.

Instead of surprised indignation, which she fully expected, his answer was quiet and pensive. "There're times I have doubts about it," he confessed. "I thought that went along with the game."

"Game?" Taryn shook her head sadly. "Marriage and love aren't a game, Reed."

"Love!" He voiced the word musingly. "I don't see what the big fuss is. I've seen the earth-shattering kind portrayed in movies and I read about it in almost every book I pick up, every song I hear on the radio, but personally I think it's all a lot of malarkey."

"You've never been in love?" she asked him incredulously.

"Not that way," he confided. "Oh, I love my family. . . ."

"But you've never loved a woman with all those 'earth-shattering' feelings you just spoke about? You've never met anyone you just *knew* you didn't want to live without?"

"No, I haven't." His gaze was fixed steadily on his cup as he spoke calmly. "I just told you, I don't believe in that kind of love."

"Boy, are you in for a surprise," she remarked playfully.

"Did you and your husband have that kind of love?"

"You bet we did," she said honestly. "And I have every intention of finding it again someday."

"Well, as I've told you before, Elaine and I will have a good marriage without all that . . . togetherness." He pushed away from the table, stood up, and stretched. "I guess I better go feed Malcolm. He was sleeping like a rock when I left the room this morning."

Taryn laughed. "He was probably exhausted from his night of chatter."

"What's on your agenda today?" he inquired pleasantly as they walked out of the kitchen.

"Martha Feagan's services are this afternoon. I have a world of things to do before then. You don't suppose you could help me with some of them, do you? Foster isn't feeling very well this morning. He

271

won't be here to help me until this afternoon. He'll have to drive the hearse to the cemetery for me."

"I can't, Taryn. . . ." Reed hated to refuse her after all she had done for him, yet he couldn't bring himself to offer his help. It would have been a different case altogether if she worked in maybe a restaurant or something. He'd be glad to fry hamburgers or scrub floors to help her out, but a mortuary . . . He shuddered. "I should start looking for someone to cut that tree off my Bronco."

"All I want you to do is run the sweeper in the front foyer for me," she chided, knowing exactly why he was refusing.

"Just run the sweeper?"

"That's all. I have a lot of paperwork I have to do and I have to be sure I have all the cards off the floral arrangements. You could do that if you'd rather," she offered, forgetting his allergies for a moment.

"Where are the flowers?" he asked cautiously.

"Well . . . you know . . . in there with Martha."

"I'll sweep." He made his choice without a second thought. "Where's the sweeper?"

"In the storage closet. Come on, I'll show you."

She hustled him down the hallway and stopped before a large door that housed the mops, brooms, sweeper, and cleaning supplies. "If you don't mind, could you dust a little, too?"

"Now wait a minute," he grumbled, dragging the large, heavy-duty sweeper out of the closet. "I

272

thought I was only supposed to run the sweeper in the foyer."

"Well, for heaven's sake! While you have it out, it's not going to hurt you to run it in the parlor, too. You wouldn't want people to come to a dusty funeral, would you?"

"Who in the world is going to notice a little bit of dust if they're coming to a funeral?" he asked in disbelief. "That's the last thing I'd have on my mind! Besides, I've already done all I can for Martha. I picked her up and put her back in that thing after the storm, didn't I?"

"I bet you don't attend funerals, period, do you?" she surmised correctly. "I bet you just let your friends leave this world without so much as a 'so long, it's been good to know you,' " she finished irritably, plugging in the sweeper and handing it to him.

"If they're *my* friends, I guarantee they're not even looking for me," he answered serenely.

"Sweep the office while you're at it." Taryn gave him a dirty look and walked away, seething at his indifference to mankind.

Reed tackled the parlor first and had it shining in thirty minutes. He carefully avoided the area where he knew the two double doors were closed, saving it until last. When he could no longer put it off, he dragged his cleaning supplies and sweeper over to Parlor B and set to work.

He was whistling under his breath, trying to keep his mind off what he knew lay on the other side of the wooden doors, when he looked up and saw the doors opening. He paused in his work, his eyes narrowing suspiciously as a large, stern-faced woman walked toward him. He had no idea who she was and he wasn't quite sure if he really wanted to.

"Pardon me," she summoned in an authoritative voice, "I was wondering if you could help me."

Reed paused, letting his sweeper run as he looked her over cautiously. What was she doing in Martha's room? The vacuum sounded as if it were sucking up rocks now as Reed leaned closer and asked in a wary voice, "What did you say?"

The woman took a deep, offensive breath, drawing in her mammoth bosom. "I said, I need your help!"

Still unable to make out her words above the clatter of the sweeper, Reed reached down and shut it off. "Now, what did you say?"

"Are you deaf?" she asked, none too kindly. "Must you respond in such a boisterous refrain? You *are* aware that there are those reposing in this house!"

"I am aware of that," he said, relenting. "Who are you?"

"I am Ms. Feagan!"

Reed's stubborn features went instantly limp. He sagged against the sweeper and stared at her with a sheepish grin on his face. "You are not," he accused weakly.

"I most certainly am!"

"No, you're not!" he insisted stubbornly, still exhibiting a disbelieving, shaky grin. "Mrs. Feagan is re-

274

posing. . . . I know she is. I helped put her there.
. . ."

"Young man, just who do you think you are?"

"Lady! I know who I am. You cut out the clowning and tell me who you are," he said in a cross voice.

"I told you, I'm Ms. Feagan and my gladiolus are dry. What are you going to do about it?" Her black, beady eyes pinned him to the spot, demanding a prompt and immediate answer.

"I'm not going to do anything about . . . that," he hedged dogmatically, not having the slightest idea of what a gladiolus was or what to do about it. "Taryn takes care of . . . you reposing people. You'll have to go ask her." He had no idea who this woman was, but if she thought she was Martha Feagan, he wasn't going to stand here trying to convince her she wasn't.

At the sound of loud, angry voices coming from the hallway, Taryn stuck her head out of the doorway and glanced toward Parlor B. "Millicent? Is there something wrong?" she called softly.

The woman and Reed were squared off facing each other like two combatants as Taryn hurriedly slipped out of the office and came over to where they were standing. "Is there a problem?" she asked.

"This brash young man *will not* get any water for the gladiolus I sent Mother yesterday," Millicent Feagan cried in a heartbroken voice. "It breaks my heart to see those lovely blooms growing more wilted every minute."

"Reed?" Taryn glanced at him in puzzlement as

she slipped her arm through his and separated the warring factions. "Why wouldn't you get Millicent some water for her mother's flowers?"

"She told me she *was* Martha Feagan!" he tattled in a distraught voice.

"I did not tell him I was Mother!" Millicent gasped, her face turning as pale as Reed's now. "I told him I was Ms. Feagan!"

"That's what I said!" he bellowed. "You told me your name was Feagan!"

"My name *is* Feagan, you idiot!" she bellowed in a most unladylike voice.

"Quiet, you two!" Taryn hissed under her breath. "Now this is ridiculous! Reed, this is Martha's daughter, Millicent. Now please go get her a pitcher of water so she can take care of the flowers." She turned to place a placating arm around the sniffling woman. "Now, please try to pull yourself together, Millicent. This has all been just a small misunderstanding. Reed didn't know that you were Martha's daughter and he's been a little edgy today," she comforted, shooting Reed a murderous glare.

"He was so rude," she whimpered self-righteously. "He didn't care one whit whether Mother's gladiolus went limp!"

"Oh, no, Millicent, he cares," Taryn crooned, leading her back through the wooden double doors. "He's really very understanding."

"See, I told you you weren't Mrs. Feagan," he gloated childishly under his breath as Millicent passed him. He was smugly determined to have the last word in this argument.

"Reed!" Taryn scolded heatedly. "Go get the water!"

"I'm going already!" He turned and marched irritably toward the kitchen.

When he returned, he set the water down in front of the doors of Parlor B and yelled for Millicent to "Come and get it!" then went straight to the office and loudly slammed the door. Minutes later, Taryn followed, closing the door quietly behind her. "That little scene was completely uncalled-for, Reed. We are trying to operate this business in a quiet, dignified manner and that does not include yelling 'Come and get it!' in our slumber rooms and slamming office doors."

"Don't start with me, Taryn," he warned in a testy voice. "You know how this place gets to me! I'm out there minding my own business when this lunatic looking like a marine drill sergeant comes waltzing out of Parlor B and announces she is Ms. Feagan! What in the hell was I supposed to do? Believe her?"

Taryn stifled a laugh, determined to keep a straight face in front of him. She was aware he was nervous in his new surroundings and she had to be tolerant with him. "I still think you could have been politer. After all, she is a customer, and her name is Ms. Feagan. She's never married."

"No kidding," he mocked. "I wonder why?"

"Reed." Taryn frowned at his lack of tact.

"Is this phone working yet?" He eyed the receiver hopefully.

"Yes, why—"

"I'm going to call Elaine."

Taryn's heart fell. "Oh, do you want me to leave?" She was beginning to notice a disconcerting pattern. Every time things got tough, he had to call his precious Elaine!

"Suit yourself, I'm not going to seduce her over the telephone," he assured her in a grumpy voice. Picking up the receiver, he dialed the long-distance operator and placed a collect call to Elaine Matthews in Santa Fe, New Mexico.

Taryn busied herself with the paperwork she had been working on earlier as he talked with his fiancée. Although he was being very casual in his conversation, Taryn felt stirrings of jealousy toward Elaine. He was talking to the woman he was going to be marrying in another few days! Berating herself for such foolish feelings, she tried to block out Reed's voice and was surprised at how successful she was. It shouldn't make any difference one way or the other whom he was talking to, or in what manner he was talking to them, she reminded herself. But, darn it, it did!

"How many times are you going to staple that piece of paper," she heard his voice ask a few minutes later.

Looking up from her work, she encountered Reed's amused face. "What?"

278

"The paper. How many times are you going to staple it?" he repeated patiently, motioning to the social security form she had absently riddled with staples.

Taryn stared blankly at the paper in her hand, then threw it back on the desk in embarrassment. "I like to be sure none of the forms are lost," she excused lamely. "Saves me a lot of trouble."

"It might save you a lot of trouble," he agreed, "but I'd sure hate to be the one you're sending it to."

"Well, you're not, so why worry? How's Elaine?" Taryn stood up and walked over to file the paper, hoping he didn't think she had been listening to his conversation and not concentrating on her work.

"She's a little ticked off, but she'll get over it." Taryn detected a strained optimism in his answer.

"Still doesn't understand your situation?" she queried lightly. "Would it help if I called her and explained?"

"I hope you're joking," he said.

Taryn shut the file cabinet and smiled innocently. "Why, no. Should I be?" She exaggeratedly batted her eyelashes at him.

Leaning back in the chair he was seated in, he propped his feet on the desk and lit a cigarette. Through a haze of smoke his eyes narrowed appreciably as he seemed suddenly to take a candid and admiring look at her for the first time. "Let's put it this way. How would you feel if your fiancé was holed up somewhere with a redhead who was built like

Raquel Welch, and that same fiancé happens to have a terrible weakness when it comes to redheads with big hazel eyes, skin like peaches and cream, a fanny that's. . . ." His voice trailed off sexily as his eyes continued to lazily explore the outlines of her thin cotton dress. ". . . that's very hard to keep his hands off."

Mixed feelings of pleasure surged through her as she made her way back over to the desk and sank down in her chair. Her heart hammered painfully against her ribs and she wondered where all the air in the room had suddenly disappeared to.

"I wasn't aware you were attracted . . . to redheads," she stammered softly, hoping he wasn't playing some silly little macho game with her.

"Come now, Taryn. Let's not play coy," he chided. "You know you're a darn attractive woman."

"I'm not being 'coy,' " she protested, trying to avoid the smoldering invitation in his gray eyes. "You haven't given me one indication you felt attracted to me."

He took a long drag off his cigarette, letting the smoke curl out in tiny little ringlets, still intently studying her. "I haven't? What do you call that kiss we shared a couple of nights ago."

She laughed in a shaky voice. "For me? Desperation! I haven't been kissed by a man in over a year and I guess I went bananas for a minute."

"Desperate widow, huh?" His smile was wicked. "Sounds interesting."

"Not that desperate," she cautioned. "Are you playing little games with me, Mr. Montgomery? Because if you are, you're wasting your time. I've made it well over a year without the companionship of a man and I haven't any plans to change my state of celibacy."

"I'm not doing anything other than sitting here smoking a cigarette," he denied in an innocent voice. "You're reading something into the conversation that isn't there, desperate widow." He winked innocently.

Taryn smiled tolerantly. "Of course. I'm so sorry for misjudging you. I'm sure you're a perfect angel."

"Maybe not perfect, but close to it," he agreed, sitting up straighter to stub his cigarette out in the ashtray. "What do you want me to do next?"

Taryn looked at him warily. "In relation to what?"

"In relation to my cleaning duties." He had changed the subject so quickly, she was taken off guard.

"My goodness. You scared me for a minute," she said, laughing. "I thought we were still talking about me." She couldn't help feeling a slight disappointment that he had given up so easily.

For a moment his gaze captured hers and held it. "I think we'd better change the subject before I start saying things a man engaged shouldn't be saying to another woman," he said matter-of-factly.

"If a man feels like he wants to say 'things' to another woman, maybe he shouldn't be engaged at all," she reminded him, reaching out to gently touch his hand. She didn't know what had gotten into her lately. She had never made a pass at a man who was engaged!

His hand closed over hers in mutual understanding as they stood facing each other in the small room. His touch sent shivers of delight racing down her spine, and for a moment she considered leaning over, wrapping her arms around his neck, and kissing him senseless! At that moment, there was nothing in the world she wanted more!

"Maybe he shouldn't," Reed relented in a voice suddenly filled with seriousness. He reached out to touch a lock of her hair reverently. "The color of your hair reminds me of the sun setting on a hot summer evening," he whispered huskily.

"Can I kiss you?" she asked impetuously, no longer able to deny her attraction to him.

By the sudden look of shock on Reed's face, you would have thought she had asked if she could pull his toenails out by the roots! "No!" he refused guiltily. He drew away quickly and fumbled nervously in his shirt pocket for another cigarette.

"Why not?" she demanded, a shadow of annoyance flickering across her face. He didn't love Elaine! He had admitted as much!

"Because, damn it, I'm engaged!" he told her in exasperation.

"That doesn't count because you don't really love Elaine," Taryn pointed out, stepping closer to his lithe, muscular physique. "If I really thought for one minute that you loved her, I wouldn't dream of doing what I'm about to do. You don't need that cigarette!" She snatched it out of his hand and threw it into the waste can.

"Have a heart, Taryn," he pleaded, warily backing away from her. But she persisted and, as her arms went up around his neck and she buried her fingers in the thick dark waves she had been powerless to take her eyes off, the fight slowly began to drain out of him. Sensing her victory, her mouth feather-touched his in flagrant seduction.

"This is miserable . . . you're supposed to respect my state of engagement. . . ."

"That's just what your engagement is—a miserable state. How long is it going to take for you to realize it?" Her mouth came down softly on his and she kissed him in a most aggressive manner. At first he obediently avoided the onslaught, but seconds later he was kissing her with a hunger that belied his indifference. Pulling her toward him, he molded their bodies closer and closer as his mouth devoured the sweetness of hers, breaking away only occasionally to catch a short, ragged breath. Taryn had no idea why she was torturing herself like this . . . their relationship could never go anywhere. But for the moment it didn't matter. She simply didn't care. He felt so good pressed against her softness, he tasted so good, he smelled so good. . . .

She knew she should protest when he began to

caress her bottom intimately, running his large hands over the delightful dips and curves as his tongue scrimmaged sensuously with hers. "It feels as good as I thought it would," he confessed with a wry grin. "Now I'm going to want to know how it feels without all this material wrapped around it." Taryn grew weak as he nipped at the corners of her mouth and pressed her tighter against his rising desire. "Don't you?"

"I know what it feels like," she said inanely, letting him have better access to her neck with his moist, warm kisses.

"Yeah . . . but I don't. We could change all that if you want to take a few minutes off from your work. . . ."

If a knock hadn't sounded on the office door then, Taryn didn't honestly know what her answer would have been. It would have been very tempting to let him find out for himself! The interruption sent them repentantly scampering apart from each other, yet it was several moments later before Taryn could manage a shaky "Come in."

Millicent Feagan stuck her head in the doorway and frowned when she saw Reed standing there. "May I have a word with you?" she asked Taryn.

"Of course." Taryn straightened her dress and hurriedly brushed by Reed. "Why don't you go fix us a sandwich?" she murmured. "We'll just have time to eat before Martha's service begins."

"All right. I'll meet you in the kitchen." She noticed his voice wasn't exactly steady as a rock either.

Millicent's problem could turn out to be a big one and Taryn was still thinking about it when she joined Reed in the kitchen ten minutes later.

"What's old picklepuss's problem this time?" Reed asked sourly, still ticked off over his earlier encounter with Martha Feagan's old-maid daughter.

"She's concerned because the singer for Martha's services hasn't shown up yet."

"Let *her* get up there and belt out a song," Reed suggested, slapping ham and cheese between slices of whole wheat bread. "That should put a little life in the service."

"Reed! That isn't funny! I could have a serious problem on my hands," Taryn admonished.

They ate their sandwiches in silence, neither attempting conversation. Taryn berated herself for acting in such a love-starved, asinine way earlier. She had no doubt that she had scared Reed to death with her blatant aggression. Even though he had responded, she still had no right to make a play for another woman's fiancé. She made a mental note to control herself in the future.

Reed said very little during the meal, asking for the pepper once and the salt twice. They both seemed relieved when the meal was over and Taryn took their plates to the sink.

"I'll just have time to freshen my makeup before

the service starts. What are you going to do this afternoon?"

"Try to get something done about my car," he returned curtly.

"Well, that's going to take some time and even if your car was all right, you wouldn't be able to leave," she pointed out. "The highways are still impassable."

"I know, but those highways have to be reopened before long and I want to be sitting there with my motor idling when they do." For the first time since their passionate encounter in the office, he looked directly at her, his silvery gray eyes growing cloudy. "I . . . have to leave, surely you realize that," he reiterated in a strained voice.

"Yes, I know you think you do." Taryn swallowed hard and refused to look at him. "I'll only be a few minutes."

When she emerged from the bathroom five minutes later, Reed was waiting for her. Silently, they walked down the hallway, both wrapped in their own thoughts.

"Oh, shoot. I forgot to feed Malcolm." Reed's footsteps faltered as they neared the small chapel where people were already somberly filing in, in honor of Martha Feagan. "I better run back up and see about him. He didn't eat much of his breakfast."

Taryn was a bit surprised at Reed's concern for Malcolm. "How much is a parrot supposed to eat?"

"I have no idea, but I noticed he just sort of pecked

around at his food this morning," Reed fretted. "I wouldn't want Sadie to come back and find him sick."

"Well, I confess I know nothing about parrots, but I don't think his pecking at his food is anything to be concerned over. I'm sure he isn't going to sit down and eat his birdseed with a knife, fork, and spoon."

"I still better go check on him. I'll slip out the back door so I won't disturb the services," he promised. Before Taryn could make any further comment, he had turned and disappeared back down the hallway.

Ten minutes later Taryn burst into the family quarters, frantically calling his name. "Reed! Where are you?" If he had already left, she didn't know what she would do!

The bedroom door flew open and Reed rushed out clutching a box of birdseed in his hand, his face a mask of anxiety. "What's wrong?"

"It's Martha! It's Martha!" she gulped, trying to catch her breath.

Reed's face turned an ashen gray. "Again? What's wrong with her now?" His eyes narrowed suspiciously. "So help me, Taryn, if she's fallen out of her casket again, she can just climb back in herself because I'm *not*—"

"*She* didn't do anything, you ninny! But the man who was supposed to sing at her service never showed up!" Taryn interrupted.

Sagging weakly against the couch, Reed tried to steady his frayed nerves. "Is that all! Well, put on a record! And *please* stop running through this damn house yelling 'It's Martha! It's Martha!' I will never be so *glad* to see a woman go to her final resting place *and* stay there!" he bellowed angrily.

"This is serious, Reed," Taryn said. "You are simply going to *have* to help me this time."

"No way," he stated bluntly. *"No way!"*

"Can you read music?" She totally ignored his growing case of hysterics.

"I refuse to answer on the grounds it might incriminate me," he said, crossing his arms stubbornly.

"Ah hah! I knew it. You can read music, can't you?"

"Very little," he snapped in a belligerent tone.

"Can you play any kind of an instrument?"

"The harp, and I do a little ballet, but I didn't pack my tights!"

"Come on, Reed! Be serious! I have a whole chapel of people sitting out there waiting for a service that was supposed to begin ten minutes ago. *You have to help me!*" she demanded in a panic-stricken voice.

Reed's face sagged in defeat. "Oh, bull! All right. I know how to play the piano! But I wouldn't if my mother hadn't made me when I was a kid," he defended himself meekly.

"Oh, thank goodness!" Taryn's voice was full of relief. "Okay. I'll play the organ and you can play the piano. Do you read music well enough to play a duet with me?"

Reed's shoulders lifted indifferently. "I took lessons for eight long miserable years."

"Oh, good, oh, good," she murmured in a relieved

tone. "I know you can sing like a lark, so we'll both play the duet and then you can sing a couple of verses of the song Martha requested, 'When They Ring Those Golden Bells.' You do know, 'When They Ring Those Golden Bells'?"

Reed's face was mirroring shock, then disbelief, as she rattled off her hasty instructions.

"Reed! Answer me. Do you know 'When They Ring Those Golden Bells'?" she persisted.

"No, I don't know 'When They Ring Them Golden Bells,' and even if I did, there's no way in the world I'm going to go out there and sing in front of all those people!"

"Oh, pooh! You really have a much nicer voice than the man who was supposed to sing in the first place," Taryn dismissed airily. "Okay, you can sing 'The Old Rugged Cross.' Surely you know that one. Everyone in the world knows that song!" she accused.

"Of course I know 'The Old Rugged Cross', but I'm not going to sing it! It's your funeral home, *you* sing it!"

"I can't sing!" she wailed. "My voice sounds like someone running their fingernails down a chalkboard! You will have to sing it, hum it, whistle it . . . I don't care. Just help me get through this catastrophe!"

"I absolutely refuse." He planted his feet solidly on the floor and stared at her in defiance. "Period. Subject closed."

"Oh, no, it isn't!" Taryn grabbed his arm and

289

started physically dragging him out the door. "You can't let me down now and I don't have time to stand here and argue with you," she fumed. "If you don't do this for me, I'll call Elaine and tell her where you are, and that you've been staying in a house with a desperate young widowed redhead the last two nights!"

"You wouldn't dare!" he bellowed, dragging his heels down the hallway. "You don't know how to get in touch with her!"

"If you don't get out there and sing, you just watch me! I can pick up the phone and place a collect call to Elaine Matthews in Santa Fe, New Mexico, just as easily as you can!"

"Let go, Taryn, I mean it! Let go!" he stormed, trying to jerk his arm loose from her stranglehold. "I'm not going out there!" he yelled as she pulled him along the empty corridor, stringing the boxful of birdseed he was carrying all over the carpet he had vacuumed earlier. *"I mean it, you crazy redhead, I won't do it!"*

CHAPTER SIX

At any other time, their entrance into the small cubicle that housed the organ and piano for Lassiter Funeral Home would have been nothing short of disgraceful, but Taryn's only concern at the moment was getting the "guest" singer into position. The service should have started a full fifteen minutes earlier and she simply couldn't delay any longer.

The rustle of papers and the heated whispers could be heard in the small, quiet chapel as the mourners turned their eyes in the direction of the sheer curtain and watched with bated expectation.

"Sit down over there and be quiet," Taryn hissed as she frantically shuffled through the music looking for the piano-organ duet she had performed many times before in this chapel.

"I'm *not* going to do it," Reed vowed in a pleading whisper. "I've never sung before anyone in my whole life, and besides, I'll sneeze my brains out around all those flowers!"

"This room is far enough away from the flowers so you shouldn't have any trouble," Taryn dismissed irritably. The pile of music in her lap slid off onto the floor as they continued to argue. "Now look what you've made me do," she jeered impatiently.

"Oh, good grief! Let me do it and let's get this insanity over with!" They both reached to retrieve the fallen music at the same time, their heads banging painfully into each other with a loud crack. They both saw stars for a full sixty seconds before Reed staggered over to the piano bench, bellowing in excruciating pain.

"Oh, damn! You've cracked my head open," he screamed in an agonized whisper.

"Me!" Taryn gingerly rubbed her head, tears smarting her eyes. "I'm not wearing this three-inch knot because it's the latest style, you know! Now shut up and take this music!" She threw a sheet of music at him and hit the first note on the organ loudly.

Every guest in the chapel jumped a good two inches out of their seats as the music blared over the intercom, signaling that the service had finally begun.

The sweet, melodious sound of the organ filled the chapel as Taryn began to play the opening refrain of a beautiful hymn, one that immediately stirred the hearts of the mourners. For several minutes she played flawlessly, watching Reed uneasily from the corner of her eye. He sat on the piano bench rubbing his head, shooting her poisonous glares. She could tell he was quietly assessing his chances of her bluffing about calling Elaine. This was the duet he had agreed to play—not sing—so she didn't have any worries yet, she told herself as her fingers moved professionally over the keys. The real test would come later when the duet was over.

When she came to the part that called for the piano solo, she held her breath and glanced in Reed's direction. Without a moment's hesitation, the sound of the piano rang out clearly and exquisitely in the hushed chapel as he played the notes of the music with an expertise that astounded her. Tiny goose bumps popped out all over her as the music swelled and filled the air with heavenly glory as the listeners were asked to "abide with me" in the most soul-stirring way Taryn had ever heard it played. His fingers moved effortlessly over the ivory keys, and only the look of strained concentration on his face reminded her he was performing under extreme coercion. Together, the organ and piano joined in harmony, and before the song was through, tears of emotion were slipping quietly down Taryn's face. She glanced sheepishly over at Reed, and her tears ceased instantly when she noticed he was glaring at her as if she had lost all her marbles this time!

"What's wrong now?" he mouthed crossly. "Did I hit a sour note?"

She waved his question away with her hand and hastily shuffled through her music once more, looking for "The Old Rugged Cross." Men! How could they be so sensitive one minute and so callous the next! She thrust his copy of the sheet music to him, and watched as he glanced at the title for a second, then began shaking his head adamantly.

Pointing her finger at him, as a parent would do to a disobedient child, she nodded her head firmly and mutinously hit the opening note on the organ.

In deliberate rebellion, Reed crossed his arms, then crossed his legs, and calmly shook his head vigorously.

Again, a little louder this time, Taryn hit the note, trying to glare him into submission.

The guests sat in the chapel, quietly awaiting the forthcoming solo, wondering how many times the opening note would be hit before there was some sort of voice answering the response.

Taryn clenched her teeth as he turned his face toward the wall, childishly continuing to steadfastly ignore her musical introduction.

"Come on, Reed!" she whispered in a pleading tone. "Do it!"

"Yeah, Reed, do it!" a gruff male voice implored in a low, impatient tone from the other side of the curtain. "For heaven's sake let's get this show on the road, fella."

When the organ sounded again, it was with such belligerence that Reed was on his feet, and the mourners cringing in their seats, as the first note of "The Old Rugged Cross" rang out loud and clear in a male voice.

The rich, deep baritone made the wait more than worthwhile as he sang the old familiar song with sweet, honest simplicity. No one could possibly guess that what he was doing wasn't a natural thing for him and that he hadn't sung at funerals all his life. On the contrary, one would have sworn the good Lord had sent one of his messengers today, straight from a heavenly choir in honor of good, kind Martha Feagan.

Only Taryn saw the fear in his beautiful gray eyes as he sang verse after verse, his voice bringing comfort to the bereaved, hope to the weary, and compassion to those who had suffered the loss of an old friend. When the last note was played, Reed slumped down on the bench next to Taryn, perspiration dripping down his face.

The intoning voice of the minister filled the small chapel now as Taryn reached over and cradled him in her arms, waiting for the tension to seep slowly out of his body. "It was beautiful," she whispered lovingly in his ear.

"That was the hardest thing I've ever done in my life," he admitted in a ragged voice. "I sure hope Martha was listening."

"I'm sure she was," Taryn comforted as she patted him on the back in tender reassurance. That *was* a dirty thing to pull on anyone, but the situation warranted drastic measures! Biting pensively at her lip, she continued to pat his back absently as she tried to come up with some tactful way to break the news to him; he was going to have to drive the hearse to the cemetery, since the injuries to Foster and his wife during the storm had been more serious than first believed. Taryn had found out about this latest development only moments before the musical crisis. After racking her brain to come up with a quick solution, she had decided to call on her grandfather's neighbor Ferris to come to her aid. Ferris would drive the family car, Reed would drive the hearse, and she would drive the flower car. It was the only thing she could come up with on such short notice.

"May I speak with you outside for a moment, please?" she whispered in a pleasant voice.

Reed looked up, his eyes mirroring relief that he wasn't going to have to sit through the services. "Sure, let's get out of here."

The sound of distant, rolling thunder could be heard as they slipped out into the dim foyer together. "Oh, no," Taryn muttered, glancing out the window in despair. "It looks like it's going to rain again."

"It's probably just a light summer shower," Reed predicted, casting a quick glimpse toward the threatening clouds playing tag with each other across the darkening sky. "Well"—he gave a wide yawn and stretched his arms above his head, trying to ease some of the remaining tension out of his tired shoulders—"guess I'll cut out and go see about my Bronco."

Taryn watched the play of his muscles against his broad chest and wondered fleetingly for a minute what he would look like with his shirt off . . . and maybe his slacks. . . .

"Hey, I wish you wouldn't look at me that way," he protested gently.

"What way?" She felt the color rising in her cheeks as she hastily averted her eyes from his.

"You know 'what way.' "

"I was just looking at you," she said defensively. "Why should that upset you?"

"Because it makes me start wishing for things that can't be," he argued impatiently.

Taryn shrugged. "Now who's reading things into a conversation . . . or an innocent look?"

"I'm going to be married Saturday, Taryn. That's a simple fact. Up until three days ago, I never dreamed I would ever question that, but the last two days—" His voice broke off in frustration. "Well, hell. The last couple of days have started me thinking, and I don't like it!"

"I'm afraid I can't help you. You have to decide how, and with whom, you'll spend your life, Reed. If it'll help any, I'll try not to look at you again until you leave," she promised sourly.

"That sounds fair. I'll try not to look at you either." He grinned guiltily, his eyes lazily surveying her delectable derriere. "Or touch," he tacked on longingly.

The sound of the minister's closing remarks filtered from beneath the chapel door, turning Taryn's attention away from Reed's suggestive teasing as she focused her thoughts back on the hour. "It sounds like the services are over."

"Yeah. I guess I'll be running along. Better check on old Malcolm sometime this afternoon," he warned. "He's down on himself again today and he's still not eating like he should."

"Uh . . . Reed . . ." She had to break the bad news to him before he got away.

He turned at the front door he was about to open and met her sheepish countenance. "Yes?"

The mourners in the chapel heard a loud, muffled *"Oh no!"* as the final prayer was issued and they filed quietly past the casket to pay their final respects to Martha Feagan.

Fifteen minutes later a huffy Reed was helping Taryn load the floral tributes into the car. "Now, you remember. The bargain is you are to personally see that the tree is cut off my car today!" he reminded her as she stuck a huge bouquet of yellow mums in his arms. He sneezed violently, then pitched them into the back of the van.

"I will, I promise," she pacified, scooping up another wreath and handing it to him. She planned on keeping her promise. After his car was freed, *then* she would think of some other way to keep him around until he could see the frivolity of entering into a marriage with someone he didn't really love! She had suddenly formed the intense, indisputable opinion it was her Christian duty to save him from the jaws of marital disaster.

"Reverend Parsons, would you like to ride in the hearse?" Taryn invited as the minister made his way

298

out of the side door. The long black limousine was sitting under the canopy, being loaded by six older men to go to the cemetery, as the rain continued to fall.

"Oh, thank you, but no. I have my own car," he called back pleasantly.

"You're sure?" The ministers usually chose to ride to the cemetery and back with the funeral director.

"No, I'll just take my own car," he refused again firmly.

"If he wants to take his own car, let him take his own car," Reed said irritably, then sneezed loudly again. "Get off the poor man's back!"

"I was only thinking of you," she pointed out. "I thought it might make it easier if you had someone to keep you company on the drive to the cemetery." What she really meant was, someone to take his mind off the cargo he was carrying, but she discreetly refrained from saying so.

Reed paused in his loading and glared at her. "You mean it's just going to be me and ol' Martha again?"

"She won't cause you any more trouble, I'll personally guarantee it. Here, take this and blow your nose!" Taryn handed him a clean handkerchief and loaded the last bouquet of flowers into the van herself. Slamming the doors closed, she dusted off her hands and anxiously surveyed the line of cars beginning to form behind the long black car. "Oh, darn. I was hoping the rain would let up before we had to start, but it looks like it's set in for the day."

"Let's just go and get it over with," Reed grumbled just as another sneeze shattered his words.

"Just keep on the main road," Taryn instructed as she hopped into the van and turned the ignition. "The cemetery's about five miles from here on the right. You can't miss it."

Reed was still sneezing as he walked to the front of the hearse and got in, casting a suspicious eye in the back of the limousine. He wanted to be sure *everything* was closed up tight!

The funeral procession pulled slowly out of the drive, following the hearse, flower car, and family car. The rain seemed to be growing heavier as the cars solemnly wove their way toward the cemetery. The procession had almost reached its ultimate goal when the minister's car lurched forward a couple of times, then stalled. The cars in the line came to a halt as Taryn rolled down her window and tried to see what the problem was. From her vantage point she could hear the minister trying to restart his car without success. Reed jumped out of the hearse and walked over to speak with the minister, both of them shaking their heads and talking rapidly. The funeral procession was beginning to tie up traffic and motorists started honking their horns as Taryn slid out of the front seat of the van and hurried over to the two men.

"What's the matter?" she asked, hurriedly brushing her wet hair out of her eyes. Her dress was soaked through already and the thin fabric was clinging provocatively to her feminine curves.

"The minister's car ran out of gas," Reed explained as his eyes distraughtly took in her revealing attire. He quickly took off his jacket and wrapped it around her shivering body.

"I'm sorry, Taryn, my gas gauge isn't working properly and I thought I still had half a tank," the Reverend Parsons apologized with a chagrined smile on his kindly features.

"It happens to the best of us," Taryn said, trying to relieve his embarrassment.

"We'll have to push the car out of the way," Reed yelled above the downpour.

Ferris got out of the family car to help the two men as they grunted and groaned and pushed on the heavy four-door sedan amid the persistent blare of irate motorists trying to get around the long line of cars. Never in her whole life had Taryn had such a horrible time trying to conduct one simple burial service!

In an effort to speed up the process, Taryn rushed over to lend her feeble muscle power to those of the men shoving on the Reverend's car.

"What are you doing?" Reed snapped as she fell in beside him and heaved with all her might. "Go get back in the van before you drown!"

"We have to get this car out of the way and the line moving again," she puffed, straining every muscle in her body. "There's going to be a riot in a few minutes if we don't!"

"We can handle it without your help!" he shouted. "Now get back in the car and for heaven's sake keep that jacket on! I don't want every man out here ogling you!"

Taryn's heart fairly sang as she dropped back and let the men work up enough speed to roll the stalled car over to the side of the road. Reed had sounded almost jealous! Everyone returned to their respective vehicles, the minister riding in the hearse with Reed this time, and they soon had the procession rolling along smoothly again. When the cars pulled into the cemetery, Taryn groaned out loud as she saw the muddy roads Reed was trying to force the hearse through. Holding her breath and crossing her fingers, she prayed Reed would be able to get the hearse up the small incline to where the green canopy was spread out over the open grave site.

The thought had no more left her mind when the back wheel of the limousine sank to the axle in a puddle of deep, black mire.

When Reed slammed out of the hearse this time, there was a murderous glint to his eye as he leaned down and grimly surveyed the embedded wheel. He was mumbling some sort of unintelligible garble as Taryn shuffled, disheartened, over to the car and slumped against the fender in disgust.

"Well, this is a fine how-do-you-do," she announced flatly.

When he turned his stormy features in her direction, she was immensely thankful she wasn't a mind reader!

"Go get Ferris and the minister again. We're going to have to try to shove it out, but I want to warn you, I think we've got about as much chance of doing it as a snowball has in hell."

Taryn went after the two rain-drenched men and the process of shoving began all over again. She got in the car and tried to assist their efforts by rocking the car back and forth, but only succeeded in spinning the wheels and throwing a wall of mud over the three men. Ferris and the Reverend Parsons took the small discomfort in stride, but Taryn was mortified at Reed's language in front of a minister!

"Go get the pallbearers and anyone else available. We're going to have to carry Martha up the hill," he announced in a tightly controlled voice as he calmly spit mud out of his mouth. The whites of his eyes were the only clean thing on him now.

Taryn hurried to gather the pallbearers. Not one of them seemed overly anxious to get out in the monsoon, but ten minutes later the entourage were staggering their way up the rain-slicked hillside as the occupants of the other cars scattered like buckshot toward the dry cover of the canopy.

Taryn winced painfully as Reed went down on his knees several times trying to regain firm footing in the wet grass. The other men were having the same traction problem as they made their way precariously up the hill, trying to balance the heavy casket between them.

When they finally reached the grave site, everyone in the crowd heaved an audible sigh of relief.

The minister withdrew his Bible from his soaked jacket and gingerly tried to separate the wet, muddy pages to begin his final message.

Reed walked over to stand next to Taryn, his hair plastered against his face like a wet, dripping mop. He sneezed twice as they both edged as far away from the flowers as they could. By now Taryn was close to a nervous breakdown from the chaos of the last thirty minutes. She knew the pandemonium that had occurred could not be attributed to lack of responsibility from the Lassiter Funeral Home, but it still broke her heart to think of how all the dignity and solemnity of the hour had been cruelly stripped from Martha's services. She could only hope Millicent would forgive her eventually. Tears of frustration sprang to her eyes as a strong arm reached out and drew her close to the comfort of his strong body. Reed held her tenderly as she laid her head on his shoulder in weariness and listened to the droning voice of the Reverend Parsons. It felt so right to be here, cuddled in his arms as the rain beat down soundly on the green canvas. His fingers gently massaged her shoulders as they bowed their heads together in silent prayer. Taryn knew it was wrong for her to long for Reed's touch, wrong even to dream about any permanent relationship with him, yet her heart told her it was so very right.

She opened her eyes at the close of the prayer and stiffened perceptibly in Reed's arms. He felt the change in her body and glanced questioningly over at her. Motioning with her eyes toward a woman who must have weighed somewhere in the vicinity of two hundred and fifty pounds, Taryn frowned worriedly. The woman was sobbing hysterically, her massive body swaying back and forth in an unsteady motion. Taryn knew to watch for just such signs, signs that told her the woman was becoming so emotional she was going to faint. It wasn't an unusual thing to occur at a grave site, but her grandfather usually took control in these situations.

"See that heavyset woman standing over there next to the flowers?" Taryn whispered to Reed.

"Is that *one* woman? I thought I was looking at twins," Reed returned in a conspiratorial whisper, meant to coax a small smile from her serious face.

"I'm afraid she's going to faint," Taryn cautioned quietly.

Reed's eyes shot nervously over to the woman and he stepped quickly away from Taryn, reaching out to offer the woman his hand for support. The next thing Taryn knew, the woman gave a loud swooning sigh and, in a wild flurry of thrashing arms and legs, collapsed on Reed, burying him under her sizable bulk among the mound of flowers piled high by the grave site. Taryn gasped out loud, nearly becoming hysterical as her eyes searched the mound of human flesh pulverizing his body in a sea of pink and red carnations. Only the violent fit of ah-choos, followed by a series of painful groans assured her he was still alive as the crowd of mourners broke apart and scurried over to dig frantically through the flowers and rescue Reed and the overwrought lady.

"Oh, my poor darling," Taryn crooned as she pushed a clump of gladiolus off his battered body and brushed frantically at a clump of dirt mashed onto his nose and forehead. "You have had a simply horrible day, haven't you?"

"I think you could be safe in assuming that," he moaned, staring up at her in a catatonic state.

"Oh, here, let me help you up." She helped him rise to his feet, supporting his limp frame against hers. "I'm going to take you home and get you out of those wet clothes and into a tub of hot water before you catch a cold on top of everything else," she babbled, leading his dazed form in the direction of the van.

"Is it over? Is Martha buried?" he asked, giving her a stupefied grin.

"Yes, darling, it's all over. I'll ask Ferris and a couple of other men to finish up here, because I think you've had all you can stand for a day. Maybe they can get the hearse out of the mud hole. But don't you worry about it one little bit! There's no way I'm going to ask you to do one more thing for me today, because it just wouldn't be fair. Can you ever forgive me? I should have never been so mean to you and made you do all these things against your will, but you have to realize I didn't have another soul I could ask, you know, with the storm and all, but I do appreciate everything you've done for me I really do."

"Thank you—"

"Oh, you're so welcome, darling." She paused and hugged his filthy neck, her affection and appreciation for him spilling over. "Now you just lean on me and I'll have you home before you know it and then I'll fix us something good to eat. What do you like? Pork chops? I have some nice pork chops I can fix and maybe some stuffing. Do you like stuffing better than mashed potatoes? Well, anyway, we can both relax now that Martha has been taken care of and we can talk. You know, I think we really need to talk about Elaine and Gary—"

"Taryn!" Reed paused and sagged against her weakly. "You're rattling again."

"Oh. I am?"

"You are."

"I'm sorry," she apologized in a remorseful little voice.

Leaning over to touch his mouth briefly to hers, he whispered in an unmistakably affectionate voice, "Take us home, Motormouth."

"I'd be happy to." She returned his kiss happily. "And, with a little luck, I just might get to keep you!"

CHAPTER SEVEN

"Squaaawk, Malcolm is a bad boy. Squaaawk, Malcolm is a bad boy!"

Malcolm swung back and forth on his perch in a high-strung manner as Reed stretched his aching body out on the bed in Martin Lassiter's bedroom later that evening. On arriving back at the funeral home, he had immediately headed for the bathroom and a hot shower. If he had to cite a day in his memory that defied all explanation, this would be *the* one.

He closed his eyes for a moment and the image of Taryn Oliver drifted enticingly before him. Now, that was strange, and just a little bit irritating to him. Why should her face pop up instead of Elaine's? True, he did have a terrible weakness for redheads and she *did* have a shape that made his eyes keep pole-vaulting over in her direction—and that cute little posterior of hers . . . His eyes flew open guiltily and he forced his mind to take another direction. Elaine was going to have his hide if he didn't get to Santa Fe in the next couple of days. It had taken her and her mother months to plan this wedding and all the prenuptial parties and events that were taking place now. Reed rolled over on his side and listened to the rising wind rattling the old house. Now why, after all these months of total indifference, was he suddenly beginning to feel the noose of marriage tightening around his throat and nearly strangling him? Premarital jitters. Everyone had them, he assured himself confidently. Elaine and his marriage would be a good one, no matter what that nerve-racking redhead said! No, he didn't love Elaine, at least not with that blinding, overpowering kind of love Taryn spoke about. But he did like her, a lot, and they would have a nice, sane life together. He chuckled softly as he quietly contemplated what his life would be if he were married to that sexy mortician he had spent the last couple of days fighting with. Desire sprang up hot and totally unexpected at the thought of Taryn and himself sharing a marriage bed. Forcing the unwilling thought out of his mind, he rolled over again and stared at the ceiling.

"Squaaawk, Malcolm wants a Fig Newton. Squaaawk, Malcolm wants a Fig Newton!" the bird demanded belligerently.

"Malcolm has six Fig Newtons lying in the bottom of his cage right now that he's not eating," Reed replied dryly. "Malcolm's going to have a boot down his throat if he doesn't shut up and let me go to sleep," he added in a no-nonsense tone.

"Squaaawk, Reed's a baaad boy, Reed's a baaad boy!"

Well, at least he's let up on himself for a while, Reed thought sleepily.

A soft knock on the door interrupted the argument. "It's open," Reed called, sitting up on the side of the bed.

"Hi." The smell of a sultry perfume filtered lightly into the room as Taryn stepped inside carrying a tube of medicated analgesic in her hand. "How's your shoulder?"

Reed's hand went up absently to his sore shoulder, having forgotten for the moment the pain he had suffered when the heavyset woman had fallen on him earlier. "It's not bad," he protested, forcing his eyes away from the sexy peignoir she was wearing. The sheer pink material wasn't that skimpy, but it still did nothing to ease his already uncomfortable state of enforced celibacy.

"I found some medicine to rub on it," she offered, strolling over to where he sat on the edge of the bed. "Want me to put some on for you?"

"No, I don't think it needs any," he hedged, edging slightly away from her. "It's doing okay."

"I thought you said it was really bothering you when we were having dinner," she pursued. She sat down on the side of the bed, her face growing amused as he scooted even farther across the bed—away from her. "What's the matter?"

"Nothing. Why?"

"Oh, no reason, I just thought I better warn you, though, if you scoot any farther away from me, you're going to land on the floor," she teased. "I thought I'm the one who's supposed to be doing the scooting. Are you afraid I'm going to attack you again?"

"No." He grinned weakly. "To be honest, I'm afraid I'm going to attack you!"

Taryn sighed softly, trying hard not to let his words mean anything, but it was so tempting. Sitting here next to him, listening to the wind howl outside the small window, lent a touch of intimacy to the room that was beginning to steal over her and make her long for more than could rightfully be hers.

"Why the big sigh?" he asked perceptively, forcing himself to look at his hands and ignore the way her beautiful hair fell loosely across her creamy shoulders.

"No reason. Are you sure you wouldn't like some of this rubbed on your shoulder?" she asked whimsically, becoming increasingly aware of the growing sexual tension that had suddenly sprung up between them.

The soft glow of the bedside lamp caught the strawberry highlights of her hair as she held the tube up for his inspection, and he felt his insides turn into one big, painful knot. In all the years he had known Elaine, she had never once made him feel like he did at this moment, all warm and mushy inside. . . . In that one brief moment, Reed suddenly began to seriously question his forthcoming marriage. He knew with swift, unexplainable clarity that he was destined to hold this woman in his arms and make love to her, and when he did, nothing in his life would ever be the same again. The sun would still rise and set, wars would rage on, the poor would go hungry, the lonely would still cry themselves to sleep at night, and the sound of a child's laughter would still touch the hearts and light the faces of all who heard; but for Reed Montgomery, life would change.

"Taryn . . ." Her gaze told him she was feeling all that he was, yet neither one spoke for a moment. Finally, Reed heaved a defeated sigh and whispered softly, "You know this is crazy. We've only known each other three days—three days! Things like this just don't happen in three days!"

There was no need to put into words what he was referring to. Taryn knew without a doubt because she had questioned the sanity of it herself. Her head nodded slowly in shame. She did know that. Here was a man who had walked into her life and turned it upside down in a scant three days, a man who belonged to someone else. But those things no longer held meaning when she looked into the deep silvery pools of his eyes and saw the longing that she herself could no longer deny.

"What are we going to do? I don't want to hurt Elaine," she whispered. And she meant it. She knew what they both were contemplating could cause great pain for all involved.

"I don't want to hurt her either," he confessed.

"What I'm feeling right now has nothing to do with her, yet the consequences will affect her."

"Maybe it's just a sexual attraction that will pass after it has been fulfilled," she suggested in a faltering voice. That was entirely possible. She had heard of such things, although she herself had never practiced the theory.

"I hadn't thought of it that way, but maybe you're right." His voice sounded somewhat relieved. "That's probably what it is." His hand moved out to hesitantly cover hers, his fingers gently massaging hers to tingling awareness. "I suppose we're doomed to find out one way or the other. . . ."

Her heart thudded painfully as he moved closer and his lips moved down to touch hers with silky softness. With a soft sigh, her arms moved up around his neck and she tilted her mouth upward to accept his kiss, which came without hesitation as he moaned softly and pulled her closer to him. His kiss was poignantly sweet, in no way demanding, only seeking to give and receive the pleasure they both knew was awaiting them. His mouth brushed hers with tantalizing slowness as he nibbled at the corners of her lips, quickly shattering the remains of any composure she might have had.

"You taste as good as you look," he murmured, trailing his mouth down the slender column of her neck. His touch was gentle and exploring, and she could tell he was keeping a tight leash on his passion. His hands sensuously touched her skin, drinking in the feel of her loveliness as his mouth found hers once more for a deep kiss. They lay back on the bed and her fingers found their way under his shirt. She longed to touch him, to discover all the mysteries she had only guessed at until now.

"You want me to take my shirt off," he murmured, stealing honeyed kisses from her willing mouth. "Or better yet, why don't you take it off for me?"

"Reed." Her body was responding to his caresses with a growing need that would soon be demanding complete fulfillment. She vaguely remembered there was one thing she had to do before she gave her love, her total being, to another man.

"What's the matter, sweetheart? Am I going too fast?" he whispered. "I know I probably am, but you can't possibly know how very much I've wanted to hold you like this. Ever since you came into my arms in the basement during the storm. Do you remember doing that . . . ? I was scared to death you would feel my need for you that day," he admitted, moving that need against her now in tantalizing persuasion of his words. "It's been there all along, Taryn, from the minute I laid eyes on you. At first it scared me. I've never felt this way about a woman, never felt the thrill or the joy of being with someone who makes me grow weak with longing when I just look at her." His voice was filled with soft wonder as he buried his hands in the thickness of her hair and inhaled its perfumed fragrance, murmuring her name tenderly.

"Reed, before we make love . . . there's something I have to do," she pleaded breathlessly, feeling her body spring achingly alive with all the feelings she had once thought were dead and gone forever.

"Now? Oh, I had forgotten about that." He assumed she would want to protect herself and he silently berated himself for not thinking of it first.

"Would you give me a few minutes alone, then come to my room?" She lovingly traced the outline of his masculine features as she gazed up into his passion-laden eyes. "There's something very important I must do."

"I'll be there in five minutes," he promised in a voice growing huskier with passion by the moment. They exchanged another long series of lingering kisses before he reluctantly rolled off her and let her go. Her knees felt like water as she made her way across the hall, her lips tingling from his passionate lovemaking.

When she entered her bedroom, she hurried over to the bed to pick up the small photograph that had been so much a part of her life the last year. She fingered the outline of her husband's face tenderly as tears gathered gently in her eyes. A tear dripped silently on the picture frame as she reached for a handkerchief and dabbed at her eyes. She dried her eyes and blew her nose soundly, then walked over and opened the bottom drawer of her dresser and started lovingly to place the photo beneath a pile of sweaters she had worn in high school. She whispered a prayer in a sheepish voice as she closed the drawer.

"Listen, God, I'm not so sure Reed feels as strongly about all this as I do so, if you aren't too busy up there and it wouldn't be a lot of trouble, I sure would appreciate your help the next few days. You know . . . make it possible for Elaine not to be hurt too badly by all this and make Reed realize he loves *me* and can't live without me. Thanks!" She leaned against the bureau and took a deep breath just as Reed knocked softly on her door.

"Come in." She hurried over to the doorway as he quietly entered the room.

"Everything all right?"

"For the first time in a very long time, everything is just fine," she assured him, taking his hand and gently leading him toward her bed. His arm came out to pull her up against him as his mouth eagerly enfolded hers. For a brief moment they held each other tightly, their mouths molding and plying hungrily. His mouth left hers after a while, moving down the curve of her face and finally settling at the base of her throat.

"Who were you talking to?" he murmured.

"Were you listening?" she scolded, shivering as his tongue traced along the swell of her breasts.

"No . . ." he replied meekly, "I had just started to knock on your door when I heard your voice. I didn't hear anything you said," he assured, "but I can't help being curious. . . ."

"I was praying and saying good-bye, darling." She

brought his face back up to cup gently between her hands.

"There will be no one sharing our bed when we make love, Reed. I promise you." Her eyes sweetly told him that her promise was sincere and straight from her heart.

Whatever differences they had quickly dissolved like cotton candy on the tongue as her arms pulled him into their loving shelter and he buried his face in the perfumed fragrance of her neck, whispering of his great, overpowering need of her. Taryn gently pushed him away and her fingers found the buttons on his shirt as she gazed warmly into his beautiful eyes. "I want to see every delicious part of you," she confessed, undoing the buttons in deliberate provocation. "You can think me shameful, but I don't care. I want to know what you feel like, look like, taste like. . . ." Her mouth followed her words as the first few buttons came loose.

"Oh, lady, I love your way of thinking," he groaned as she slipped the last button through the loop. The shirt came off, then the belt, his socks, his slacks, and then she was finally down to the delectable, mouth-watering icing on the cake.

"To think, I thought you might be *shy* about this," he said as he grinned in a silly, smug, completely chauvinistic way.

She showed him just how totally wrong he could be, shattering that infuriating confidence of his to smithereens as she rid him of the last vestige preventing her ultimate pleasure. Her eyes darkened passionately as she surveyed the wondrous treasure she had discovered. A light coating of golden brown hair covered his athletic physique and he was built exactly as she had imagined he would be. The soft smattering of hair weaved its way across his broad chest, down his arms, and along the length of his powerful thighs. Taryn knew without a doubt she was going to overindulge on "dessert" tonight as her mouth nibbled smoothly along his broad shoulder muscle. Tonight would be a special time in their lives and she longed to make it as memorable for Reed as it would be for her.

Reed moaned as her mouth became more aggressive, and his hands slipped the filmy pink robe from her shoulders and let it float gently to the floor. Seconds later her gown joined the sheer fabric and he gathered her satiny body up to nest provocatively between his taut thighs.

"You're making me crazy, do you know that?" he murmured, letting her feel his awesome need for her, as his hands began slowly to acquaint themselves with her gentle swelling curves.

Their kisses turned hot and hungry now as he laid her on the bed and his hands moved eagerly over her, exploring every bit of unfamiliar terrain. Kissing her breasts to soft, budding fullness, he suddenly seemed to have lost all previous control of his emotions as he moved to claim her, filling her with his elemental power, blocking out all rational thought as they soared together in a world of ecstasy that was so beautiful, so awesome, it took their breath away. The joy they were bringing each other sang through their veins as she met his ardor with her own until the world dissolved into a million tiny stars for them, casting them out into a heavenly void.

Taryn buried her face in his broad chest, placing heated kisses on his warm, moist skin, her hands tenderly guiding him back to the real world as he slumped against her, still murmuring her name.

Only the sound of the wind could be heard as they lay locked in each other's arms, lovingly exchanging sweet, languorous kisses.

"You don't happen to have any ketchup with you, do you?" Reed murmured in a shaken voice.

"Ketchup? Are you serious? What do you want with ketchup at a time like this?" she asked incredulously.

"Well, I think I'm just about ready to eat my words," Reed admitted shyly.

Taryn leaned on her elbow and playfully kissed the tip of his nose. "You mean those famous last words about not having ever experienced that formidable, devastating power of love? *Those* words?"

Reed's eyes grew clouded as he rolled on his back and stared thoughtfully up at the ceiling. "Love? I'm still not sure about that, Taryn. Love is such a . . . 'forever after' word."

"And you're not ready to accept that kind of love," she finished in a small, troubled voice.

"Does that bother you?"

"Not really. I think everyone has to reach a point in their lives when they're willing to let go of their love and place it in someone else's hands. That isn't an easy thing to do. In fact, it's very scary. But, Reed, you—are—willing to place your life in Elaine's hands, so why does the thought of placing it in my hands scare you?"

"I'm willing to place my life in her hands, Taryn, not my love. There's a big difference."

"That sounds very cold and callous, Reed, and I happen to know you're not that way at all."

"Maybe I am, Taryn. All my adult life I've had to think of someone else's wants and needs and I'm just darn tired of having other people chart my destiny. For once in my life I'd like to be able to make my own decisions. Can you understand that?" His voice sounded accusing, almost as if he were blaming her for the unsavory predicament he now found himself in.

"Well, don't blame me, Reed. I'm not the one making you marry a woman you don't love just so you can have a topnotch position in her daddy's law firm," she reminded him curtly.

Her angry words took him by surprise. "That's a rotten thing to say!"

"Rotten, but true. You said yourself you were marrying Elaine for the position in her father's company."

"I'm not marrying her solely for that reason," he

protested. "Elaine and I have a lot of things in common. We've known each other for years. We like the same movies, the same type food, we have the same taste in music—"

"And, I suppose, her parents have to haul their money to the bank in a dump truck," she interjected curtly.

"They're not hurting, if that's what you're getting at, but that has nothing whatsoever to do with my decision," he told her tensely. "I have always made my own way in the world and I always will!"

"Are you sleeping with her?" Taryn knew his answer was only going to bring her pain, but she asked him anyway.

Reed reached over and pulled her onto his chest, kissing her into silence. When they parted a long time later, he chose to answer her question the kindest way he knew possible. "If I were sleeping with her, I'd never tell you or anyone else. That happens to be a very personal thing between a man and woman, don't you agree?"

"You are! I knew it," she accused him.

"Now, look! What about Gary? The idea that you loved another guy enough to marry him doesn't exactly thrill me either!"

"That doesn't count," she justified meekly. "That was before I ever knew you existed. What I felt for Gary is so much different from what I'm feeling for you, Reed. There's no comparison, actually. Gary and I met and had a whirlwind romance. We were married a short three weeks after we met and he died six weeks after the marriage. Sometimes I look back on that time of my life and think that it was all a dream. What we shared was quick and explosive and wonderful, but sometimes . . . sometimes I have to think really hard to remember what he kissed like, or how he smelled, or even what color his eyes were or how his voice sounded. I was so crushed and bitter over his death and I wanted so desperately to hang on to what we had, but lately . . . ?" She paused and absently ran her hands through the hair on Reed's chest. "I've been so darn lonely."

"It sounds to me like you were deeply in love with him," Reed murmured.

"I was. In a wild, crazy, totally unexplainable way, because that was the kind of guy he was, wild, crazy, and completely unexplainable. There have been times in the last year that I've wondered if our attraction for each other would have lasted. Gary was a natural and free spirit. I like things more steady and down-to-earth. Who knows, after the shine wore off our marriage, we may have woken up one day to find out we really didn't have anything at all."

Reed's eyes searched her face and found her words to be genuine and honest. "And you think we could have something more lasting . . . the 'forever after' kind people are always talking about?"

"I think it wouldn't hurt to explore that possibility," she admitted, tracing the outline of his lips with the tip of her long, perfectly shaped nail.

"The thought doesn't scare you?"

"What? 'Forever after' love?" She laughed. "I deal in the 'forever after' every day of my life," she teased him.

He gave an exaggerated groan as he nipped at her finger with his strong white teeth. "Now, there's another problem we haven't discussed. Your nerve-racking occupation."

"What about it?"

"Taryn, honey, even if we didn't have all these other obstacles standing in the way of our relationship, there is *no* way on earth that I could live in a funeral home on a day-to-day basis. These last few days have me walking around wishing for an extra set of eyes in the back of my head, and if I had to live through one more day like today . . ."

"Silly!" She stopped his flow of words with persuasive kisses. "Let's not even think about that problem until we're able to solve some of the larger ones.

"Reed?" she asked a few minutes later. "Do you realize, until a few minutes ago we actually didn't know anything about each other? I don't even know where you live!"

Reed sat up and propped the pillow on the headboard and reached for a cigarette out of his shirt pocket and lit it. Drawing Taryn back into the shelter of his arm, he began to fill in the empty pages of his life for her. "That's simple enough to clear up. I've lived in Kansas City since I graduated from law school. Elaine . . ." He paused and drew her closer as he felt her stiffen again at the mention of his fiancée's name. "Elaine and I have worked in the same law office for the last couple of years. When her dad found out about our engagement, he offered both of us a position in his firm. Since it didn't make any difference to me where we lived, I let Elaine make the decision. Naturally, she chose to go home. She wanted to have the wedding in Santa Fe anyway since her grandparents' health prevented them from making the trip to Kansas City, so she left for home a couple of months ago to plan the wedding and look for an apartment while I stayed behind and cleared up last-minute business. As you already know, I was headed to Santa Fe when the storm caught me."

Taryn had never felt so miserable as she listened to his somber words. "I wish I hadn't asked. It makes the wedding and Elaine seem so real now," she managed to say beyond the tight lump in her throat.

"They *are* real," he replied solemnly, absently stroking her hair. "I want you to know I don't make a habit of this sort of thing, Taryn, this is the first time I've been with another woman since I became seriously involved with Elaine."

"I'm sorry. I feel so cheap." She buried her head in his shoulder and fought with her warring feelings. Tonight would only be a brief, sweet remembrance. She now realized it was just too late in Reed's life to change his plans.

"Cheap! Don't you ever let me hear you say that again," he demanded in an astonished tone. "Wha happened tonight was not a cheap, tawdry roll in the hay, Taryn, and I won't have you dirtying it up with those kinds of thoughts."

"What happened was wrong, Reed, and I'm afraid I instigated it to the fullest. I seriously thought you didn't love Elaine and I could save you from making what I consider the mistake of your life. Not only for you but for Elaine, too. But I see now that it doesn't matter. You have to do what you have to do."

"I'm confused," he confessed. "I have no idea which way to turn or what to do next."

Taryn knew she shouldn't do it, but her arms automatically tightened around his neck and she began slowly to kiss away the look of pain that now clouded his face.

He reached over and put out his cigarette, then drew her back into his arms. "You're one lovely lady and I'll never forget this night," he promised, capturing her mouth with almost savage intensity this time.

Their kisses turned fiery once more as their passion returned in full force. Reed had just kissed his way down to Taryn's navel, all thoughts of right and wrong put aside for the time being, when the phone rang in the other room.

"Let it ring," he urged, taking her breath away with a demanding kiss that caused her insides to quiver.

"I can't," she moaned. "It might be business."

"Business? This time of night?"

"We're on call twenty-four hours a day. You stay

right here and don't you dare go away," she warned, reaching for her housecoat. "I mean it, don't move!" It might be wrong, but they could only be hung for their crime once!

"I'm lying here nude in a house that's old and creaking, with a downstairs that is a funeral parlor, and the pretty redheaded mortician I'm in the process of making mad, passionate love to is creeping around in her nightgown answering telephones that're going to lead to God only knows what this time, and you honestly feel it's necessary to tell me not to go anywhere? Don't worry. I'll be here," he promised her dryly.

"Make sure you do." She stole one final kiss filled with enough promise to keep a man in bed for the next six months if asked, then rushed to answer the persistently ringing phone.

CHAPTER EIGHT

"Boo!" Taryn sneaked up behind the man standing in front of the kitchen sink rinsing off a head of lettuce, and poked him playfully in the ribs.

Reed let out a nervous yelp and jumped two feet off the floor as a head of lettuce flew straight up in the air then dropped to the ground and landed at his bare feet.

"Will you cut that out!" he demanded impatiently, leaning over to pick the head back up and toss it in the sink.

Taryn giggled and wrapped her arms around his waist. "I'm sorry, did I frighten you?"

"You little witch, you know you scared the pants off me creeping around yelling boo!" Reed turned around to face her and drew her back to him for a long, welcoming kiss, his actions belying his grumpy words.

"You were supposed to stay right where you were," she reminded him, kissing his eyes and nose and face. "I went back to bed and you were gone."

"I got hungry," he complained with a grin.

"What in the world are you wearing?" She stood back and surveyed his attire, laughter welling up in her. He was wearing her old blue chenille housecoat, and although it was big on her, it couldn't come close to fitting his broad, muscular frame. The front of the robe gaped open shamefully as he turned around and around, preening for her like a conceited peacock. "How do you like it? Turn you on?"

"Where are your pants?" she asked in mock despair, enjoying every minute of his risqué performance.

"I just told you. You scared them off me." He shrugged innocently, pulling her back in his arms for another hungry kiss.

"Why are you wearing *my* housecoat, you idiot?"

"I didn't want to get dressed, since I knew we'd be going back to bed, so I put the robe on to come out here and fix a sandwich. Now that you're back, I seem to have lost my appetite . . . for food, that is." He affectionately nuzzled her neck, drawing her into the confines of the robe with him. "What took you so long? I missed you."

"Oh, the call was from the clinic."

"Everything all right?"

"Yes, it wasn't concerning Grandpa. It was . . . business." She caught her breath as his tongue licked sensuously at her ear, poking playfully in and out, sending shivers racing down her spine.

"Don't you think we should mosey on back upstairs and get back to what we were doing before the phone interrupted us?" he whispered in a low, suggestive voice. His hands had found what they were seeking and she was beginning to be caught up in a new web of growing arousal. "I can skip my sandwich," he coaxed her with a series of persuasive kisses.

"We can't. I have to leave," she confided in a regretful voice.

"Leave?" He pulled back a fraction and curiously searched her face. "For where?"

"The clinic."

"I thought you said everything was all right with your grandfather."

"It is, silly," she assured, kissing him one final time before she reluctantly stepped out of his embrace. "I told you. I have to go there on . . . business."

Enlightenment slowly crept over his puzzled countenance as his arms dropped back to his sides in disappointment. "Oh. *That* kind of business."

"Yes, *that* kind of business. I don't suppose you'd consider going with me again?" She grimaced, and braced herself for the explosion that would surely follow.

Heaving a tired sigh, he ran his fingers through his hair and silently pondered the question for a moment. Finally he asked in a reluctant voice, "What would I have to do this time?"

"Nothing, really. Just help me lift . . . something on a stretcher," she hedged.

He walked back to the sink and tore off a chunk of

lettuce, chewing thoughtfully on it as he carefully mulled her request over in his mind. "I suppose you'll have to go by yourself if I don't?"

"That's right. I can manage if you don't think you feel up to it, though," she added quickly. After all, he had done more for her today than even Gary would have done, she reminded herself.

He leaned against the sink and crossed his arms, bringing a lopsided grin to Taryn's face once more as she surveyed his disreputable attire showing off every ounce of his impressive masculine traits.

"What are you laughing about now, Redhead?"

"You and your ridiculous housecoat."

His grin took a definite turn to wicked as he noticed the path her eyes were taking. "Am I becoming nothing but a common, ordinary sex object to you already?"

She tilted her head and soberly contemplated what he so smugly felt assured had brought her to that captive state. "Ummm . . . sex object maybe, but common, ordinary . . . naw, even with my limited experience, I don't think so." Her grin was as wicked as his now.

"Come here, Ms. Oliver," he ordered softly as his eyes darkened in renewed passion.

"I don't think I should." She slowly backed away from him, her smile growing broader. "Something tells me you are going to try to delay my call to work."

"Don't try to play games and run from me. I'll

come after you," he challenged, still using that low, sexy voice.

"Not necessarily. It depends in what direction I run," she countered. "Now, should I choose to run toward the front parlor, I'd probably be more than safe. . . ."

He took a step forward and caught her back into his arms, pulling her down on the kitchen chair with him.

"Let go! I don't have anything on under my robe," she protested, feeling the warmth and firmness of his masculinity meet her bare bottom.

"What a shame," he said in a voice that didn't have one shred of regret in it.

For the next five minutes they kissed and touched and murmured in happy, contented sighs. It was Reed's turn to pull away this time as he groaned and stood up, scooping her up in his arms, whispering against her mouth, "Let's take a quick bath, then get started on your business, so we can get back to *our* business."

"You're going with me!" she squealed in delight. "Oh, thank you!" Her arms clasped tightly around his neck, and as they walked up the stairs they kissed heatedly. She knew his going with her to the clinic was a tremendous concession for Reed to make, and her love for him grew by leaps and bounds.

Walking into the hall bathroom, he turned on the bathtub faucets with his mouth still welded to hers. Their robes were quickly discarded and they spent the next few minutes playfully washing each other, pausing only long enough to steal long, languid kisses.

"You know what you're doing to me, don't you?" he murmured in a husky tone as they slid down in the warm water and let it surround them completely. He shifted to pull her wet body on top of his, moving intimately against her.

"No, what?" she asked innocently, her teeth playfully biting his shoulder. She knew the effect she was having on him and silently reveled in her power.

"You're forcing me to do something I don't think I should do . . . at least not right now," he argued in a practical voice.

"I'm not doing anything," she denied innocently, nibbling on his earlobe and moving in rhythm with his swaying body.

"Then you want me to go ahead and do it?" he prodded, fully aware of her intent to torment him.

"That's up to you," she returned primly, running the tip of her tongue around the outline of his bottom lip. He surged against her and they kissed for a few moments. "You're going to have to make up your mind," she encouraged as their lips finally parted. "It's growing very late . . . we really should be going."

"Well, if you're sure . . ." He reached down and pulled out the stopper, letting the soothing water drain away. Still passionately kissing her, he waited until the tub was empty, then replaced the plug and turned the cold water on full blast. Her eyes widened as she realized what he had done, and she screamed as the malicious rush of cold water seeped up around their bodies.

"What are you doing!" she screeched.

"Cooling us down so we can go to work," he returned in a totally innocent voice. "What did you think I meant?"

"Ohhh . . . you idiot!" She slapped him across the face with her wet washcloth and exited the tub in a fit of temper. He was right behind her, laughing deviously as he scooped her up in a towel and briskly rubbed her dry. Before he was through, her anger was long forgotten and they were trading passionate kisses once more.

"You sure do have a lot of freckles," he commented, surveying her rosy pink body as he handed the towel to her and motioned for her to return the favor.

"I know." She began to rub his back briskly. "At the slightest hint of sun they pop out like dandelions!"

His hand reached out and stilled her flying hands, his face turning serious for the first time as he looked into her eyes.

Her smile grew tender as she lovingly ran her fingers through the wet, dark waves of his hair. "What is it? Why are you looking at me like that?" she prompted softly.

"I'd like to see you when those freckles fade," he stated simply, "in the winter and in the fall. . . ."

Her hazel eyes dropped bashfully away from his silvery gray ones. "Isn't this something? You know, I've never done anything this crazy and wild in my whole life," she confessed.

Tipping her face gently back up to meet his, he smiled. "I know. And, if it helps any, I haven't either."

"What do you think? You think we both have gone completely out of our gourds?" she asked with a perky tilt of her head.

"That's very possible." He nodded. "In fact, that thought has entered my mind more than once in the last three days."

Another lingering kiss was shared before they finally parted to get dressed. When Reed came downstairs fifteen minutes later, Taryn was waiting for him. He looked so breathtakingly handsome in a pair of light blue dress jeans with a dark blue shirt tucked neatly in the waistband that it took all the willpower she could muster not to run over and throw herself in his arms.

While she was dressing, she had come to the conclusion that she was going to have to start restraining herself around him. Their impetuous actions were only going to make it harder on both of them when the time came for him to leave. And, she knew without a doubt, that time would come.

Reed walked over to the chair where she was sitting and leaned down and kissed her. "You look cute. I've never seen you in jeans before."

"Thanks. You look cute too. Much better than that horrible bathrobe you were wearing earlier," she teased, carefully avoiding his gaze.

"You think so?"

"I think so."

Stealing another quick kiss, he took her hand and pulled her to her feet. "Well, we might as well go and get your new . . . customer." With one arm draped casually around her waist, he walked with her through the kitchen and out the back door. The night air was warm and balmy as they strolled out to the four-car garage and opened the door.

"I suppose we're taking the hearse," he said, frowning.

"No, we can take the van if you'd rather."

"That's up to you, honey." He called her "honey" with such ease, it was as if they had known each other all their lives.

"The hearse," she decided, knowing that it would be more practical.

"I'll drive," he announced, holding out his hand for the keys. Gratefully handing them to him, she hurried around and got in on the passenger side.

The car roared to life and Reed backed it smoothly out of the drive. Seconds later they were driving down the main road leading to the clinic.

"You remembered! I didn't think you would," she

complimented, surprised he had recalled the way without having to have his memory refreshed.

"Oh, I'm truly amazing," he admitted with a sexy wink. "Haven't you noticed that yet? Hey! What are you doing way over there?" He reached over and pulled her close to his side. "This is where gorgeous redheads belong."

Taryn had to agree it was as his arm came around her, and she snuggled her head on his shoulder in contentment. This was not very ethical, she had to admit, but it was certainly very nice.

The clinic came in view too quickly to suit either one of them. Reed parked the limousine according to Taryn's instructions beside a side door leading into the clinic. Reaching into the back, he helped her withdraw a cot and wheel it in the doorway.

"The patient's name is Ralph Morliss," Taryn mused, referring to the slip of paper she held in her hand.

They wheeled the cot down the dimly lit hallway. "Why don't you take the stretcher into room two eighteen and get Mr. Morliss ready while I stop at the nurses' desk and let them know we're here."

"Now, look!" The cot came to a screeching halt. "Don't push your luck, Redhead. Consider yourself darn lucky I even consented to come, let alone send me in one of those rooms by myself!"

"Oh, all right," she said. "Wait here and I'll be back as soon as I get things squared away." She walked off down the hall in the direction of the nursing desk, leaving Reed leaning indolently against the wall.

Five minutes later he realized that he was starving. His earlier thoughts of a sandwich had been aborted in favor of more appealing things, but now his stomach told him it needed food—fast! Glancing down the hallway, he saw a nurse emerge from a small room down the corridor carrying a soft drink and a candy bar. Digging in his jeans pocket for some loose change, he walked down the hall and bought a package of corn chips and a can of soda pop and walked back to where the cot was standing. The snack did nothing to appease his appetite, and when Taryn failed to appear ten minutes later, he returned to the small room and bought two more candy bars and another bag of corn chips.

She had been gone for over twenty minutes when he started to grow impatient. *The smell of the hospital is beginning to make me sick,* he thought, forgetting to take into account the two bags of corn chips, two candy bars, and the can of soda pop he had just devoured.

Summoning up the nerve to get started on the task of transporting Ralph Morliss to the waiting cot, he wheeled the stretcher up to the nurses' desk and brought it to an abrupt halt. The nurse on duty glanced up expectantly.

"What room is Morliss in?" he mumbled. He couldn't remember what room number Taryn had mentioned earlier.

The nurse's eyes lit up appreciatively at the handsome man peering skittishly over the desk at her. "Why, hello," she purred. "May I help you?"

"Hello. What room is Morliss in?" he repeated, his fingers anxiously twisting the edge of the white sheet lying on the cot.

The nurse stood up and came around to look up at the tall, good-looking stranger. She had been a nurse for fifteen years in this clinic and she had never seen anything this magnificent standing in front of her desk before. "I'm sorry, what patient did you want to see?" she asked again, stalling for more time to make his acquaintance.

Reed had not failed to miss the female-predator gleam in her eye and it made him more nervous than he already was. Where in the devil had Taryn disappeared to!

"What's your name, handsome?" The nurse smiled a sultry silent invitation.

She might be looking for a good time, but he wasn't. At least, not with her! He didn't like blondes *or* nurses! Losing all patience with the situation he found himself in, he barked out his request once more. "Morliss! What room's Morliss in, lady!"

Flinching at his gruff demeanor, the nurse snapped up a chart, her eyes hurriedly scanning the list, seething quietly under her breath. *He may be cute, but he sure has a nasty disposition!* "Morris is in room two twenty!" she snapped.

"Thank you!" Wheeling his cart around in a

haughty manner, he resisted the urge to thumb his nose at the pushy nurse as he streaked back down the hallway, pushing the cot at a dead run. One of its wheels had begun to wobble unevenly, making a loud clacking noise as he worked his way down the quiet hallway, trying to read the door numbers in the dim lighting. The cot slowed, then rolled to a halt in front of room 220.

Hordes of nervous butterflies rose up in his stomach as he thought about what awaited him beyond the closed door. Taking a deep breath, he cautiously pushed the door open and groaned softly when he saw the room was pitch-black and that Taryn was nowhere to be seen.

He shrugged, deciding his task might be easier if he didn't have to look at what he was putting on the cart. He carefully wedged the cot through the doorway and then tiptoed over to the bed. He stood on his toes and tried to peek at the figure lying on the bed through the faint ray of light shining from the window. His heart sank. This one was another big one. *Well, Montgomery, you're not going to get the job done by standing around dreading it,* he chided himself. *Let's get this thing over with.*

He brought the cot to the side of the bed. Reed stood for a moment assessing the still form sprawled on the bed, trying to figure out the best way to go about this. He shook his head in disbelief. How had he ever gotten himself in this mess to begin with? If it wasn't for the fact he had fallen head over heels in love with that redhead . . . His thoughts came to a sudden halt. In love with the redhead? Was he in love with the redhead?

The fact hit him hard and fast. He *was* in love with Taryn Oliver! He shook his head again as if to clear out the stunning thought. When had *that* happened and what was he going to do about it? Great balls of fire! He had only known her three days . . . three miserable days! Maybe his feelings for her were a direct result of his new surroundings. No, that's not it, he thought miserably, he *was* in love with her, plain and simple, but was it too late to do anything about it? Putting the disturbing puzzle aside for the time being, he went back to his immediate dilemma: how to get Mr. Morliss on the cot without touching him. Reed wasn't sure it could be done, but he *was* sure he was going to try everything within his power to accomplish that feat.

Stifling a sneeze, he pulled the ends of the bottom sheet out, then pulled the top sheet over the entire body, creating a makeshift sling. *You would think someone had already done all this!* he grunted, silently bemoaning the fact that it was impossible to get good help anymore!

Now he had a nice neat bundle. The only problem was how to switch it over to the cart. Ralph was pretty hefty, so Reed was going to have all he could do to make the switch alone. Climbing up on the bed, he braced one leg on the rail and started to ease the sheet slowly toward the cart. He paused for a moment. Had Morliss moved? A cold sweat beaded across his forehead as he sat perfectly still for a moment, barely breathing. No. It was only his overactive imagination. Taking another deep breath, he tugged at the sheet again, this time managing to move the body an inch or two in the right direction. Where in the *hell* was Taryn! He wiped at the perspiration dripping down his neck now. He should have waited, he decided. He just wasn't cut out for this sort of thing. Well, it was too late to back out now. A couple more good heaves should see the job finished, then he could get out of here. He sneezed once more, nearly knocking over a bouquet of flowers sitting on the nightstand next to the bed. Why, dear Lord, if I had to fall in love, did it have to be with a mortician?

Straddling the broad bundle now, Reed grunted and shoved once more just as "Morliss" sat straight up and let out an ear-piercing scream.

"What is going on? *Help! Mugger! Pervert!*" the bundle shouted at the top of its lungs in a high feminine screech.

Reed was so stunned, his first instinct was to pass out cold. Instead, his basic instincts took over and he slapped his hand over the screaming woman's mouth, trying to still the angry shrieks of hysteria.

"Quiet down! I'm not a pervert, lady. I'm from the funeral home!" he shouted above her screaming voice.

The screams turned from frightened to horrified now as the woman grabbed a pillow and began battering him around his shoulders, as if he were a punching bag.

"Funeral home! *Help! Somebody please help me!*" she roared at the top of her lungs.

The two rolled off the bed in a tumble of sheets, flogging arms and pillows amid loud screams and bellows of pain as the woman soundly thrashed Reed's cowering body, repeating over and over in a shrill, authoritative voice that *she* wasn't ready for a mortician yet!

The door flew open and the room flooded with light as two nurses ran in and began to separate the dueling duo.

"Mrs. Morris! Mrs. Morris, please calm down!" One of the nurses grabbed the pillow out of the over-wrought woman's hands, but not before she could prevent her from getting in one more sound whack, knocking Reed flat on his back as he struggled to get up.

"He's from the funeral home!" Mrs. Morris protested, starting after him again. "He was trying to get me on that horrible . . . cart!"

It took both nurses to protect Reed this time as he staggered dazedly to his feet.

"It was a mistake, lady! Just a simple mistake!" he groaned weakly, cowering behind one of the nurses.

From out of nowhere Taryn suddenly appeared in the doorway, her face growing distressed as she quickly assessed the situation. "Oh, Reed, what's going on!"

Reed was by her side, clinging to the hem of her jacket, much as a small child would, as he incoherently tried to babble his side of the story. By now the hallway had begun to fill with people, all of them craning their necks to see what the commotion was about.

The nurses were trying to work Mrs. Morris's considerable bulk back on the bed as the woman bellowed hysterically that all she had was minor surgery and she couldn't be in need of a mortician yet!

"I was only trying to help," Reed protested in a numb state as Taryn gently led him out of the room. "How was I to know I was in the wrong room? I thought I would surprise you and have Ralph Morliss all loaded and ready to go. So I went to the desk and asked the nurse, 'What room's Morliss in?' and she batted her fake eyelashes at me and said 'What's your name, handsome' and I sure wasn't in any mood for a flirty, blond-headed nurse, so I said, 'Morliss, what room is Morliss in,' and she said, 'Room two twenty.' I swear to you, Taryn, she said room *two twenty,* so I went down there and started to load . . . that thing on the cot and all of a sudden this crazy person was screaming and batting me over the head with her pillow shouting, *'Help! Mugger! Pervert!'* and I kept trying to tell her I wasn't there to rob her *or* to attack her, for cripes sake! But she kept screaming and banging me over the head with her pillow." He paused and rubbed his head in bewilderment. "My stomach hurts. Do you have any Pepto-Bismol with you?"

Taryn stopped and put her arms around him and gave him a reassuring hug. "Do you realize you're rattling on just like I do?"

"*Oh, no!* You have me doing it too? I want to go home, Taryn," he pleaded in a voice like a frightened child's.

"I know, darling, I'll take you home. You sit right down here and wait while I go finish what we came to do, then we'll go home."

"Are you coming back for me this time?" he demanded impatiently, sounding for the world like a spoiled little boy. "You didn't come back earlier, you know!"

"I just stepped in to check on Grandpa and Sadie and I completely forgot the time," she apologized sheepishly. "Would you like a soda pop or a candy bar while you wait? There's a vending machine down the hallway. I can have the nurse bring you something—"

"You keep *her* away from me," he cut in sharply.

"All right. All right! I'll hurry," she promised quickly.

Placing a quick kiss on his forehead, she left him sitting in the hallway staring blankly into space. She should have been more careful about the time. Just when she thought she was finally making progress with his paranoid fears of her profession, this had to happen!

Thirty minutes later she had both men safely loaded in the limousine and was on her way back home. One was feeling absolutely no pain, the other was sick to his stomach and extremely cranky, and *she* had a splitting headache!

CHAPTER NINE

It was growing very late when Taryn finished her work and slowly climbed the stairway back to her bedroom. The clock on the mantel was striking the hour of three as she yawned, then automatically began to unbutton her blouse as she entered her bedroom. Reed had disappeared the moment they arrived home. She had assumed he was going to bed, although he hadn't said where he was going. For one brief moment she hoped he had decided to sleep in her bed, then quickly berated herself for such thoughts. This madness between them had to stop.

The soft moonlight streaming through the window lit her pathway into her small bath as she shed the remainder of her clothes and slipped into the shower. Ten minutes later she turned off the bathroom light and rubbed moisturizer on her face as she walked over to the bed. She paused and smiled as she saw the strong masculine length of Reed burrowed under the light blanket. A strong arm came out to draw her under the cover as she slid willingly into the bed and cuddled against his warm body.

"Do you know it's three in the morning?" he asked in a drowsy voice.

"Yes, I think so. 'It's three in the mor-r-r-rn-n-ing,' " she sang dutifully, wrapping her arms around him and snuggling deeper against him.

"You feel good," he murmured, running his hands up her gown and gently massaging her cool bottom, "but you were absolutely right. Your voice stinks."

"Ummm . . . you feel good too," she acknowledged, fortifying her words with her eager hands. "And I never fib . . . well . . . almost never. What are you doing in my bed?"

"After the day I've put in, I wouldn't sleep in this house alone for love nor money," he stated flatly. "On top of that, I wanted to be with you. Any objections?"

"None, and I agree. You have had a horrible day," she granted with a tired sigh. "Maybe tomorrow will be better."

Neither one wanted to think about tomorrow as their mouths found each other and they kissed lazily, their tongues teasing and touching, then searching deeper, extracting the sweetness waiting therein. It occurred to Taryn that they both seemed perfectly happy to lie in each other's arms, seeking nothing more than the exquisite pleasure of being together. There was a sexual attraction neither one could deny, nor did they want to. But for the moment their needs went deeper than those of the flesh and they drifted off to sleep in each other's arms kissing and holding one another tightly.

Early the next morning, the sound of birds singing woke Taryn up first. She lay for a moment trying to memorize Reed's handsome features, realizing that today could be the last they would spend together. In fulfilling her promise, Taryn had spoken with Ronnie and he had pledged to have the tree removed no later than noon today and would assess the damage. Reed had decided to borrow a car from the garage and the highways had been reopened late last night, so there would no longer be any reason for Reed to delay his departure.

She reached over and gently touched his hair. She loved the way it looked so tousled and boyish in his sleep. He was lying on his back, his arm slung over her chest. His mouth looked soft and so very kissable, she thought yearningly. There were tiny age lines beginning to form around his eyes, those beautiful silvery gray eyes that looked at her with such puzzlement at times, such unidentifiable longing at others. Her fingertip lightly traced the outline of his sleeping features, trying to indelibly score on her mind the man who had captured her heart in such a brief interval. Funny, there had only been two men in her life who had made love to her, and both had done so in a ridiculously short span of time. Soon Elaine would be lying in his arms, waking up to him every morning, accepting his kisses, having his children.

Elaine Montgomery. Mrs. Reed Montgomery. Tears rose up in Taryn's eyes. Mr. and Mrs. Reed Montgomery. Reed and Elaine Montgomery. Why was she doing this to herself? Wasn't it hard enough just lying here looking at him without torturing herself with things that were beyond her control?

The arm that had been lying on her chest closed slowly over her rib cage and brought her over against him. Turning on his side, he buried his face in her hair and whispered in a sleepy voice, "Hasn't anyone ever told you you can get in a lot of trouble looking at a man that way?"

Sure that her voice would betray her emotions, she could only shake her head and wipe hurriedly at the tears slipping down her cheeks. "I . . . I thought you were asleep."

"I was until a finger started running across my face," he murmured. "What time is it?"

"Close to six."

"Oh, good . . . too early to get up," he groaned, drawing her tighter into his embrace. His mouth began to search her neck languorously, nuzzling it in affection. "Don't you agree?"

"I never get up this early," she confessed. "In fact, I hate getting up mornings, period."

"You do? I do too." His mouth lazily captured hers. "Since we both hate getting up, let's just stay here for a while," he whispered persuasively. "I had great plans, but I fell asleep before I could proceed with them."

If she was any sort of decent person at all, this was where she should politely explain that what had occurred between them the night before was nice, and most likely unavoidable given the circumstances, but this was a new day and their madness must come to a halt. If she was to be fair to Elaine and not take advantage of a situation that was beyond Reed's or her control, she would force those words out of her mouth.

"Reed. Last night," she began.

"Did I happen to mention what great legs you have?" he asked softly, rubbing his hands along the silky texture of her thighs.

"Reed, about last night," she tried again, shivering as the hand moved to the inside of the silky softness and stroked suggestively.

"They are, you know. I'd like to see you in a bikini . . . one of those little skimpy things that barely leaves anything to a man's imagination." His voice was deep and hypnotic as his hands roamed over her in a tantalizing search of her pleasure points. "Do you have one of those?"

"I have a nice, serviceable one-piece," she returned, trying to keep her mind on business. "Reed, about last night. It was wonderful—"

"I agree. It was more than wonderful." He began to ravish her mouth with persistent kisses. "You already know how your hair turns me on, and your eyes, and the taste of your skin, and the sound of your voice when you whisper my name. Whisper my name again, Taryn," he ordered softly.

"Reed," she whispered, not in answer to his request, but out of her own need to get his attention.

"You say it so right. I've never heard a woman say it the way you do, all soft and breathless." His hands had found her full breasts and he paused to kiss each one thoroughly and lovingly, cradling their softness with such gentleness that it took her breath away.

"We shouldn't," she protested as she fervently returned his kisses now, her fingers threading through the dark waves of hair and pulling his mouth tighter against hers. "This has to stop, Reed."

"No, it doesn't," he murmured, moving his large body possessively over hers. "Don't spoil things, Taryn," he begged in a husky voice, showering hungry kisses along her eyes and jawline. "Let me love you . . . not just make love to you . . . let me share what's in my heart right now. I love you, don't you realize that by now? I know it's crazy and unexplainable and I haven't the slightest idea what we're going to do about it, but I love you."

The joy in her heart was so great she thought it would burst as she recognized the truth in his words. "I love you too, Reed."

"Honest?" He lifted his gaze to meet hers, a look of awe shimmering in his passion-laden gray depths. "I know you loved Gary and you're probably not over him yet, but would it ever be possible for another man to take his place in your heart?"

"No, you could never take his place," she confessed in a voice so filled with love he couldn't help but believe what she was about to say. "You'll have a place all your own."

"I've . . . I've never been in love before," he admitted, fingering a lock of her softly perfumed hair. "It feels strange to love someone so damn much it hurts."

"Don't you love your family?"

"Sure, but it's not the same. I haven't seen Mom and my three sisters for a while. Just wait until you meet them, honey, they're going to love you as much as I do . . ." His voice faltered and his eyes grew troubled as he realized what he had said. "Taryn . . . dear God, what am I going to do?" he murmured in a defeated voice.

"You're going to make love to me," she answered simply and honestly.

His thumbs grazed along the outline of her lips as he smiled, his eyes darkened to a smoldering gray. "We're going to make love to each other," he corrected. His mouth nudged hers open, tasting it, exploring it, then closing over it.

The feel of his hair-roughened chest pressed against the sensitive warmth of her bareness sent erotic sensations tumbling through her as she arched closer to his long, hard, powerful body. He deepened the kiss, his tongue tantalizing, demanding the response she so freely gave now.

"We were made for each other," he whispered, his

voice husky with passion. "Can't you feel how perfectly we fit together?"

Her answer was lost in Reed's groan of pleasure as his hands slid under her thighs and he lifted her body up to merge with his in searing, blinding pleasure.

Their lovemaking was urgent and fiery, tender and gentle, hungry and unquenchable, then slowed so they could take their time, drawing out the exquisite pleasures they were bringing to each other. Soft murmurs of gratification were muffled by long, agonizingly sweet kisses until they finally exploded into a single fireball, shattering out into the universe in a wondrous blaze of glory.

"Taryn, Taryn, my sweet, sweet Redhead," Reed whispered, kissing her over and over again as they floated slowly back to earth.

A soft weakness had invaded her bones now as she lay in his arms, showering his face with soft kisses. She didn't want to talk now, she didn't even want to think, she only wanted to lie in his embrace and feel his warmth against hers. His earlier words came back to drift meaningfully through her drowsy state. He had said it felt strange to love someone until it actually hurt. Well, she was feeling that "hurt" right now. So badly that she wanted to throw him in a shopping bag and run away with him somewhere where Elaine could never find him.

The sound of his soft breathing told her he was sleeping once more, as she drew the blanket back over them and cradled his head closer to her breast.

Her arms wrapped around Reed's neck more tightly as she stole one final kiss from his slack mouth, and snuggled back down in her pillow for another couple of hours sleep.

The air was strained later that morning as Reed and Taryn sat in the sunny breakfast nook eating their breakfast. Ronnie had knocked on the door ten minutes earlier and informed them the tree had been removed and that Reed's car was at the garage and the borrowed car was ready to go.

The subject of his imminent departure had not been broached, yet both knew the time was drawing near.

"More coffee?"

"No, thanks." Reed lit a cigarette and picked up the paper, glancing through it. "Boy, this thing's loaded with information," he mused. "Listen to this. 'Althea Burch and her daughter, Trealla, spent the afternoon shopping in Meadorville the day the storm hit. Trealla was purchasing her dress for the spring dance that was to be held this Friday evening in the Meadorville High gymnasium. Due to storm damages, the dance will now be held in the basement of the Legion Hall. Althea, along with Myrtle Mosely and Alice Woody, will be chaperoning the gala affair.' " He laid the paper down and gave Taryn a sexy wink. "Now that's one 'gala affair' I hate to miss."

Plucking the cigarette out of his mouth, she ground it out and pitched it in the wastebasket amid grunts of protest from him. "Stop making fun of our newspaper," she chided. "Where else can you get that sort of earthshaking news for fifteen cents?"

"Fifteen cents? Are you serious?" He picked up the paper again to examine the price and found that she was right. "I didn't think such bargains existed in the world today."

"There's a lot of things in this world you're not aware of," she said curtly. Now she had done it! She had been determined not to bring up any personal subject concerning her and Reed. If he had something to say, she wanted him to say it on his own, without any encouragement from her.

His face softened and he reached over and took her hand. "That may be, but I've learned a couple of things in the last few days that I wasn't aware of before."

Taryn drew her hand away from his, somehow sensing his next words. "You really are going to leave this morning, aren't you?" she asked softly.

"Taryn, don't look at me that way. You know I have to, don't you?" he prodded gently.

"Yes," she replied, forcing her gaze painfully away from his.

"I can't just ignore what's waiting for me in Santa Fe. What kind of person would I be to leave a woman standing at the altar?" His troubled eyes pleaded with hers for understanding.

"I'm aware of that, but I can't stand to think of you marrying someone you don't really love. . . . Oh,

Reed, don't you see that you'll be hurting Elaine as much as yourself if you step into a marriage bred of convenience?"

"Taryn . . . don't. Don't upset yourself. . . ."

"Don't upset myself!" She sprang to her feet in anger. "Don't you upset me! If you must go, then go! Don't stay around and torture me with trivial mishmash over what your duties to Elaine are!" Her face was flushed and angry as she faced him defiantly.

"I was afraid this would happen." Reed groaned and buried his hands in his hair in exasperation. "Can't you see I'm between the devil and the deep blue sea? What do you want me to do, Taryn? Pick up the phone and tell Elaine to 'dump her punch' because on the way to *our* wedding four days ago I found a redheaded mortician I've fallen crazy in love with? She wouldn't believe that in a million years!"

"Yes, that's exactly what I want!"

"No!" They glared at each other belligerently. "I won't do it that way. I'll have to go to her . . ."

Taryn didn't wait to hear him finish the sentence. She turned on her heel and marched toward the front parlor, muttering something under her breath.

"Stop grumbling, darn it!" Reed bellowed, helplessly trailing her through the house. "If you want to talk, say it so I can hear it!"

"Believe me, you wouldn't want to hear it," she yelled, tossing her red hair in defiance.

"Taryn, stop this nonsense and come back here. I want to talk to you—"

The loud slam of a door cut off his brusque demand. He glanced up and groaned in despair again. She had disappeared into Parlor B!

"Come out here, right now!" he ordered curtly through the closed door.

"You come in here if you want to talk to me" came her sharp, muffled reply. He could tell by her voice she was crying.

Mumbling obscenities under his breath, he hesitantly pushed the door open a crack and peered into the cool interior of the slumber room where Ralph Morliss lay reposing.

"Get out here!" he ordered.

"No!" She continued to arrange a spray of red roses, calmly ignoring him.

"You know I'm not coming in there. Get your fanny out here now!"

"No. Good-bye, Mr. Montgomery. Be sure and give Elaine my fondest regards!"

"I am going to get my car, then I'm leaving. Are you going to come out here and discuss this in a civilized manner or not?" His voice held grim authority now.

"Not," she answered crossly.

"Then I'm leaving!" He turned on his heel and started away, then whirled back around once more and opened the door a crack. "Don't forget to feed the damn bird!"

The door slammed closed again and she heard him march away in disgust.

Reed was gone by the time she came out of the parlor five minutes later. Her heart ached that their parting had to be so stormy, but she couldn't stand the pain of saying good-bye. He had certainly fooled her. After last night and his ardent confession of love, she could have sworn he *was* ready to tell Elaine to "dump her punch" or whatever. Men! Her eyes turned accusingly upward. "Men!" she reiterated aloud testily.

She forced herself to go into the office and try to concentrate on some forms that needed her attention. Her mind kept drifting back to Reed and Elaine and she began to simmer. It was simply not fair! He loved her, not Elaine! Why should she give up so easily and let another woman have him? Granted, Elaine had nabbed him first, but she should have made him love her enough that *nothing* could interfere with that love.

Taryn threw the pen she was using down on the desk and stood up, a call to arms resounding in her head. She had to stop Reed from leaving town! All she needed was a little more time to convince him of his madness.

Hanging a GONE TO LUNCH sign on the front door, she raced out the back, grabbing a set of keys on the way out. She noted with disgust that they were the keys to the hearse and knew Grandpa would skin her alive for taking it, but this was surely considered an emergency in anyone's books.

The big limousine was cumbersome to back out of

the drive, nevertheless she managed and was soon speeding down the road in front of the funeral parlor, plotting her devious course of action. She spotted Reed driving a car that was pulling into the street a few blocks ahead of her. Pushing down harder on the accelerator, she gained momentum on his vehicle and shot past him, waving happily at his surprised glance in her direction.

Minutes later the black hearse was idling smoothly in front of Reed's borrowed car as they sat at the stoplight waiting for the red light to change.

Reed had chosen to ignore her, aloofly turning his head away as she peered in the rearview mirror, innocently waving at him.

Good! There was Pryor, the town sheriff, sitting opposite her at the stoplight. This was going to work out splendidly, she congratulated herself as she raced the motor a fraction and slipped the transmission into reverse. This was going to cost her a pretty penny, but it was going to be worth it.

The light changed to green and she waved brightly to Pryor as he passed. When he was safely by, she stomped her foot down on the accelerator and prayed her grandpa wouldn't find out about this. The black car shot backward and a loud crunching sound filled the air as she came to a sudden halt, the back of the hearse buried in the borrowed car's grill.

Bounding hurriedly out of the car, she put on a sober face and marched over to where Reed was standing, angrily surveying the spewing radiator.

"What in the hell do you think you're doing!" he shouted, slamming his hands on his hips in agitation.

"Me! What do you think you're doing! You rear-ended me!" she accused hotly.

"Me! Are you crazy! I wasn't even aware the light had changed!"

"Well, of all the nerve. You hit me from behind and then try to stand here and tell me I am responsible. Well, this is unbelievable," she sputtered.

"I don't know what you're trying to pull, but you're not going to get away with it," Reed announced flatly, grimly surveying his mangled bumper and gaping radiator. "You hit me!"

"Here comes Pryor. We'll let him decide," she declared calmly.

"We certainly will!" Reed agreed.

The sheriff's car pulled up behind the two vehicles and Pryor got out, ambling slowly over to the scene of the accident. "Morning, Ms. Taryn," he greeted politely.

"Good morning, Pryor," she returned angelically. "I'm afraid Mr. Montgomery hit me in the rear."

"I'm going to stomp your rear if you don't stop lying!" Reed interjected swiftly. "Officer, this redheaded lunatic backed into me while we were sitting at that stoplight!"

"Backed into you, huh?" Pryor rubbed his jaw and solemnly contemplated the wrecked vehicles. "Backed into you, you say?" His voice sounded doubtful.

"That's right," Reed agreed with an earnest nod of his head. "I was sitting here minding my own business when all of a sudden she came flying back and took the whole front end out of the car."

"Honestly, Reed." Taryn placed her hands on her hips and looked at Pryor tolerantly. "Now, think, Pryor. Why in heaven's name would I be *backing* up at a stoplight? Don't you think that sounds like a desperate man who's trying to get out of a ticket?"

Pryor glanced from one opponent to the other. "Seems like that, don't it?" He took off his ten-gallon hat and scratched his head in puzzlement. "Nope, don't believe anyone would be backing up at a stop-sign," he agreed reluctantly.

"Hey, you two!" Reed crossed his arms stubbornly. "I happen to be a lawyer and I will personally see you in court if you try to pull this on me! She hit me!" he flared in exasperation.

"Well." Pryor dragged out his ticket pad and started writing. "I'll be there. Just let me know when you're comin'."

"Taryn!" Reed's mouth dropped open and his arms sagged weakly back to his side as he realized he was about to be ticketed for something he didn't do. "I'm going to pop him in the mouth, you crazy woman! Tell him the truth!"

"Can you add, 'threatening an officer of the law' to that offense?" she asked Pryor helpfully.

"I'm being framed!" Reed shouted in disbelief as a

ticket was ripped off the pad and slapped firmly in his hand.

"Thirty dollars, or thirty days!" Pryor said flatly.

"I don't believe this!" Reed shouted as the sound of a horn broke into the heated discussion. Pryor, Reed, and Taryn glanced up to see a late-model convertible pulling up to the curb.

"Oh, brother! That's all I need," Reed groaned, slumping against the car.

"Reed, who is she?" Taryn asked, her voice growing fearful as she stepped closer to him and surveyed the pretty woman climbing out of the convertible and running toward the accident. Her heart grew numb as she awaited the inevitable, distressing answer.

"It's Elaine . . . and her mother," he confirmed tightly.

Moments later Elaine was throwing her arms around Reed and showering his face with kisses as she inquired whether he was hurt or not.

"Darling, Mother decided we should drive down and pick you up ourselves. We've had a heck of a time. We only knew the name of the town, but a nice man at the service station told us where your car had been trapped by the tree, but it was gone when we got there . . . it's just luck we noticed the accident here at the stoplight," Elaine explained, fussing with his windblown hair. "Are you all right? I've been so worried!"

Taryn didn't wait to hear Reed's comment as she

turned away from the painful scene, holding the tears back until she could make her way to the car. Elaine was here. She was real, and Taryn could no longer pretend she didn't exist. She was here, kissing the face that Taryn loved so very much . . . and she was pretty . . . very, very pretty.

"Ms. Taryn, do you need any help getting home?" Pryor shouted, surprised at her abrupt departure. "We need to fill out a report. . . ."

"Later," she called. "I'll stop by the office later. . . ."

Her hands trembled violently as she tried to start the hearse, feeling as if she was going to be sick any minute.

"Taryn!" She could hear Reed shouting to her as her motor sprang into life and she put the car in gear.

He suddenly appeared at the window, reaching in to still her hands, his gray eyes filled with such desolation that it only made her cry harder.

"Don't, Taryn, please don't do this," he pleaded huskily. "Give me time . . . I'll try to work this thing out . . ." he promised, tears forming in his eyes now too.

"Let me go, Reed. I don't think I can stand this. . . ." She took great gulping sobs of air as she tried to make her words come out intelligently. She had to get away from him before she broke down completely.

"Look at me, Taryn, are you all right?" His hand

tightened in concern as he brought her face forcefully up to meet his.

His fingers brushed hers, sending a sharp electrical current between them as she made herself look at him one last time. His face was tense, the tired lines around his eyes etched deeper than she remembered. For one crazy moment, she thought about kissing those lines away, trying to ease the pain she saw written on his face.

"Don't do this," he whispered in a barely audible voice. "I love you, Taryn."

Taryn swallowed her pride and grabbed his hand, burying her face in its familiar warm scent. "Don't go with her, Reed. I'll be anything you want me to be! I'll be the other woman if that's what it takes. I'll share you with her if that's what it takes to keep you, because I love you so very much and I don't think I can stand losing you." She broke down sobbing heartbrokenly.

"No, don't, sweetheart." His hand tightened possessively on hers as Elaine's voice called impatiently to him.

Taryn turned tear-filled eyes up to meet his tortured gaze. "I'll give up being a mortician. I'll be anything in the world you want me to be if only you won't leave me." She had no idea where her pride had flown, but suddenly she was willing to offer anything if she didn't have to suffer this horrible loss.

He was so moved by her words, he could no longer

speak as Elaine's voice called out sharply again, "Reed! Are you coming?"

"You don't have to change, Taryn. You're everything in the world I want." He turned and strode away from the car, wiping self-consciously at his eyes with the sleeve of his jacket before Taryn could offer one final plea.

She sat for a moment pondering his words deep in her heart. She was everything he wanted. That's what he had said! The thought lifted her heavy burden. "God?" she called softly, turning her eyes toward the heavens. "Was he really telling me the truth or was he just trying to make things easier for me?" She thought for a minute and suddenly her spirits felt noticeably lighter. He'd sounded sincere! She frowned. Yet, if that were true, why was he getting into the car with the woman he was supposed to marry in four days? Her eyes shot upward once more. "I hope you have got this thing firmly in hand, because I've definitely lost control!" she conceded.

She drove away before she started crying again as Reed helped Pryor shove the damaged car over to the curb, then joined Elaine and her mother.

CHAPTER TEN

It was all over. Reed Montgomery and Elaine Matthews were married. It was late Saturday afternoon as Taryn climbed the small hill overlooking the cemetery and set Malcolm's birdcage down under the giant oak tree. The emerald-green leaves rustled pleasantly in the light breeze as she stood gazing over the lush countryside trying to will her mind to accept that fact. After all was said and done, he'd still gone ahead and married a woman he didn't love.

"He'll regret it," she told the bird solemnly.

Malcolm swung back and forth on his perch dejectedly. He had been unusually quiet the last few days. Taryn supposed he missed Sadie. Her stay in the hospital had been extended and she wouldn't be home until Monday.

She sighed and sat down on the ground next to his cage and idly offered him a Fig Newton, which he promptly refused. Having missed a few meals herself lately, she shrugged and bit into the cookie.

"He will, you know," she continued, chewing absently on the gooey filling. "One of these days Reed will wake up and look around and realize what a horrible mistake he's made."

"Squawk, Reed's a baaad boy. Reed's a baaad boy!" Malcolm confirmed.

"No, he isn't," Taryn said curtly, forgetting for a moment she was conversing with a bird. "Reed's wonderful. Don't talk badly about him. At first I had hard feelings toward him too. I thought he should have been wise and brave enough to stand up for what he wanted, but when you stop to think about it, Malcolm, that would have been an awful lot to ask of a person. It was very hard for me to trust my heart and admit that I could fall in love in three short days, so I can see what an impossible situation he found himself in. You know, Elaine planning a big wedding and all. And her father expecting him to be a part of his firm. I can see that," she confessed, glumly taking another bite of cookie. "Now, be honest. Can't you?"

Malcolm continued swinging, offering no comment to her question.

She sat watching the workman remove the canvas awning spread over the new grave site where they had laid Ralph to rest this afternoon. Unlike Martha's, the service had been peaceful and reverent. Reed would have liked that, she pondered sadly. No, he wouldn't, she corrected truthfully. He would have hated every minute and his allergy would have bothered him.

Tonight would be his wedding night. The cookie

turned to sawdust in her mouth as she stood up and angrily flung the remains over the hillsides.

"Oh, God." The pain closed in on her and made her cry out in exasperation. "Make him come driving up right now and tell me it's all over, that he told Elaine he couldn't possibly marry her because he's in love with *me* and we're going to get married and buy a chicken ranch and have lots of children and live happily ever after . . ." Her voice trailed off brokenly as she heard a car pull in the cemetery and stop. She squinted against the sun, trying to make out who the new arrival was. Her hazel eyes slowly grew round as dinner plates as she saw Reed's tall form climbing out of a new car. Her hand went over her mouth in disbelief, her eyes turning sheepishly toward the heavens. "Gosh," she breathed in a voice filled with reverence. "I was beginning to think you weren't listening!"

Reed glanced up toward the hillside and saw her standing there. His smile was warm, yet it contained a certain sternness as he placed his hands on his hips and shouted, "Are you ready to tell the truth about backing into me yet?"

"Uh . . ." She was having a horrible time finding her voice, hardly daring to believe he was actually standing down there shouting at her! "You . . . ran into me . . . I think," she called back nervously. What was he doing here? Oh, Lord. Surely he and Elaine hadn't stopped by on their honeymoon!

"Oh, no, I didn't!" he stated adamantly. He began

to make his way up the hillside as she sought to find some air for her lungs. "Thirty bucks, lady. That little fib cost you thirty bucks, plus the repair bill on the car that the garage loaned me." He reached the top of the hill with one hand waving a bill in front of her startled face. "What do you have to say in defense of your despicable actions?" he asked her in a stern voice.

"You . . . you're not wearing a wedding band," she noted hopefully.

Reed glanced down at the empty third finger of his left hand. "No, you haven't given me one yet. Now, back to problem number one. Why in the hell did you tear the whole front end out of that car!"

"You didn't marry Elaine this afternoon?" she pursued, her voice lifting slightly with the first faint rays of hope.

"No, I can't marry Elaine. I'm in love with you."

"Just like that. You're in love with me?"

"Well, not just like that. It took four whole days," he told her solemnly. "Now, why did you back into me?"

"Because I didn't want you to leave. Was she upset?"

"Wouldn't it have been simpler and a lot less costly just to ask me not to leave? I planned on coming back," he said patiently. "If you had let me explain that day instead of running into that slumber room and hiding, I would have told you I planned on going to Santa Fe to explain to Elaine the best way I knew

369

now what had happened, and to break the engagement. And, yes, she was a bit miffed. Don't plan on getting *her* business when she goes."

"You're not engaged anymore?"

"I didn't say that."

"You didn't break the engagement?" Her face fell as hard as her hopes.

"I'm still engaged," he confirmed easily.

She frowned at him sullenly. "To whom?"

"To youwhom," he mispronounced teasingly.

Her frown softened. "To . . . me?"

"To you." He grinned. "Why do you find that so surprising? Isn't it perfectly natural for a man who hates the mere thought of cemeteries, ghosts, ghouls, Halloween, dogs howling at full moons, and witches —not to mention driving hearses, singing at funerals, and slinking around hospitals picking up dead bodies —to find himself stranded in a town with a redheaded mortician whom he falls head over heels in love with in three—actually I think it was closer to two—days? He's willing to give up a lucrative law practice making a staggering amount of money each year, to leave a lovely woman whom he's been friends with for as long as he can remember stranded at the church altar with her punch already made and in the bowl waiting for the seven hundred guests the bride and groom have invited. He throws *all* that away without so much as a second thought and races back here in a new car he just drove out of the showroom to plead with this lovely mortician to marry him. What's so strange about that?" he asked calmly.

"Oh," she scoffed weakly, "Elaine didn't really have her punch made and she wasn't actually standing at the altar . . . was she?" Taryn would have felt terrible if Reed had been that callous. The price of ingredients for punch was sky-high nowadays! she agonized, her practical side surfacing now.

"Squawk! Reed's a baaad boy! Squawk, Reed's a baaad boy." Malcolm had suddenly decided to voice his opinion.

"Shut up, Malcolm, this is between me and the lady," he advised the bird sternly. "No, it hadn't quite reached that point yet," Reed continued, reaching out to hesitantly touch the strands of her titian hair ruffling gently in the spring breeze. "I'll bet you thought I wasn't coming back, didn't you, Red?"

She nodded, her eyes devouring his familiar features lovingly. "Pinch me," she demanded softly.

He reached out and tenderly pinched the end of her nose.

"I felt that!" Her smile was radiant as the tips of her trembling fingers ran adoringly over the hollows and planes of his face, drinking in his unique scent, the feel of his skin against hers. "I'm not dreaming, am I? You're here, you're real. . . ."

"I'm here, and I'm real." Their gazes caught and held silently for a moment, both so overcome with emotion for the moment, they couldn't speak.

"I'm sorry I took so long in coming back, but I couldn't leave Elaine alone to face all the things that had to be done to cancel the wedding," he apologized, sensuously stroking the corners of her mouth with his thumbs. "I know I should have called to tell you that I had broken the engagement, but I wanted you in my arms when I told you."

"Oh, Reed," she sighed, drowning in her happiness yet acutely feeling Elaine's pain. "Was she very . . . hurt?"

The gray of his eyes clouded for the briefest of moments. "I can't say that it was easy on either one of us, Taryn. True, I wasn't in love with Elaine, but I do admire and respect her and her parents."

"When did you tell her?"

"The day she came to get me. When we arrived in Santa Fe, we went straight to her parents' home and that's when I broke the news to all of them. They were very polite and I think her parents just might have understood, but I'm afraid it didn't ease Elaine's pain . . . or humiliation. In any other circumstances, I would have never done that sort of thing to anyone . . . but through it all I kept remembering what you had said to me once. You said, there comes a time for people when they have to decide how they want to live their lives, and with whom. Do you know I had never candidly stopped to ask myself that question? I had always sort of flowed along with the tide, taking each day as it came and never really thinking about the future or what I wanted? Until I made love to you and felt that overpowering need to have you beside me for the rest of my life, I continued to ignore what I wanted. It was just easier to please everyone else." His eyes darkened to a passionate slate gray as he surveyed the lovely features he had seen over and over in his dreams the last four nights. "But once I held you in my arms and experienced how wonderful love—not like—could be, of the joy you could bring into my life, I was forced to ask the question and come up with the only possible answer. I love you, redheaded Taryn Oliver. Today, tomorrow, next year, forever after . . . and *in* the forever after, if you'll let me."

They shifted nearer to each other, their mouths moving closer and closer together as they talked. Taryn was dying for him to kiss her, but he seemed willing to let his eyes express his feelings for the moment, love radiating out of their smoky depths.

"Are you ready to let me take care of you from now on?" he asked in a hopeful voice, his breath gently caressing her cheeks as he touched his face to hers. "I know you'll never forget Gary, but I promise to love you as much or more than he did."

"Oh, darling, of course I'll never forget Gary, and no matter what you think, I have put him in his rightful place, Reed. You're all I ever have or ever will want.

"Reed," she murmured, snuggling closer to his broad chest. "When are you going to kiss me?"

"Not until I can't stand it another second, which

isn't far away," he confirmed, avoiding her tempting mouth that was clearly aching to be kissed. "Once I start kissing you, I won't be stopping for a while and we still have things to be decided."

"Did you kiss Elaine good-bye?" she asked, wishing she hadn't.

Reed's grin was defiantly guilty. "One kiss," he defended. "Surely you're not going to be jealous over one kiss out of the fifty million I plan on giving you in the next couple of hours alone!"

"I certainly *am* jealous, and that had better be the last time you ever kiss another woman, or you're a dead duck, Reed Montgomery," she stated adamantly.

He flinched painfully. "Dead duck. That brings us to the next problem that needs to be discussed."

"Such as?" she asked with disappointment, refusing to relinquish her tight hold around his neck.

"Such as, were you serious about living anywhere with the man you loved?"

"Indubitably, dear! Where do you want to live?"

"Well, there is this beautiful piece of land about twenty miles from here. I noticed it on the way out of town the other day. . . ."

"You mean the land out by the new highway . . . the one that has the lovely old two-story house that sits back in the woods?"

"Yeah! You know the one I'm talking about?" he asked excitedly. "The one with all the white fences surrounding the land?"

"Yes! I love the place myself! I called the realtor yesterday and it's priced very reasonably," she assured.

"You called about it? Why?"

Taryn's grip around his neck increased. "Well, I was thinking if my prayers were answered and you *did* come back, the land would make a lovely chicken ranch."

"You did! That's exactly what *I* was thinking!" He picked her up in his arms and swung her around and around, both of them laughing with delight.

"You would really give up being a mortician and live on a chicken ranch with me?" he asked happily.

"I'd *be* a chicken for you, if that's what you wanted!" she exclaimed, hugging him with exuberance. "But what about you? Do you honestly want to give up being a lawyer after all the hard years you've spent in law school?"

"I really don't think either one of us has to give up our profession," he replied, with a broad grin. "Surely Meadorville, population six hundred and forty-three, can up their total by one more and have room for a small law office in their sprawling metropolis. Then in the evenings I can come home to you and we can have our chickens until our children come along. In the meantime, you can still help your grandfather with his . . . business." He paused and squeezed her with authority. "As long as you don't involve me in any of your emergencies. I love you, but there's a limit to what my nerves can take!"

"Oh, I won't ever ask you to help me again," she promised, bringing her mouth closer to his once more. "Can we kiss now?"

He cocked his head and smiled at her wickedly. "Can't wait, huh?"

"Reed . . . kiss me!"

"Not yet," he procrastinated, enjoying the look of childlike disappointment covering her face. He walked over to the birdcage and leaned down. "Are you feeling any better about yourself yet, fella? What you need is a good woman to set your feathers on fire. Maybe a redheaded one like I have," he suggested helpfully, handing the bird a Fig Newton.

Turning back to Taryn, he smiled and held out his arms in warm welcome. "And now I would be more than happy to give you that kiss . . . and a hundred more besides. Come here, Redhead, and let's show him what can happen to a guy when he falls in love."

Taryn flew into his arms and they kissed hungrily, their hands exploring and touching each other with fervor. The kisses were sweet, then demanding, then poignant, both pouring out their love for the other, both finding it hard to believe that they were together once more, this time never to be parted again.

"Squawk! Reed *is* baaad boy!" Malcolm reminded primly as Reed's hand slipped beneath her blouse and lovingly caressed her feminine softness.

"You don't know the half of it, Malcolm," he chuckled wickedly as Taryn's face blushed a rosy pink. His hands intimately began to take possession of every inch of her silken skin as he drew her closer in his arms. "Before I take you home and make love to you until *your* feathers burn, there's one more thing I'd like to do," he whispered suggestively.

"Anything," she offered devotedly.

Reed affected a low, gentlemanly bow. "I would like to have the honor of dancing with my best girl." He held out his arm politely. "Milady. If I might?"

Taryn curtsied and demurely accepted his hand.

Reed turned and bowed again to Malcolm. "Sir, you will join us?" He picked up the birdcage and winked at Taryn sexily. "I hope you don't mind, but you know how sensitive he can be."

"I quite understand," she returned with formal consent.

Holding the birdcage with one finger, he placed his large hands lightly in hers and they began to slowly waltz under the spreading oak, their gazes locked adoringly. Amid the rustle of the leaves, he began to sing to her, his beautiful baritone voice ringing out loud and clear over the quiet hillside. To the melody of "Let Me Call You Sweetheart," he whirled her and Malcolm around the grassy meadow as the birds in the trees twittered noisily in sweet accompaniment.

There were a few parts in the song he improvised, making up his own words to tell her of his love. Taryn found herself giggling, then flushing bright red at times with his racy lyrics, but she thought it was the most lovely dance she had ever had.

When their feet finally slowed, they came together in a long, smoldering kiss as Malcolm settled down contentedly to swing back and forth on his perch, enjoying his Fig Newton for the first time in a week.

"Take me home, Taryn." Reed raggedly made the familiar plea against the sweetness of her mouth as she drew him closer to her heart.

"Yes, darling. And, this time, I will keep you."

As he buried his face in the perfume of the hair he loved so very much, she turned her eyes once more toward the blue of the heavens. Making a perfect round circle with her thumb and forefinger, she lifted the salute gratefully as her mouth silently formed the words *Thanks!*

**Two complete love stories
in each collector's volume!**

THE BEST OF JOAN HOHL

SNOWBOUND WEEKEND/GAMBLER'S LOVE.
Two cold strangers warm up to each other in a romantic
ski lodge in *Snowbound Weekend*. In *Gambler's Love*, the
odds are against Vichy Sweigart as she risks all she has for
the love of a handsome gambler.

_____2726-7 $3.95

**THE TAWNY GOLD MAN/MORNING ROSE,
EVENING SAVAGE.** In *The Tawny Gold Man*, Anne
Moore longs to rekindle the passion she shared with Judd
Cameron, who once vowed to love her always. Then
shrewd Tara gets more than she bargained for when she
marries a rich man she doesn't love in *Morning Rose,
Evening Savage*.

_____2738-0 $3.95

LEISURE BOOKS
ATTN: Customer Service Dept.
276 5th Avenue, New York, NY 10001

Please send me the book(s) checked above. I have enclosed $ _____
Add $1.25 for shipping and handling for the first book; $ .30 for each book
thereafter. No cash, stamps, or C.O.D.s. All orders shipped within 6 weeks.
Canadian orders please add $1.00 extra postage.

Name _____

Address _____

City _____ State _____ Zip _____

Canadian orders must be paid in U.S. dollars payable through a New York
banking facility.   ☐ Please send a free catalogue.

SIZZLING CONTEMPORARY ROMANCE...

BY MAGGI BROCHER

Behind the walls of a nunnery, a penniless Irish girl brought forth her illegitimate baby. Leaving her tiny son in the care of the sisters, she vowed that one day she would return. But married to a wealthy politician, she surrounded herself with the trappings of power and money, determined to forget the past. She had built her life on a foundation of lies — until her shocking secret was trumpeted to the world, and the walls came tumbling down.

_____2477-2 $3.95US/$4.95CAN

LEISURE BOOKS
ATTN: Customer Service Dept.
276 5th Avenue, New York, NY 10001

Please send me the book(s) checked above. I have enclosed $ _____
Add $1.25 for shipping and handling for the first book; $ .30 for each book thereafter. No cash, stamps, or C.O.D.s. All orders shipped within 6 weeks. Canadian orders please add $1.00 extra postage.

Name _____

Address _____

City _____ State _____ Zip _____
Canadian orders must be paid in U.S. dollars payable through a New York banking facility.   ☐ Please send a free catalogue.

JOAN SMITH

"JOAN SMITH IS ON A HOT STREAK!"
—Romantic Times

DESTINY'S DREAM. A woman shrouded in a mystery and surrounded by whispers of scandal, lovely Flora Sommers was the talk of the town. Though sought after by the peers of London, only one man could pierce her haughty reserve to touch her wild, willing heart. In his strong arms she knew the sweetness of surrender, the shattering fulfillment of physical passion. He stole her innocence and forged her strange destiny, but would he ever make her dreams of love come true?

_____2628-7 $3.95 US/$4.95 CAN

LEISURE BOOKS
ATTN: Customer Service Dept.
276 5th Avenue, New York, NY 10001

Please send me the book(s) checked above. I have enclosed $_____
Add $1.25 for shipping and handling for the first book; $ .30 for each book thereafter. No cash, stamps, or C.O.D.s. All orders shipped within 6 weeks. Canadian orders please add $1.00 extra postage.

Name _____

Address _____

City _____ State _____ Zip_____

Canadian orders must be paid in U.S. dollars payable through a New York banking facility.   ☐ Please send a free catalogue.

JOAN SMITH

AUTHOR OF OVER
FIVE MILLION BOOKS IN PRINT!

Joan Smith is a winner of the *Romantic Times* Reviewers' Choice Award, and is the bestselling author of over forty novels.

EMERALD HAZARD. Fresh from the lush green countryside, young Moira Dauntry enchanted all of London society with her exquisite beauty. But it was the enticing wildness of her spirit that lured the city's most dashing lord, James Raeburn, to her side. After a single night of danger, desire and deception, he offered her his ring, and all her dreams were about to come true. Yet when he found she was nothing but an illegitimate serving girl, her hopes for happiness were destroyed . . . but their love would survive and flourish forever.

_____2704-6 $4.50 US/$5.50 CAN

LEISURE BOOKS
ATTN: Customer Service Dept.
276 5th Avenue, New York, NY 10001

Please send me the book(s) checked above. I have enclosed $_____
Add $1.25 for shipping and handling for the first book; $ .30 for each book thereafter. No cash, stamps, or C.O.D.s. All orders shipped within 6 weeks. Canadian orders please add $1.00 extra postage.

Name _____

Address _____

City_____ State_____ Zip_____

Canadian orders must be paid in U.S. dollars payable through a New York banking facility.   ☐ Please send a free catalogue.

THRILLING GOTHIC ROMANCE BY THE AUTHOR OF MORE THAN FIVE MILLION BOOKS IN PRINT!

JOAN SMITH

A Whisper on the Wind

Soon after her glorious marriage to the dashing Fraser Audry, young Rosalie suddenly felt that something was terribly wrong. People she had never met treated her as an old friend and people kept bringing up a past she knew they'd never shared. Her uneasiness turned to desperate fear as she chased phantom clues that led nowhere. Rosalie sought comfort in the arms of her husband, but an ominous whisper on the wind warned her not to trust even her own heart.

__2950-2 $3.50 US / $4.50 CAN

LEISURE BOOKS
ATTN: Customer Service Dept.
276 5th Avenue, New York, NY 10001
Please add $1.25 for shipping and handling of the first book and $.30 for each book thereafter. All orders shipped within 6 weeks via postal service book rate.
Canadian orders must reflect Canadian price, when indicated, and must be paid in U.S. dollars through a U.S. banking facility.

Name _____

Address _____

City _____ State _____ Zip _____

I have enclosed $ _____ in payment for the books checked above.

Payment **must** accompany all orders.   ❏ Please send a free catalogue.

SPEND YOUR LEISURE MOMENTS WITH US.

Hundreds of exciting titles to choose from—something for everyone's taste in fine books: breathtaking historical romance, chilling horror, spine-tingling suspense, taut medical thrillers, involving mysteries, action-packed men's adventure and wild Westerns.

SEND FOR A FREE CATALOGUE TODAY!

Leisure Books
Attn: Customer Service Department
276 5th Avenue, New York, NY 10001